KU-488-380

Nicholas Monsarrat

'H.M.S. Marlborough Will Enter Harbour'

Leave Cancelled
Heavy Rescue

A MAYFLOWER BOOK

GRANADA
London Toronto Sydney New York

Published by Granada Publishing Limited in 1972
Reprinted 1973, 1975, 1979, 1982

ISBN 0 583 12096 2

First published in Great Britain
by Cassell & Co Ltd (as *Depends What
You Mean By Love*) 1947.
Reprinted five times
Published by Panther Books 1956
Reprinted thirteen times

Granada Publishing Limited
Frogmore, St Albans, Herts AL2 2NF
and
36 Golden Square, London W1R 4AH
866 United Nations Plaza, New York, NY 10017, USA
117 York Street, Sydney, NSW 2000, Australia
100 Skyway Avenue, Rexdale, Ontario, M9W 3A6, Canada
61 Beach Road, Auckland, New Zealand

Printed and bound in Great Britain by
Cox & Wyman Ltd, Reading
Set in Monotype Times

Granada ®
Granada Publishing ®

By the same author

Foreword

These three short stories, dealing with differing aspects of love in wartime, were written at intervals during the past two years. It was my original intention to publish the second one, *Leave Cancelled*, as a separate volume, but my publishers disagreed for reasons concerned in varying degrees with production difficulties and professional caution. I dare say they were right. I must, however, remark that *Leave Cancelled*, published as a separate novel in America, dodged in and out of the best-sellers lists for more than six months, sold 60,000 copies, and earned, in a mid-Western journal, the singular heading "Briton Slave To Sex". This proves something, though I am not sure what.

N.M.

"H.M.S. Marlborough will enter Harbour"

CHAPTER 1

THE sloop, *Marlborough*, 1,200 tons, complement 8 officers and 130 men, was torpedoed at dusk on the last day of 1942 while on independent passage from Iceland to the Clyde. She was on her way home for refit, and for the leave that went with it, after a fourteen-month stretch of North Atlantic convoy escort with no break, except for routine boiler-cleaning. Three weeks' leave to each watch – that had been the buzz going round the ship's company when they left Reykjavik after taking in the last convoy: but many of them never found out how much truth there was in that buzz, for the torpedo struck at the worst moment, with two-thirds of the ship's company having tea below decks, and when it exploded under the forward mess-deck at least sixty of them were killed outright.

H.M.S. *Marlborough* was an old ship, seventeen years old, and she took the outrage as an old lady of breeding should. At the noise and jar of the explosion a delicate shudder went all through her: then as her speed fell off there was stillness, while she seemed to be making an effort to ignore the whole thing: and then, brought face to face with the fury of this mortal attack, gradually and disdainfully she conceded the victory.

The deck plating of the fo'c'sle buckled and sagged, pulled downwards by the weight of the anchors and cables: all this deck, indeed, crumpled as far as the four-inch gun-mounting, which toppled forwards until the gun muzzles were pointing foolishly to the sea; a big lurch tore loose many of the ammunition lockers and sent them cascading over the side. Until the way of her sixteen knots fell off, there were crunching noises as successive bulkheads took the weight of water, butted at it for a moment, and then gave in: and thus, after a space, she lay – motionless, cruelly hit, two hundred miles from home.

So far it had been an affair of metal: now swiftly it became an affair of men. From forward came muffled shouting – screaming, some of it – borne on the wind down the whole length of the ship, to advertise the shambles buried below. The dazed gun's crew from "A" gun, which had been directly over the explosion, climbed down from their sagging platform and drew off aft. There was a noise of trampling running feet from all over the ship: along alleyways, up ladders leading from the untouched spaces aft: confused voices, tossed to and fro by the wind, called as men tried to find out how bad the damage was, what the orders were, whether their friends had been caught or not.

On the upper deck, near the boats and at the foot of the bridge-ladders, the clatter and slur of feet and voices reached its climax. In the few moments before a firm hand was taken, with every light in the ship out and only the shock of the explosion as a guide to what had happened, there was confusion, noisy and urgent: the paramount need to move quickly clashed with indecision and doubt as to where that move could best be made. The dusk, the rising sea, the bitterly cold wind, which carried an acrid smell in sharp eddying puffs, were all part of this discordant aftermath: the iron trampling of those racing feet all over the ship bound it together, co-ordinating fear into a vast uneasy whole, a spur for panic if panic ever showed itself.

It never did show itself. The first disciplined reaction, one of many such small reassurances, to reach the bridge was the quartermaster's voice, admirably matter-of-fact, coming up the wheel-house voice-pipe: "Gyro compass gone dead, sir!" The midshipman, who shared the watch with the First Lieutenant and was at that moment licking a lip split open on the edge of the glass dodger, looked round uncertainly, found he was the only officer on the bridge, and answered:

8

"Very good. Steer by magnetic," before he realized the futility of this automatic order. Then he jerked his head sideways, level with another voice-pipe, the one leading to the Captain's cabin, and called: "Captain, sir!"

There was no answer. Probably the Captain was on his way up already. God, suppose he'd been killed, though . . . The midshipman called again: "Captain, sir!" and a voice behind him said: "All right, Mid. I heard it."

He turned round, to find the comforting bulk of the Captain's duffle coat outlined against the dusk. It was not light enough to see the expression on his face, nor was there anything in his voice to give a clue to it. It did not occur to the midshipman to speculate about this, in any case: for him, this was simply the Captain, the man he had been waiting for, the man on whom every burden could now be squarely placed.

"Torpedo, sir."

"Yes."

The Captain, moving with purpose but without hurry, stepped up on to the central compass platform, glanced once round him – and sat down. There was something special in the act of sitting down, there in the middle of the noise and movement reaching the bridge from all over the ship, and everyone near him caught it. The Captain, on the bridge, sitting in the Captain's chair. Of course: that was what they had been waiting for. . . . It was the beginning, the tiny tough centre, of control and order. Soon it would spread outwards.

"Which side was it from?"

"Port, sir. Just under 'A' gun."

"Tell the engine-room what's happened. . . . Where is the First Lieutenant?"

"He must have gone down, sir. I suppose he's with the Damage Control Party."

Up the voice-pipe came the quartermaster's voice again: "She won't come round, sir. The wheel's hard a-starboard."

"Never mind." The Captain turned his head slightly. "Pilot!"

A figure, bent over the chart table behind him, straightened up. "Sir?"

"Work out our position, and we'll send a signal."

"Just getting it out now."

The Captain bent forward to the voice-pipe again. "Bosun's Mate!"

"Sir?"

"Find the First Lieutenant. He'll be forrard somewhere. Tell him to report the damage as soon as he can."

"Aye, aye, sir."

That, at least, was a small space cleared. . . . Under him the ship felt sluggish and helpless; on the upper deck the voices clamoured, from below the cries still welled up. He looked round him, trying in the increasing darkness to find out who was on the bridge. Not everyone he expected to see, not all the men who should have collected at such a moment, were there. The signalman and the bridge messenger. Two look-outs. Bridger, his servant, standing just behind him. Pilot and the Mid. Someone else he could not make out.

He called: "Coxswain?"

There was a pause, and then a voice said: "He was below, sir."

"Who's that?"

"Adams, sir."

Adams was the Chief Bosun's Mate, and the second senior rating on board. After a moment the Captain said:

"If he doesn't get out, you take over, Adams. . . . You'd better organize three or four of your quartermasters, for piping round the ship. I'll want you to stay by me. If there's anything to be piped you can pass it on."

"Aye, aye, sir."

There was too much noise on the upper deck, for a start. But perhaps it would be better if he spoke to them over the loudhailer. Once more the Captain turned his head.

"Yeoman!"

Another pause, and then the same definitive phrase, this time from the signalman of the watch: "He was below, sir."

A wicked lurch, and another tearing noise from below, covered the silence after the words were spoken. But the Captain seemed to take them in his stride.

"See if the hailer's working," he said to the signalman.

"I've got the position, sir," said Haines, the navigating officer. "Will you draft a signal?"

"Get on to the W/T office and see if they can send it, first."

"The hailer's all right, sir," said the signalman. "Batteries still working."

"Very good. Train the speaker aft."

He clicked on the microphone, and from force of habit blew through it sharply. A healthy roar told him that the thing was in order. He cleared his throat.

"Attention, please! This is the Captain speaking." His voice, magnified without distortion, overcame the wind and the shouting, which died away to nothing, "I want to tell you what's happened. We've been torpedoed on the port side, under 'A' gun. The First Lieutenant is finding out about the damage now. I want you all to keep quiet, and move about as little as possible, until I know what the position is. . . . 'X' gun's crew will stand fast, the rest of the watch-on-deck clear away the boats and rafts ready for lowering. Do *not* start lowering, or do anything else, until I give the order over this hailer, or until you hear the pipe. That is all."

The speaker clicked off, leaving silence on the bridge and all over the upper deck. Only the voices hidden below still called. He became aware that Haines was standing by his elbow, preparing to speak.

"What is it, Pilot?"

"It's the W/T office, sir. They can't transmit."

"Who's down there?"

"The leading tel., sir. The P.O. tel. was below." (That damned phrase again. If those two messes, the Chiefs' and the Petty Officers', were both written off, it was going to play hell with organizing the next move, whatever it was.) "But he knows what he's doing, sir," Haines went on. "The dynamo's been thrown off the board, but the set's had a hell of a knock anyway."

"Go down yourself and make sure." Haines, as well as being navigating officer, was an electrical expert, and this was in fact his department.

"Ay, aye, sir."

"Midshipman!"

"Sir?"

"Pass the word to the Gunnery Officer –"

"I'm here, sir." Guns' tall figure loomed up behind him. "I've been looking at 'A' gun."

"Well?"

"It's finished, I'm afraid, sir."

Guns knew his job, and the Captain did not ask him to elaborate. Instead he said:

"I think we'll try a little offensive action while we're waiting, in case those — come up to take a look at us." He considered. "Close up on 'X' gun, go into local control, fire a spread of starshell through this arc" – he indicated the port bow and beam – "and let fly if you see anything. I'll leave the details to you."

"Aye, aye, sir."

Guns clumped off down the ladder on his way aft. It was one of his idiosyncrasies to wear street-cleaner's thigh boots with thick wooden soles, and his movments up and down the ship were easily traceable, earning indeed a good deal of fluent abuse from people who were trying to get to sleep below. As the heavy footfalls receded aft, the Captain stood up and leant over the port side of the bridge, staring down at the tumbling water. There was nothing to be seen of the main area of the damage, which was hidden by the outward flare of the bows; but the ship had less freedom of movement now – she was deeper, more solidly settled in the water. They must have taken tons of it in the ripped-up spaces forward: the fo'c'sle covering them looked like a slowly crumbling ruin. It was about time the First Lieutenant came through with his report. If they had to –

"What's that?" he asked suddenly.

A thin voice was calling, "Bridge, Bridge," from one of the voice-pipes. He bent down to the row nearest to him, but from none of them did the voice issue clearly. Behind him the midshipman was conducting the same search on his side. The voice went on calling, "Bridge, Bridge, Bridge," in a patient monotone. It was the Captain's servant, Bridger, who finally traced it – a voice-pipe low down on the deck, its anti-spray cover still clipped on.

The man bent down to it and snapped back the cover. "Bridge here."

A single murmured sentence answered him. Bridger looked up to the Captain. "It's the Engineer Officer, sir, speaking from the galley flat."

The Captain bent down. A waft of bitter fume-laden air met his nostrils. "Yes, Chief?"

"I'm afraid Number One got caught by that last bulkhead, sir."

"What happened? I heard it go a little while back."

"We thought it would hold, sir." The level voice, coming from the heart of the ruined fo'c'sle, had an apologetic note, as if the speaker, even in that shambles, had had the cool honesty to convict himself of an error of judgment. "It did look like holding for a bit, too. Number One was with the damage control party, between the seamen's mess-deck and the bathrooms. They'd shut the water-tight door behind them, and were just going to shore up, when the forrard bulkhead went." Chief paused. "You know what it's like, sir. We can't get at them without opening up."

"Can't do that now, Chief."

"No, sir."

"Can you hear anything?"

"Not now."

"How many were there with the First Lieutenant?"

"Fourteen, sir. Mostly stokers." There was another pause. "I took charge down here, sir. We're shoring up the next one."

13

"What do you think of it?"

"Not too good. It's badly strained already, and leaking down one seam." There was, now, a slightly sharpened note in the voice travelling up from below. "There's hell of a mess down here, sir. And if this one goes, that'll mean the whole lot."

"Yes, I know." The Captain thought quickly, while overhead and to port the sea was suddenly lit up by a cold yellow glare – the first spread of star-shell, four slowly dropping lights shadowing their spinning parachutes against the cloud overhead. Very pretty. . . . The news from below could hardly have been worse: it added up to fully a third of the ship flooded, all the forward mess-decks cut off, fourteen men drowned at one stroke, and God knows how many more caught by the original explosion. "Look here, Chief. I don't want any more men lost like that. You must use your own judgment about getting out in a hurry. See how the shoring up goes, and let me know as soon as you can if you think it'll hold."

"All right, sir."

"We're firing star-shell at the moment, to see if there's anything on the surface. 'X' gun may be firing independently, any time from now on."

"All right, sir."

"Take care of yourself, Chief."

He could almost hear the other man smiling at what was, from the Captain, an unexpected remark. "I'll do that, sir."

The voice-pipe went dead. Walking back to his chair, the Captain allowed himself a moment of profound depression and regret. The First Lieutenant gone. A good kid, doing his first big job in the Navy and tremendously keen to do it properly. With a young wife, too – the three of them had had dinner at the Adelphi in Liverpool, not two weeks ago. There was a bad letter to be written there, later on. And the loss might make a deal of difference to the next few hours.

The star-shell soared and dropped again. Sitting in his

14

chair, waiting for Chief's report, listening to the green seas slapping and thumping against the side as *Marlborough* sagged downwind in the wave troughs with a new, ugly motion, he was under no illusions as to what the next few hours might bring, and the chances of that "bad letter" ever being written by himself. But that was not what he was now concentrating on: that was not in the mapped-out programme. . . . This was the moment for which the Navy had long been preparing him: for years his training and experience had had this precise occasion in view; that was why he was a commander, and the Captain of *Marlborough* when she was hit. Taking charge, gauging chances, foreseeing the next eventuality and if necessary forestalling it – none of it could take him by surprise, any more than could the chapter headings of a favourite book. When the moment had arrived he had recognized it instantly, and the sequence of his behaviour had lain before him like a familiar pattern, of which he now had to take the tenth or twentieth tracing. He had not been torpedoed before, but no matter: tucked away in his mind and brain there had always been a picture of a torpedoed ship, and of himself as, necessarily, the key figure in this picture. Now that the curtain was drawn, and the image became the reality, he simply had to play his assigned part with as much intelligence, skill, and endurance as he could muster. The loss of the First Lieutenant and over half the ship's company already was a bitter stroke, both personally and professionally: it would return in full force later; but for the moment it was only a debit item which had to be fitted into the evolving picture.

"Signalman!"

"Sir."

"Get the Gunnery Officer on the quarter-deck telephone."

A pause. More star-shell, reflected on a waste of cold tumbling water, dropped slowly till they were drowned in darkness again. There wasn't really much point in going on with the illumination now: the U-boat probably thought they had other ships in company ready to counter-attack, and had sheered off. She had, indeed, cause to be satisfied, without pursuing the advantage further. . . .

"Gunnery Officer on the telephone, sir."

The Captain took the proffered receiver. "Guns?"

"Yes, sir?"

"I'm afraid Number One has been killed. I want you to take over."

"Oh – all right, sir."

Hearing the shocked surprise in his voice, the Captain remembered that the two of them had been very good friends. But that, again, was something to be considered later: only the bald announcement was part of the present pattern. He continued:

"I think you had better stay aft, as if we were still at full action stations. Chief is in charge of damage control forrard. Stop star-shelling now – I take it you've seen nothing."

"Nothing, sir."

"Right. You'd better have all the depth-charges set to safe – in fact have the primers withdrawn and dropped over the side. And I want someone to have a look at our draught-marks aft."

"I've just had them checked, sir. There's nothing to go on, I'm afraid: they're right clear of the water."

"Are the screws out of the water too?"

"Can't see in this light, sir. The top blades, probably."

"Right. Get going on those depth-charges."

The Captain handed back the receiver, at the same time saying to the signalman: "Get your confidential books in the weighted bags ready for ditching. And tell the W/T office to do the same."

"Aye, aye, sir."

"Bridger."

"Yes, sir."

"Go down and get the black hold-all, and come back here."

"Aye, aye, sir." Bridger's tough, unemotional expression did not alter, but his shoulders stiffened instinctively. He

16

knew what the order meant. The black hold-all was, in his own phrase, the scram-bag: it held a bottle of brandy, morphine ampoules, a first-aid kit, some warm clothes, and a few personal papers. It had been tucked away in a corner of the skipper's cabin for nearly three years. It was as good as a ticket over the side. They'd start swimming any moment now.

The report from aft about the draught-marks had certainly quickened the tempo a little: his orders to Bridger and to the signalman were an endorsement of this. But quick tempo or slow, there was still the same number of things to be fitted into the available time, the same number of lines in the pattern to be traced. Now, in the darkness, as he turned to the next task, very little noise or movement reached the bridge from anywhere in the ship: only a sound of hammering from deep below (the damage control party busy on their shoring job), a voice calling, "Take a turn, there", as the whaler was swung out, the endless thump and surge of the waves driving downwind – only these were counter-distractions in the core of heart and brain which the bridge had now become. Indeed, the Captain was much less conscious of these than of the heavy breathing of Adams, the Chief Bosun's Mate, who stood by his elbow as close and attentive as a spaniel at the butts. Adams had heard the order to Bridger, and had guessed what it meant: it had aroused, not his curiosity – matters were past such a faint reaction as curiosity now – but the same tough determination as the Captain himself had felt. They were both men of the same stamp: seamen first, human beings afterwards; the kind of men whom *Marlborough*, in her extremity, most needed and most deserved.

"Mid!"

"Yes, sir?"

"Go along to the sick bay, and –"

One of the voice-pipe bells rang sharply. The midshipman listened for a moment, and then said: "That's the doctor now, sir."

17

The Captain bent down. "Yes, doc?"

"I want to report about casualties, sir."

"What's the position?"

"I've got nine down here, sir. Burns, mostly. One stoker with a broken arm. I got a stretcher-party organized, and brought them down aft."

"I was hoping there'd be more."

"Afraid not, sir."

"Do you need any hands to help you?"

"No, I'm all right, sir. I've got one sick-berth attendant – Jamieson was caught forrard, I'm afraid – and the leading steward is giving me a hand."

"Very well. But you'll have to start moving them, I'm afraid. Get them on the upper deck, on the lee side. Ask Guns to lend you some hands from 'X' gun."

There was a pause. Then the doctor's voice came through again, more hesitantly. "They shouldn't really be moved sir, unless –"

"That's what I meant. You understand?"

"Yes, sir."

"Send the walking cases up to the boat deck, and see to the others yourself. Divide them up between the two boats. I'll leave the details to you."

"Very well, sir."

Thank God for a good doctor, anyway – as bored, cynical, and impatient as most naval doctors were for three-quarters of their time, with nothing to do but treat warts and censor the mail, and then, on an occasion like this, summoning all the resource and skill that had been kept idle, and throwing them instantly into the breach. The doctor was going to be an asset during the next few hours. So, indeed, was every officer and man left to the ship.

He would have liked to muster the remaining hands, to see how many the explosion had caught and how many he had left to work with; but that would disrupt things too much, at a time when there must be no halting in the desperate race to save the ship, or, at least, as many of the re-

18

maining lives as possible. But as he sat back in his chair, waiting for what he was now almost sure must happen, the Captain reviewed his officers one by one, swiftly tabulating their work at this moment, speculating whether they could be better employed. Number One was gone, of course. Guns in charge aft. Haines in the wireless office (time he was back, incidentally). Chief working the damage control party – that was technically his responsibility anyway, and here was a first-class Chief E.R.A. in charge the engine-room. The Mid here on the bridge. The doctor with his hands full in the sick bay. Merrett – the Captain frowned suddenly. Where the devil was Merret? He'd forgotten all about him – and indeed it was easy to overlook the shy, newly-joined sub who had startled the wardroom on his first night by remarking: "My father went to prison as a conscientious objector during the last war, so he's rather ashamed of me in this one," but had then relapsed into the negative, colourless attitude which seemed natural to him. Where had he got to now?

The Captain repeated the query aloud to the midshipman.

"I haven't seen him at all, sir," the latter answered. "He was in the wardroom when I came on watch. Shall I call them up?"

"Yes, do."

After a moment at one of the voice pipes, the midshipman came through with the answer: "He was there a moment ago, sir. They think he's on the upper deck somewhere."

"Send one of the bosun's mates to –" The Captain paused. No, that might not be a good move. "See if you can find him, Mid, and ask him to come up here."

When the midshipman had left the bridge the Captain frowned again. Why in God's name had Merrett been in the wardroom a moment ago? What was he doing there at a time like this? Any sort of alarm or crisis meant that officers went to their action stations automatically: Merrett should have gone first to "A" gun, where he was in charge, and then, as that was out of action, up to the bridge for orders. Now all that was known of him was that he had been in the ward-

19

room, right aft. The Captain hoped there was a good explanation, not the attack of nerves or the breakdown of self-control he had been guessing at when he sent the midshipman to find Merrett. He could understand such a thing happening – the boy was barely twenty, and this was his first ship – but they just could not afford it now.

His guess had been right: so much became obvious as soon as Merrett was standing in front of him. Even in the darkness, with the exact expression on his face blurred and shadowed, he seemed to manifest an almost exalted state of terror. The movements of foot and hand, the twitching shoulders, the slight, uncontrolled chattering of the teeth, the shine of sweat on the forehead – all were here a distillation of fear which would, in full daylight, have been horrible to look at. So that was it. . . . For a moment the Captain hesitated, trying to balance their present crucial danger, and his own controlled reaction to it, against the almost unknown feelings of a boy, a landsman-turned-sailor, confronted with the same ordeal; but then the over-riding necessity of everyone on board doing his utmost, swept away any readiness to make allowances for failure in this respect. The details, the pros and cons, the fine-drawn questions could wait; nothing but one hundred per cent effectiveness would suffice now, and that was what he must re-establish.

"Where have you been?" he asked curtly.

Merrett swallowed, looked across the shattered fo'c'sle to the wild sea, and drew no comfort or reassurance from it. He said, in a dry, strained voice. "I'm sorry, sir. I didn't know what to do, exactly."

"Then you should come and ask me. Do you expect me to come and tell you?" It was rough: it was, in Merrett's present state, brutally so but it was clearly dictated by the situation they were in. "Where were you when we were hit?"

"I'd just gone up to 'A' gun, sir."

"Must have shaken you up a bit." So much allowance, and no more, did the Captain make for what he could only guess at now – youth, uncertainty, self-distrust, perhaps an inherited horror of violence. "But I don't want to have to send for individual officers at a time like this. You understand?"

"Yes, sir." It was a whisper, almost a sigh. He'd been drinking whisky, too, the Captain thought. Well, that didn't matter as long as it had the right result; and this, and the tonic effect of giving him a definite job to do, could be put to the test now.

"Very well. . . . There's something I want you to do," he went on, changing his tone in such a way as to indicate clearly that a fresh start could now be made. "Go down to the boat-deck and see how they're getting on with the boats. They're to be swung out ready for lowering, and all the rafts cleared away as well. You'd better check up on the boats' crew, too: remember we've only got this one watch of seaman to play with so far as we know. You'll want a coxswain, a stoker, and a bowman told off for the motor-boat, and a coxswain and a bowman for the whaler. Got that?"

"Yes, sir."

It seemed that he had: already he was making some attempt to take a grip on his body, and his voice was more under control. Watching him turn and make for the bridge-ladder, the Captain felt ready to bet that he would make a good job of it. The few minutes had not been wasted.

But they had been no more than an odd, irrelevant delay in the main flow of the current; and now, in quick succession, as if to re-establish the ordained pace of disaster, three more stages came and were passed. Bridger appeared with the black hold-all, and with something else which he handed to the Captain almost furtively. "Better have this, sir," he said, as the Captain's hand closed over it. It was his safety-light, which he had forgotten to clip to his life-jacket – one of the small watertight bulb-and-battery sets which were meant to be plugged in and switched on when in the water. The Captain took it with a grunt and fastened it on, his eyes turning instinctively to the black expanse of water washing

21

and swirling round them. Yes, better have the light ready. . . .

Then Haines came up the ladder from below, starting to speak almost before he was on the bridge:

"I'm afraid they were right about the W/T set, sir," he began. "It's finished. And the main switchboard has blown, too. Even if we got the dynamo back on the board –"

"All right, Pilot," said the Captain suddenly. And then, to the figure he had discerned at the top of the ladder, the third messenger of evil, he said, "Yes, Chief?"

The engineer officer did not speak until he was standing close by the Captain, but there was no hesitation about his opening words. "I don't think it's any good, sir." He spoke with a clipped intensity, which did not disguise any exhaustion of spirit. "That bulkhead – it might go any minute, and she'll probably break in two when it happens. That means a lot more men caught, sir."

"You've shored up completely?"

"Yes, sir. But the space is too big, and the bulkhead was warped too much before we got the shores to it. It's working badly already. I can't see it holding more than another hour, if that."

"It's the last one worth shoring," said the Captain, almost to himself.

"Yes, sir." Chief hesitated. "I've still seven or eight hands down in the engine-room, I'd like to get them out in good time. Is that all right, sir?"

Chief was looking at him. They were all looking at him – Haines, the midshipman, the signalman, Adams, the lookouts, the hard-breathing Bridger – all waiting for the one plain order which they now knew must come. Until that moment he had been refusing to look squarely at this order as it drew nearer and nearer: he could not believe that his loved ship must be given up, and even now, as he hesitated, and the men round him wondered, the idea still had no sort of reality about it. For this man on whom they all relied, this man to whom they attributed no feelings or qualities apart from the skill and forethought of seamanship, was not quite

22

the stock figure, the thirty-eight-year-old R.N. commander, that they took him to be.

True, he fitted the normal mould well enough. He had always done so, from Dartmouth onwards, and the progress from midshipman to commander had followed its appointed course – twenty years of naval routine in which a mistake, a stepping-out-of-line would have denied him his present rank. He never had stepped out of line; he had been, and still was, normal about everything except this ship; but for her he had a special feeling, a romantic conception, which would have astounded the men waiting round him. It was not the Navy, or his high sense of duty, or the fact that he commanded her, which had given him this feeling: it was love.

The old *Marlborough*. . . . The Captain was not married, and if he had been it might not have made any difference: he was profoundly and exclusively in love with this ship, and the passion, fed especially on the dangers and ordeals of the past three war-years, left no room for a rival. It had started in 1926 when she was brand new and he had commissioned her: it had been his first job as First Lieutenant, and his proudest so far. She had been the very latest in ships then – a new sloop, Clyde-built, twin turbines, two four-inch guns (the twin mountings came later), and a host of gadgets and items of novel equipment which were sharp on the palate. . . . There had been other ships, of course, in the sixteen years between; his first command had been a river gun-boat, his second a destroyer: but he had never forgotten *Marlborough*. He had kept an eye on her all the time, checking her movements as she transferred from the Home Fleet to the Mediterranean, thence to the China Station, then home again: looking up her officers in the Navy List and wondering if they were taking proper care of her: making a special trip up to Rosyth on one of his leaves, to have another look at her; and when, at the outbreak of war, he had been given command of her, it had been like coming home again, to somebody dearly loved who was not yet past the honeymoon stage.

She was not, in point of fact, much of a command for a commander, even as the senior ship of an escort group, and he could have done better if he had wished. But he did not wish. Old-fashioned she might be, battered with much hard driving, none too comfortable, at least three knots slower than the job really demanded; but she could still show her teeth and she still ran as sweet as a sewing machine, and the last three years had been the happiest of his career. He was intensely jealous of her efficiency when contrasted with more up-to-date ships, and he went to endless trouble over this, intriguing for the fitting of new equipment "for experimental purposes", demanding the replacement of officers or key-ratings if any weak point in the team began to show itself. In three years of North Atlantic convoy work he had spared neither himself not his ship's company any of the intense strain which the job imposed; but *Marlborough* he had nursed continuously, so that the prodigious record of hours steamed and miles covered had cost the minimum of wear.

He knew her from end to end, not only with the efficient "technical" eye of the man who had watched the last five months of her building, but with an added, intimate regard for every part of her, a loving admiration, an eye tenderly blind to her short-comings.

Now she was going. No wonder he could not phrase that final order, no wonder he stared back almost angrily at the Chief, delaying what he knew must happen, waiting for the miracle to forestall it.

Up to the bridge came a new, curious noise. It came from deep within the fo'c'sle, a blend of thud and iron clang which coincided with the ship's rolling. Something very solid must have broken adrift down there, either through the shock or the unusual level of their trim, and was now washing to and fro out of control. Chief, his face puckered, tried to place it: it might have been any one of a dozen bits of heavy equipment in the forward store. The big portable pump, most likely. There must be the hell of a mess down there. Men and

24

gear smashing up together – it hardly bore thinking of. And the noise was unnerving; it sounded like the toll of a bell, half sunk, tied to a wreck and washing with the tide. A damned sight too appropriate.

The Captain said suddenly: "I'll come down and look at that bulkhead, Chief. Haines, take over here." He turned to Adams. "You come with me. Bring one of the quarter-masters, too."

There might be some piping to do in a hurry.

The journey down, deck by deck, had the same element of compulsion in it as, in a nightmare, distinguishes the random lunatic journey which can only lead to some inescapable horror at its end. The boat-deck was crowded: two loaded stretchers lay near the whaler, the figures on them not more than vague impressions of pain in the the gloom: Merrett was directing the unlashing of a raft near by: on the lee side of the funnel a dozen hands, staring out at the water, were singing "Home on the Range", a low-pitched chorus. The small party – Captain, Chief, Adams, the quartermaster – made their way aft, past the figures grouped round "X" gun, and down another ladder. At the iron-deck level, a few feet from the water, all was deserted. "I sent the damage control party up, as soon as we'd finished, sir," the Chief said, as he stepped through the canvas screen into the alley-way leading forward. "There was nothing else for them to do."

Under cover now, the four of them moved along the rock-ing passage: Chief's torch picking out the way, flicking from side to side of the hollow tunnel against which the water was already lapping. Under their stumbling scraping feet the slope led fatally downwards. The clanging toll seemed to advance to meet them. They passed the entrance to the en-gine-room: just within, feet straddled on the grating, stood a young stoker, the link with the outside world in case the bridge voice-pipe failed. To him, as they passed, the Chief said, "No orders yet. I'll be coming back in a minute," and the stoker drew back into the shadows to pass the message on. Then they came to a closed water-tight door, and this they eased slowly open, a clip at a time, so that any pressure of water within would show immediately. But it was still dry . . . the door swung back, and they stepped inside the last watertight space that lay between floating and sinking.

It was dimly lit, by two battery lanterns clipped to overhead brackets: the light struck down on a tangle of joists and beams, heel-pieces, wedges, cross-battens – the work of the damage control party. The deck was wet underfoot, and as *Marlborough* rolled some inches of dirty water slopped from side to side, carrying with it a scummy flotsam of caps, boots and ditty-boxes. The Captain switched on his torch, ducked under a transverse beam and stepped up close to the bulkhead. It was, as Chief had said, in bad shape; bulging towards him, strained and leaking all down one seam, responding to the ship's movements with long-drawn-out, harsh creaking. For a single moment, as he watched it, he seemed to be looking through into the space beyond, where Number One and his fourteen damage control hands had been caught, the forbidden picture – forbidden in the strict scheme of his captaincy – giving place to another one, conjured up in its turn by the clanging which now sounded desperately loud and clear; the three flooded mess-decks underneath his feet, the sealed-off shambles of the explosion area. Then his mind swung back, guiltily, to the only part of it that mattered now, the shored-up section he was standing in, and he nodded to himself as he glanced round it once more. It confirmed what he had been expecting but had only now faced fairly and squarely: Chief had done a good job, but it just wasn't good enough.

He turned quickly. "All right, Chief. Bring your engine-room party out on to the upper deck. Adams! Pipe 'Hands to stations for –' "

The words "Abandon ship" were cut off by a violent explosion above their heads.

For a moment the noise was so puzzling that he could not assign it to anything: it was just an interruption, almost supernatural which had stopped him finishing that hated

26

sentence. Then another piece of the pattern clicked into place, and he said: "That was a shell, by God!" and made swiftly for the doorway.

Outside, he called back over his shoulder, "Chief – see to the door again!" and then started to run. His footsteps rang in the confined space: he heard Adams following close behind him down the passage way, the noise echoing and clattering all round him, urging him on. Reaching the open air at last was like escaping from a nightmare into a sweating wakefulness which must somehow be instantly co-ordinated and controlled. As he went up the ladder to the boat-deck there was a brilliant flash and another explosion up on the bridge, followed by the sharp reek of the shellburst. Damned good shooting from somewhere . . . something shot past his head and spun into a ventilator with a loud clang. He began to run again, brushing close by a figure making for "X" gun shouting, "Close up again! load star-shell!" Guns, at least, had his part of it under control.

He passed the space between the two boats. It was here, he saw, that the first shell had struck: the motor-boat was damaged, one of the stretchers was overturned, and there were three separate groups of men bending over figures stretched out on deck. He wanted to stop and find out how bad the damage was, and, especially, how many men had been killed or hurt, but he could not: the bridge called him, and had the prior claim.

It was while he was climbing quickly up the ladder that he realized that the moon had now risen, low in the sky, and that *Marlborough* must be clearly silhouetted against the horizon. If no one on the upper deck had seen the flash of the submarine's firing, the moon ought to give them a line on her position. Guns would probably work that out for himself. But it would be better to make sure.

Now he was at the top of the ladder, his eyes grown accustomed to the gloom, his nostrils assailed by the acrid stink of the explosion. The shell he had seen land when he first came out on deck had caught the bridge fair and square, going through one wing and exploding against the chart-house. Only two men were still on their feet—the signalman and one of the look-outs: the other look-out was lying, head-less, against his machine-gun mounting. Adams, at his shoulder, drew in his breath sharply at the sight, but the Captain's eyes had already moved farther on, to where three other figures – who must be Haines, the midshipman, and the messenger – had fallen in a curiously theatrical grouping round the compass platform. The light there was too dim to show any details: the dark shambles could only be guessed at. But one of the figures was still moving. It was the mid-shipman, clinging to a voice-pipe and trying to hoist him-self upright.

He said quickly, "Lie still, Mid," and then: "Signalman, give me the hailer," and lastly, to Adams: "Do what you can for them." He caught sight of the young, shocked face of the other look-out staring at him, and called sharply: "Don't look inboard. Watch your proper arc. Use your glasses." Then he switched on the microphone, and spoke into it:

"X gun, X gun – illuminate away from the moon – illu-minate away from the moon." He paused, then continued: "Doctor or sick-berth attendant report to the bridge now – doctor or sick-berth attendant."

Pity had inclined him to put the last order first: the instinct of command has told him otherwise. But almost before he stopped speaking, the sharp crack of "X" gun came from aft, and the star-shell soared. Guns had the same idea as himself.

Adams, who was kneeling down and working away at a rough tourniquet, said over his shoulder:

"Shall I carry on with that pipe, sir?"

"No. Wait."

The U-boat coming to the surface had altered everything. The ship was now only a platform for "X" gun, and not to be abandoned while "X" gun still had work to do.

As the star-shell burst and hung, lighting up the grey moving sea, the captain raised his glasses and swept the arc of water that lay on their beam. Almost immediately he saw the U-boat, stopped on the surface, broadside on to them and not more than a mile away. Before he had time to speak over the hailer, or give any warning, there was a noise from aft as Guns shouted a fresh order and then things happened very quickly.

"X" gun roared. A spout of water, luminous under the star-shell, leapt upwards, just beyond the U-boat and dead in line – a superb sighting shot, considering the suddenness of this new crisis. There was a pause, while the Captain's mind raced over the two possibilities now open – that the U-boat, guessing she had only a badly crippled ship to deal with, would fight it out on the surface, or that she would submerge to periscope depth and fire another torpedo. Then came the next shot, to settle all his doubts.

It came from both ships, and it was almost farcically conclusive. The flash of both guns was instantaneous. The U-boat's shell exploded aft, right on "X" gun, ripping the whole platform to pieces; but from the U-boat herself a brilliant orange flash spurted suddenly, to be succeeded by the crump of an explosion. Then she disappeared completely.

"X" gun, mortally wounded itself, had made its last shot a mortal one for the enemy.

Silence now over all the ship, save for a faint moaning from aft. The Captain reached for the hailer, and then paused. No point in saying anything at this moment: they would be looking after "X" gun's crew, what was left of them, and there was no more enemy to deal with. He listened for a moment to Adams's heavy breathing as he bent over the midshipman, and then turned as a figure showed itself at the top of the bridge-ladder.

"Captain, sir."

"What is it?"

"S.B.A., sir. The doctor's gone aft to the gun."

"All right. Bear a hand here. Who's that behind you?"

"It's me, sir," said Bridger's voice from the top of the ladder. "I was helping the S.B.A."

"Were you up here when the second shell landed?"

"No, sir – just missed it." Bridger sounded competent and unsurprised, as if he had arranged the thing that way. "I went down to give them a hand when the first one hit the boat-deck, sir."

"How much damage down there?"

"Killed three of the lads, sir." The sick-berth attendant's voice breaking in was strained and rather uneven. "Mr. Merrett's gone, too. He was just by the motor-boat."

Another officer lost. Guns had probably been killed, too. That meant – the Captain checked suddenly, running over the list in his mind. Number One, caught by that bulkhead. Haines and the midshipman finished up here; Merrett gone, dying typically in a quiet corner, escaping his notice. Guns almost certainly killed at "X" gun. That meant that there were no executive officers left at all: only Chief and the doctor. If they didn't abandon ship – if somehow they got her going again – it would be an almost impossible job, single-handed. . . . He put the thought on one side for the moment, and said to the sick-berth attendant:

"Take over from Petty Officer Adams. Have a look at the others first, and then get the midshipman aft to the ward-room."

He waited again, as the man got to work. The heavy clanging from below, which had stopped momentarily when the gun was fired, now started once more. Presently the doctor came up to the bridge, to report what he had been expecting to hear – that Guns, and the whole crew of seven, had been killed by the last shot from the U-boat. Even though he had been prepared for it, it was impossible to hear the news with indifference. But for some reason it confirmed a thought which had been growing in his mind, ever since the U-boat had been sunk. They were on their own now, and the only danger was from the sea. His loved *Marlborough* had survived so much, had produced such a brilliant last-minute counterstroke, that he could not leave her now. Reason told him to carry on with the order he had given

30

down below, but reason seemed to have had no part in the last few minutes: something else, some product of heart and instinct, seemed to have taken control of them all. That last shot of "X" gun had been a miracle. Suppose there were more miracles on the way?

Adams, straightening up as the sick-berth attendant took over, once again tried, respectfully, to recall the critical moment to him:

"Carry on with that pipe, sir?"

"No." The Captain, divining the uncertainty in the man's mind, smiled in the darkness. "No, Adams, I hadn't forgotten. But we'll wait till daylight."

CHAPTER 2

THERE were fourteen hours till daylight: fourteen hours to review that decision, to ascribe it correctly either to emotion or to a reasonable assessment of chance, and to foresee the outcome. What struck the Captain most strongly about it was the unprofessional aspect of what he had done. Down there in the shored up fo'c'sle, he had made a precise, technical examination of the damage and the repairs to it, and come to a clear decision: if the U-boat's shell had not hit them, and interrupted the order, they would now be sitting in the boats, lying off in the darkness and waiting for *Marlborough* to go down. But something had intervened: not simply the absolute necessity of fighting the U-boat as long as possible, not even second thoughts on their chances of keeping the ship afloat, but something stronger still. It was so long since the Captain had changed his mind about any personal or professional decision that he hardly knew how to analyse it. But certainly the change of mind was there.

He could find excuses for it now, though not very adequate ones. Daylight would give them more chance to survey the damage properly. (But he had done that already.) With the motor-boat wrecked by the first shell-burst, there were not enough boats for the crew to take to. (But some of them would always have to use rafts anyway, and if *Marlborough* sank they would have no choice in the matter.) They had a number of badly wounded men on board who must be sheltered for as long as possible, if they were not to die of neglect or exposure. (But they certainly stood more chance of surviving an orderly abandonment of the ship, rather than a last minute emergency retreat.) No, none of these ideas had really any part in it. It boiled down to nothing more precise than a surge of feeling which had attacked him as soon as the

U-boat was sunk: a foolish emotional idea, product both of the past years and of this last tremendous stroke, that after *Marlborough* had done so much for them they could not leave her to die. It wasn't an explanation which would look well in the Report of Proceedings; but it was as near the truth as he could phrase it.

The answer would come with daylight, anyway: till then he must wait. If the bulkhead held, and the weather moderated, and Chief was able to get things going again (that main switchboard would have to be rewired, for a start), then they might be able to do something: creep southwards, perhaps, till they were athwart the main convoy route and could get help. It was the longest chance he had ever taken: sitting there in his chair up on the bridge, brooding in the darkness, he tried to visualize its successive stages. Funnier things had happened at sea. . . . But the final picture, the one that remained with him all that night, was of a ship – his ship – drawing thirty-two feet forward and nothing aft, drifting helplessly downwind with little prospect of surviving till daylight.

No one ashore knew anything about them, and no one would start worrying for at least three days.

With the ship, ignoring and somehow isolating itself against this preposterous weight of odds, there was much to do; and with no officers to call on except the doctor, who was busy with casualties, and the Chief, whom he left to make a start in the engine room, the Captain set to work to organize it himself. He kept Bridger by him, to relay orders, and a signalman, in case something unexpected happened (there was a faint chance of an aircraft on passage being in their area, and within signalling distance): Adams was installed a virtual First Lieutenant; and from his nucleus the control and routine of the ship was set in motion again.

The bulkhead he could do nothing about: Chief set to work on the main switchboard, the first step towards raising steam again, and the leading telegraphist was working on the wireless transmitter; the boats and rafts were left in instant readiness, and the more severe casualties taken back under cover again. (A hard decision, this; but to keep them on the upper deck in this bitter weather was a degree nearer killing them than running the risk of trapping them below.) Among the casualties was the midshipman, still alive after a cruel lacerated wound in the chest and now in the sick bay waiting for a blood transfusion. The bodies of the other three who had been killed on the bridge – Haines, the look-out, and the bridge messenger – had been taken aft to the quarter-deck, to join the rest, from "X" gun's crew and the party on the boat-deck, awaiting burial.

Then, after a spell of cleaning up, which included the chaos of loose gear and ammunition round "A" gun, which had been directly over the explosion, the Captain told Adams to muster what was left of the ship's company and report the numbers. He was still in his chair on the bridge, sipping a mug of cocoa, which Bridger had cooked up in the wardroom pantry, when Adams came up with his report, and he listened to the details with an attention which he tried to rid of all personal feeling. These crude figures, which Adams, bending over the chart-table light, was reading out, were men, some of them well known and liked, some of them ship-mates of two and three years' standing, all of them sailors; but from now on they must only be numbers, only losses on a chart of activity and endurance. The dead were not to be sailors any more: just "missing potential", "negative assets" – some damned phrase like that.

Adams said: "I've written it all down, sir, as well as I could." He had, in his voice, the same matter-of-fact imper-sonal tone as the Captain would have used: the words "as well as I could" might have referred to some trifling clerical inconvenience instead of the difficulty of sorting out the living, the dead, and the dying in the pitch darkness. "There's the ones we know about, first. There's three officers and twelve ratings killed – that's the Gunnery Officer, Lieutenant Haines, and Mr. Merrett, and the gun's crew and the ones on the boat-deck and the two up here. The surgeon-lieutenant has one officer and sixteen men in the sick bay. We'll have to count most of them out, I'm afraid, sir. Nine of them were out of the fo'c'sle. Then there's" – he paused – "one officer and seventy-four men missing." He stopped again, expecting the Captain to say something, but as no word came from the dark figure in the chair he went on: "Then what we've got left, sir. There's yourself, and the surgeon-lieutenant, and the engineer – that's three officers, and twenty-eight men out of the Red Watch, the one that was on duty."

"Twenty-eight. Is that all?"

"That's all, sir. They lost seven seamen at "X" gun, three by the boats, and two here. Then there's seven of them down in the sick bay. That's forty-seven altogether."

"How are the twenty-eight made up? How many seamen have we?"

Adams straightened up and turned round from the table. This part of it he evidently knew by heart. "There's myself, sir, and Leading Seaman Tapper, and seven A.B.s: the quartermaster and the bosun's mate, that were in the wheel-house: and Bridger. That's twelve. Then there's the hands who were on watch in the W/T office: the leading tel. and two others, and two coders. That makes seventeen altogether. The signalman up here, eighteen. The S.B.A., nineteen. The leading steward, twenty."

"Any other stewards?"

"No, sir."

It didn't matter, thought the Captain: no officers, either.

"The rest were all engine-room branch, sir," Adams went on. "Eight of them altogether."

"How are they made up?"

"It's pretty good, sir, as far as experience goes. The Chief E.R.A. and one of the younger ones, and a stoker petty officer and five stokers. If it was just one watch they'd be all right. But of course there's no reliefs for them, and they'll have to be split into two watches if it comes to steaming." Adams paused, on the verge of a question, but the Captain, seeing it coming, interrupted him. He didn't yet feel ready to discuss their chances of getting under way again.

"Just give me those figures again, Adams," he said, "as I say the headings. Let's have the fit men first."

Adams bent down to the light once more. "Yourself and two officers and twenty-eight men, sir."

"Killed and wounded?"

Adams added quickly: "Four officers and twenty-eight."

"And missing, the First Lieutenant and seventy-four." He had no need to be reminded of the item: that "seventy-four" would stay with him always. Not counting the accident to Number One's damage control party, there must have been sixty men killed or cut off by the first explosion. All of them still there, deep down underneath his feet. Twenty-eight left out of a hundred and thirty. Whatever he was able to do with the *Marlborough* now, the weight of those figures could never be lightened.

"Will I make some more cocoa, sir?" said Bridger suddenly. He had been waiting in silence all this time, standing behind the Captain's chair. The numbers and details which Adams had produced, even though they concerned Bridger's own messmates, were real to him only so far as they affected the Captain: this moment, he judged instinctively, was the worst so far, and he tried to dissipate it in the only way open to him.

The Captain's figure, which had been hunched deep in the chair, straightened suddenly. He shook himself. The cold air was stiffening his legs, and he stood up. "No, thanks, Bridger," he answered. "I'm going to turn in, in a minute. Bring up my sleeping-bag and a pillow, and I'll sleep in the asdic hut."

"Aye, aye, sir." Bridger clumped off at a solid workmanlike pace, his heavy sea-boots ringing their way down the ladder. The Captain turned to Adams again. "We'd better work out a routine for the time between now and daylight," he said briskly. "We can leave the engine-room out of it for the moment: they're busy enough. You'd better arrange the seamen in two watches: the telegraphists and coders can work with them, except for the leading tel. – he can stay on the set. Send half the hands off watch now: they can sleep in the wardroom alleyway or on the upper deck, whichever they prefer. The rest can carry on with cleaning up."

"The doctor may want some help down there, sir."

"Yes – see about that too. . . . Keep two look-outs on the upper deck for the rest of tonight: tell them they're listening for aircraft as well. We'll show an Aldis lamp if we hear anything, and chance it being hostile. You'd better put the signalman up here, with those instructions; and pick out the most intelligent coder, and have him work watch-and-watch with the signalman. That's about all, I think. See that I'm called if anything happens."

"Do you want a hand to watch that bulkhead, sir?"

"No. The engine-room will cover that: they're nearest. About meals. . . ." The Captain scratched his chin. "We'll just have to do our best with the wardroom pantry. There were some dry provisions in the after store, weren't there?"

"Corned beef and biscuits, sir, and some tinned milk, I think. And there's plenty of tea. We'll not go short."

"Right. . . . That'll do for tonight, then. I'll see what things are like in the morning: there'll be plenty of squaring up to do. You'll have to get those bodies sewn up, too. If we do get under way again," the Captain tried and failed, to say this in a normal voice, "you'll have to work out a scheme of guns' crews and look-outs and quartermasters."

"Better take the wheel myself, sir."

The Captain smiled. "It won't exactly be fleet manœuvres, Adams."

The expected question came at last. "How much chance have we got, sir?"

"Hard to say." He answered it as unemotionally as he could. "You saw the state that bulkhead was in. It might go any time, or it might hold indefinitely. But even very slow headway would make a big difference to the strain on it, unless the bows stay rigid where they are, and take most of the weight. Almost everything depends on the weather."

As he said this, the arrangements he had been making with Adams receded into the background, and he became aware of the ship again, and of her sluggish motion under his feet. She was quieter now, certainly: no shock or grinding from below, no advertisement of distress. But he could feel, as if it were going on inside his own body, the strain on the whole ship, the anguish of that slow cumbersome roll down-wind. Earlier she had seemed to be dying: this now was the rallying process, infinitely painful both to endure and to watch. Long after Adams had left the bridge, the Captain still stood there, suffering all that the ship suffered, aware that the only effective anaesthetic was death.

It was an idea which at any other time he would have dismissed as fanciful and ridiculous, unseamanlike as a poet talking of his soul. Now it was natural, deeply felt and deeply resented. His professional responsibility for *Marlborough* was transformed: he felt for her nothing save anger and pity.

Just before he turned in, Chief came up from below to report progress. He stood at the top of the ladder, a tired but not dispirited figure, and his voice had the old downright confidence on which the Captain had come to rely. He had been in *Marlborough* for nearly three years; as an engineering lieutenant he, too, could probably have got a better job, but he had never shown any signs of wanting one.

"We've made a good start on the switchboard, sir," he began. "We ought to get the fans going some time tomorrow." There was nothing in his tone to suggest the danger, which he must have felt all the time, of working deep down below decks at a time like this. "The boiler-room's in a bit of a mess – there's a lot of water about – but we'll clear that up as soon as we can get pressure on the pumps."

"What about the bulkhead, Chief?"

"It's about the same, sir, I've been in once myself, and I've a hand listening all the time outside the next watertight door. There's nothing to report there." He turned, and looked behind him down the length of the ship, and then up at the sky. "She seems a lot easier, sir."

"Yes, the wind's going down." The phrase was like a blessing.

"By God, we'll do it yet!" Chief, preparing to go down again, slurred his feet along the deck and found it sticky. "Bit of a mess here," he commented.

"Blood," said the Captain shortly. "They haven't cleaned up yet."

"We're going to be pretty shorthanded," said Chief, following a natural train of thought. "But that's tomorrow's worry. Good night, sir."

"Good night, Chief. Get some sleep if you can."

But later he himself found sleep almost impossible to achieve, weary as he was after nearly nine hours on the bridge. He lay in his sleeping-bag on the hard floor of the asdic hut, feeling underneath him the trials and tremors of the ship's painful labouring. It was very cold. Poor *Marlborough*, he thought, losing between waking and sleeping the full control of his thoughts. Poor old *Marlborough*. We shouldn't do this to you. None of us should: not us, or the Germans, or those poor chaps washing about in the fo'c'sle. No ship deserved an ordeal as evil as this. Only human beings, immeasurably base, deserved such punishment.

Bridger woke him at first light, with a mug of tea and an insinuating "Seven o'clock, sir!" so normal as to make him smile. But the smile was not much more than a momentary flicker. Under him he felt the ship very slowly rolling to and fro, without will and without protest: she seemed more a part of the sea itself than a separate burden on it. The weather must have moderated a lot, but *Marlborough* might be deeper in the water as well.

Cold and stiff, he lay for a few minutes before getting up, collecting his thoughts and remembering what was waiting for him outside the asdic hut. It would be bitterly cold, possibly wet as well: the ship would seem deformed and ugly, the damage meeting his eyes at every turn: the blood on the bridge would be dried black. All over the upper deck there would be men, grey-faced and shivering, waking to face the day: not cheerful and noisy as they usually were, but dully astonished that the ship was still afloat and that they had survived so far; unwilling, even, to meet each other's eye, in the embarrassment of fear and disbelief of the future. And there were those other men down in the fo'c'sle, who would not wake. There were the burials to see to. There was the bulkhead.

He got up.

The bulkhead first, with the Chief and Adams. The rating outside the watertight door said: "Haven't heard anything, sir," in a noncommittal way, as if he did not really believe that they were not all wasting their time. He was a young stoker: sixteen men in his mess had been caught forward: no hope of any sort had yet been communicated to him. Noting this, the Captain thought: I'll have to talk to them, some time this morning. . . . Inside, things were as before: there was a little more water, and the atmosphere was now thick and sour: but nothing had shifted, and with the decrease in the ship's rolling the bulkhead itself was rigid, without sound or movement.

"I think it's even improved a bit, sir," said the Chief. He ran his hand down the central seam, which before had been leaking: his fingers now came away dry. "This seems to have worked itself watertight again. If we could alter the trim a bit, so that even part of this space is above the water-line, we might be able to save it."

"That's going to be today's job," said the Captain, "moving everything we can aft, so as to bring her head up a bit. I'll go into details when we get outside."

On his way back he visited the boiler- and engine-rooms. The boiler-room was deserted, and already cooling fast: here again the forward bulkhead was a tangle of shores and joists, braced against the angle-pieces that joined the frames.

"What about this one?" he asked.

"Doesn't seem to be any strain on it, sir," Chief answered. "I think the space next to it – that's the drying-room and the small bosun's store – must still be watertight."

The Captain nodded without saying anything. He was beginning to feel immensely and unreasonably cheerful, but to communicate that feeling to anyone else seemed frivolous in the extreme. There was so little to go on: it might all be a product of what he felt about the ship herself, and unfit to be shared with anyone.

The engine-room was very much alive. Two men – the Chief E.R.A. and a young telegraphist – were working on the main switchboard: the telegraphist, lying flat on his back behind it, was pulling through a length of thick insulated cable and connecting it up. Two more hands were busy on one of the main steam valves. There was an air of purpose here, of men who knew clearly what the next job was to be, and how to set about it.

The Chief E.R.A., an old pensioner with a smooth bald head in odd contrast with the craggy wrinkles of his face, smiled when he saw the Captain. They came from the same Kentish village, and the Chief E.R.A.'s appointment to *Marlborough* had been the biggest wangle the Captain had ever undertaken. But it had been justified a score of times in the last two years, and obviously it was in the process of being justified again now.

"Well, Chief?"

"Going on all right, sir. It won't be much to look at, but I reckon it'll serve."

"That's all we want." The Captain turned to the engineer officer. "Any other troubles down here?"

"I'm a bit worried about the port engine, sir. That torpedo was a big shock. It may have knocked the shaft out."

"It doesn't matter if we only have one screw. We couldn't go more than a few knots anyway, with that bulkhead."

"That's what I thought, sir."

The Chief E.R.A., presuming on their peace-time friendship in a way which the Captain had anticipated, and did not mind, said:

"Do you think we'll be able to steam, sir?"

Everyone in the engine-room stopped work to listen to the answer. The Captain hesitated a moment, and then said:

"If the weather stays like it is now, and we can correct the trim a bit, I think we ought to make a start."

"How far to go, sir?"

"About five hundred miles." That was as much as he wanted to talk about it and he nodded and turned to go. With his foot on the ladder he said: "I expect we'll be able to count every one of them."

The laughter as he began to climb was a tonic for himself as well. It hadn't been a very good joke, but it was the first one for a long time.

The sick bay next. The doctor was asleep in an armchair when he came in, his young sensitive face turned away from the light, his hands splayed out on the arms of the chair as if each individual finger were resting after an exhaustive effort. The sick-berth attendant was bending over one of the lower cots, where a bandaged figure lay with closed, deeply circled eyes. There were eight men altogether: after the night's turmoil the room was surprisingly tidy, save for a pile of bloodstained swabs and dressings which had overflowed from the waste-basket. The tidiness and the sharp aseptic smell were reassuring.

He put his hand out, and touched the sleeping figure.

"Good morning, Doctor."

Soundlessly the doctor woke, opened his eyes, and sat up. Even this movement seemed part of some controlled competent routine.

"Hallo, sir."

"Busy night?"

"Very, sir. All right, though."

"Just what you were waiting for?" The Captain smiled.

The doctor looked at the Captain, and smiled back, and said: "I haven't felt so well for years."

It must be odd to feel like that, about what must have been the goriest night of his life. But it was natural, if you were proud and confident of your professional skill, and for three years you felt you had been utterly wasted. This young man, who had barely been qualified when war broke out, must now feel, with justice, that the initials after his name had at last come to life.

The Captain looked round the sick bay. "Where are the rest of them? Adams said you had sixteen."

"Four died." It was extraordinary how the simplicity of phrase and tone still conveyed an assurance that the lives had been fought for, and only surrendered in the last extremity. "I've spread the rest over the officers' cabins, where they'll be more comfortable. There's one in yours, sir."

"That's all right. . . . How's the midshipman?"

"Bad. In fact going, I'm afraid, sir. That chest wound was too deep, and he lost too much blood. Do you want to take a look at him? He's in his own cabin."

"Is he conscious?"

The doctor shook his head. "No. I've had to dope him pretty thoroughly. That's the trouble: if I go on doping him he'll die of it, and if I let him wake up there's enough shock and pain to kill him almost immediately. That's why it's no good." Again the simple tone seemed able to imply an infinity of skill and care, which had proved unavailing.

"I won't bother, then." The phrase sounded callous, but he did not bother to qualify it: he was suddenly impatient to leave this antiseptic corner, and get to work on the ship. She, at least, was still among the living: no dope, no ordered death-bed for her. He had skill and care of his own sort. . . .

As he came out on the quarter-deck he checked his step, for there, arranged in neat rows, which somehow seemed a caricature of the whole idea of burial, were the sewn-up bodies which he must later commit to the deep. Nineteen of them: three officers and sixteen men. There had not been enough ensigns to cover them all, he noted: here and there three of them shared one flag, crowding under it in a pathetic

43

last minute symbolism . . . Adams, who had been waiting for him, straightened up as he emerged. He had only been bending down to adjust one of the formal canvas packages; but the Captain had a sudden ghoulish fancy that Adams had been giving it the traditional "last stitch" – the needle and thread through the nose, by which the sailmaker used to satisfy himself that the body he was sewing up was beyond doubt that of a dead man. The Captain looked away, and up at the sky. It was full light now: a grey cold day, the veiled sun shedding the thinnest watery gleam, the waste of water round them reduced to a long flat swell. The passing of the storm, or some lull in its centre had brought a windless day for their respite.

Chief, who had waited behind in the engine-room, now joined them, and together the three men crossed the upper deck towards the fo'c'sle. The Captain led the party, picking his way past the bloody ruin of "X" gun, and the men who were at work cleaning up. He was conscious of them looking at him; conscious of a suppressed, heightened tension among them all: conscious for example, that Leading Seaman Tapper, not an outstanding personality, had this morning assumed a new, almost heroic bearing. As the only leading seaman left alive, he was already rising to the challenge. . . . With the coming of daylight all these men had won back what the stoker, working and waiting below decks, still lacked: hope in the future, confidence in themselves and the ship. "The ship is your best lifebelt" – a phrase in his Standing Orders for damage control returned to him. By God, that was still true; and all the men up here trusted and believed it.

Presently they were standing on the fo'c'sle by "A" gun. From here the deck, buckled and distorted, led steeply downwards, till the bullring in the bows was not more than three or four feet from the water: and even allowing for this downward curve of the deck, *Marlborough* must be drawing about twenty-eight feet instead of her normal sixteen. Obviously, the first essential was to correct this if possible: not only to

44

ease the pressure forward when they started moving, but also to bring the screws fully under water again.

The Captain stepped forward carefully till he was standing directly over the explosion area: there he leant over the rail, staring down into the water a few feet away. From somewhere below an oily scum oozed out, trailing aft and away like some disgusting suppuration; but of the wound itself nothing could be seen. Unprofessionally, he was glad of that: it was sufficiently distressing to note the broad outlines of *Marlborough's* plight on this cold, grey morning, without being confronted with the gross details. He realized suddenly that this must now be treated as a technical problem, and nothing more, and after a quick look round the rest of the fo'c'sle he turned back to the Chief and Adams.

"I've got three ideas," he said briskly. "You may have some more. . . . For a start, we'll get rid of as much as possible of this" – he tapped one of the lowered barrels of "A" gun, askew on its drooping platform. "It wouldn't be safe to fire them anyway, so we can ditch the barrels – and even the mounting itself if we can lift it clear."

"The derrick can deal with the barrels, sir," said Adams. "I don't know about the rest."

"We'll see. . . . Then there are the anchors. We can either let them run out altogether, with their cables, or else let the anchors go by themselves, and manhandle the cable aft as a counter-weight. What do you think, Chief?"

"The second idea is the best one, sir. But without steam on the windlass we can't get the cable out of the locker."

"We'll have to do that by hand." The Captain turned to Adams again. "We've still got one of those weapons, haven't we? – the ratchet-and-pawl lever?"

"Yes, sir. It's a long job though."

"I know." They had once had to weigh anchor by this archaic method, a long time ago, bringing in the cable link by link, half a link to each stroke of the lever, which needed four men to operate it. It had been an agonizingly slow process, taking nearly six hours and everyone's temper. Now

45

they would have to do it to each cable in turn. . . . "But it's worth it, to get some of the weight aft. Then there's the windlass itself. If we pull it to pieces and use a sheer-legs to lift the heavy parts, we might get rid of a lot of weight that way."

The Engineer Officer nodded, rather abstractedly. It would be his job later to account for all this, item by item, in triplicate at least, and the whole thing was a horrid distortion of the principles of storekeeping. But he put the thought to one side, and produced an idea which must have been professionally more acceptable.

"I was wondering about the fore-peak, sir," he began. "You know we've kept it flooded for the last two trips, to balance the weight of those extra depth-charges aft. We can't pump it out now, because the suction-line is broken. But if we took this cover-plate off" – he pointed to the small plate screwed to the deck, right up in the bows— "and made sure the compartment was still isolated, we could pump it out by hand. That would give us some buoyancy just where we need it."

The Captain nodded quickly. "Good idea, Chief. You'll have to go carefully, though, in case the bulkhead's gone and it's all part of the explosion area. By the way, what's the fuel situation going to be, with all this part isolated?"

"Oh, we'll have plenty, sir, especially if we're only steaming on one boiler. We've still got the two big tanks aft."

"Right. . . ." He looked out at the sea again, and then at his watch. It was nearly nine. "I'll read the burial service in half an hour, Adams, if you'll have everything ready by then. Then you can make a start on the weight-lifting programme – the gun first, and then the anchors. Can you spare any stokers, Chief?"

"Maybe two, sir."

"The fresh air will be a nice change for them. . . ."

His spirits were rising.

But there was nothing artificial, no formal assumptions of mourning, in what he felt half an hour later, as he opened his prayer book, gave "Off caps" in a low, almost gentle voice, and prepared to read the service. All that remained of his ship's company stood in a rough square on the quarterdeck: at their feet the nineteen bodies, in their canvas shrouds, seemed like some sinister carpet from which they could not take their eyes. There were altogether too many of them: barely did the living outnumber the dead, and if the men in the fo'c'sle were reckoned the living were only curious survivals of a vanished time. . . . That pause in the service, when he said, "We do now commit their bodies to the deep," and then waited, as the burial party got to work and the nineteen bodies made their successive splashes, their long dive – that pause seemed to be lasting for ever.

The men in the stained sea-boots and duffle coats stood silent, their hair ruffled, watching the bodies go: flanking him, the doctor and the Chief completed the square of witnesses. The rough canvasses scraped the deck as they were dragged across; the bodies splashed and vanished; the ship rolled, and all their feet shifted automatically to meet it; a seaman coughed; the silence under the cold sky was oppressive and somehow futile. He himself, with an appalling clarity of feeling, was conscious of cruel loss. These had been his own men: to see them "discharged dead" in this perfunctory, wholesale fashion only deepened the sense of personal bereavement which was in his face and his voice as he took up the reading again.

When it was done he put the book away and faced his ship's company: in their expression, too, was something of the wastage and sadness of the moment. It was not what he wished to dwell on, but he could not dismiss it without a word: that would have been as cruelly artificial as using the dead men to whip up hatred, or additional energy for the task ahead. It was no time for anything save sincerity.

"I shall never need reminding of this moment," he began, "and I know that is true for all of you too. We have lost good men, good shipmates, and there are many more whom we cannot even reach to give them a proper burial. We can't

47

forget them, any more than we can forget the three officers and sixteen men we've just seen over the side. But," he raised his voice a little, "one of the hardest things of war is that there is never any spare time to think about these things, or to mourn men like these as they deserve. That has to come later: there's always something to do; and in this case it's going to be the toughest job any of us has ever undertaken. I may as well tell you that I nearly gave the order to abandon ship last night: for the moment the weather has saved us, and we must do our utmost to profit by it. I'm not going to hold out too much hope: but if the weather holds, and the bulkhead, which is taking most of the strain, doesn't collapse, and if I can correct the trim, we stand a good chance of getting in – or at least of going far enough south to meet other ships." He smiled. "You can see there are a lot of 'ifs' about this job. But it would be a hundred times worth trying, even if our lives didn't depend on it. I myself am going to do my utmost to get this ship in, and I'm counting on every man to back me up. Remember there are only thirty-one of us altogether, and that means a double and triple effort from each one of you. . . . We'll stand easy now, and then get to work. And keep this idea in the back of your minds: if we do get *Marlborough* in, it will be the finest thing any of us have ever done."

He wanted to say more: affected as he had been by the burials, he wanted to dwell on this aspect of sacrifice, and on *Marlborough* as a measure of its validity and as something dear to them all. But he was afraid of sounding theatrical: better perhaps to leave it like this, a challenge to their endurance and seamanship, and look to the outcome.

When he returned to the bridge he took out the deck-log and began to make an entry concerning the death and burial of his men. It was while he was adding the nineteen names and ratings that he noticed it was morning of New Year's Day.

CHAPTER 3

ALL that day they lay there, the ship's only motion a sluggish rolling. But within her the movement and the noises were cheerful. The ditching of "A" gun barrels and the greater part of the mounting was easy: the breaking and moving of the anchor cables a long-drawn-out effort which lasted well after dark. But the cables, hauled in sections along the upper deck and stowed right aft among the depth charges, made an appreciable difference to their trim: so did the jettisoned windlass, which disappeared overboard bit by bit, as in some mysterious conjuring trick. (It was too heavy and unwieldy to move aft.) But the pumping out of the fore-peak (the triangular section which makes the bows) was the most successful of all. It acted as a buoyancy chamber where it could exert the most leverage, and it brought the bows up cheerfully. Altogether, by the time the programme was fulfilled, the draught forrard had improved to twenty-four feet, and the screws aft were deep enough to get a firm grip of the water. Of course, she would steer like a mongrel waving its tail: but that wouldn't matter. There was no one watching.

One curious accident attended the lightening process. As *Marlborough's* draught forrard began to alter decisively, two bodies, released by some chance movement of the hull, floated out from the hole in the port side. They drifted away before they could be recovered: they were both badly burned, and both sprawling in relaxed, ungainly attitudes as though glad to be quit of their burden. The Captain, looking down from the bridge, watched them with absorbed attention, obsessed by the fancy that they were a first instalment of the sacrifice which must be paid before the ship got under way. He heard a rating on the fo'c'sle say: "That second one was Fletcher – poor bastard," and he felt angry at the curt

49

epitaph, as if its informality might somehow weaken the magic. He could not remember having had thoughts like that since he was a small boy. Perhaps it was the beginnings of feeling really tired.

For him it had been a long day, and now at dusk, with the prospect of another night of drifting, he felt impatient to put things to the test. He had been all over the ship again: he had seen the midshipman and two ratings who were also dying: he had looked at the radio set (from which the leading tel. had at last stood back and said: "It's no good sir — there's too much smashed"), he had made a third examination of the bulkhead, where they had been able to insert another shore and a felt-and-tallow patch, to take up the slack as the pressure on it relaxed. He had directed the work on the cables, Adams being busy on "A" gun. Now he had nothing to do but wait for Chief's report from the engine-room: the hardest part of all. He had the sky to watch, and the barometer, low but steady; and that was all. The main ordeal still lay ahead.

It was nine o'clock in the evening before the Engineer Officer came up with his report: the Captain was sitting in the deserted wardroom aft, eating the corned beef hash which was now their staple diet and remembering other parties which this room had witnessed, when there were eight of them, with Number One's wife and Gun's fiancée and one of the Mid.'s colourful young women to cheer them. Now the dead men and the mourning women outnumbered the living: no charm, no laughter could enliven any of the absent. . . . Impatiently he ground a half-smoked cigarette into his plate, cursing these ridiculous thoughts and fancies, unlike any he could remember, which were beginning to crowd in on him. There was no time to spare for such irrelevancies: he had one supreme task to concentrate on, and anything else was a drain on energy and attention alike.

Chief came in, shedding a pair of oily gauntlets, looking down apologetically at his stained white overalls.

"Well, Chief?"

"Pretty good, sir." He crossed to the pantry hatch and

hammered on it, demanding his supper. Then he sat down in his usual place at the foot of the table, and leant back. "The switchboard's done, and they're working on the dynamo now: it had a bad shake up, but I think we'll manage." He was obviously very tired, eyelids drooping in a grey, lined face. The Captain suddenly realized how much depended on the man's skill. "I'll be flashing up when I've finished supper."

"How long before we can steam?"

"Can't say to the nearest hour, sir. It'll be some time tomorrow, unless we run into more snags. There's the boiler-room to pump out, and a lot of cleaning up besides. It'll only be one screw, I'm afraid. The other's nearly locked; the shaft must be badly bent."

"It doesn't matter."

Bridger came in with the Chief's supper, and for a little while there was silence as he ate. Then, between bites, he asked:

"How's the midshipman, sir?"

"Pretty nearly gone. God knows what keeps him alive. His chest's in an awful mess."

Chief looked round the room, and said "It's funny to see this place empty."

There was silence again till he had finished eating. They shared the same thought, but it was less discomforting to leave them unspoken. Bridger, coming in with the Chief's coffee, broke the silence by asking the Captain:

"Will you be sleeping down here, sir?"

"No, in the asdic hut again."

"Will you see Petty Officer Adams, sir?"

"Yes. Tell him to come in."

There was a whispering in the pantry, and Adams came in cap in hand. "Same routine tonight, sir?" he asked.

"Yes, Adams. Two look-outs, and the signalman on the bridge. I'll be in the asdic hut."

"Aye, aye, sir."

"Things seem to be going all right. We should get going some time tomorrow."

Adams's severe face cracked into a grin. "Can I tell the hands, sir?"

"Yes, do." The Captain stood up, and began to put on his duffle coat. "How about some sleep for you, Chief?"

The Chief nodded. "As soon as I've finished up, sir. There'll be a bit of time to spare then." Relaxing, with coffee-cup in hand, he looked round the wardroom. "New Year's Day, I wish we had the radio. It feels so cut off."

"With luck you'll have your bedtime music tomorrow." He went out, stepping over the dozen sleeping men who crowded the alleyway, and made his way forward to the bridge again. With luck tomorrow might bring everything they were waiting for.

The sea was still calm, the glass unwaveringly steady.

He awoke suddenly at five o'clock, startled and uneasy. For a moment he puzzled over what had disturbed him: then he realized gratefully what it was. The lights had come on, and the little heater screwed to the bulkhead was glowing. It meant that the dynamos were now running properly, and the switchboard, which the Chief had been reserving for the engine-room circuit, was able to deal with the full load. With a surge of thankfulness almost light-headed, he got up and went over to the side table. On it lay a chart and pair of dividers, ready for a job which, impelled by yet another of those queer fancies, he had sworn not to tackle until this moment had arrived. The course for home. . . . He took out his pencil and prepared to calculate.

The only mark on the chart was Pilot's neat cross (too damned appropriate) marking their estimated position when the torpedo struck them, with the time and date – 1630/31/12. From this he started to measure off. Distance to Clyde – 520 miles. Distance to the nearest of the Faeroes – 210 miles, and nothing much when you got there. Distance to the nearest point of Britain – the Butt of Lewis, 270 miles. And just round the corner, another thirty miles or so – Stornoway. . . . That was the place to make for, he knew. It had no big repairing facilities, but it would be shelter enough, and they would be able to send tugs to bring them the rest of the way home. Stornoway – 300 miles. Say three knots. A hundred hours. Four days. Good enough.

Now for the course. The magnetic course, it must be: the master gyro-compass had been wrecked, and they would have to depend on the magnetic compasses, trusting that the explosion and the shifting of ballast had not put them out. South-east would do it. South-east for four days. Butt of Lewis was a good mark for them (he checked it on the chart): a flashing light, visible fourteen miles. That would bring them in all right. And what a landfall. . . .

When he finally laid down his pencil he was still in the same state of exaltation as had possessed him when he saw the lights come on. The desire to sleep had vanished: impelled to some sort of activity, he left the shelter of the asdic hut and began to pace up and down outside. By God, once they got going there would be no stopping them. . . . What did four days matter? – they could keep going for four weeks if it meant *Marlborough* making harbour in the end. There was no depression now, no morbid brooding about sacrifices or the cost in men. It was *Marlborough* against the sea and the enemy, and tomorrow would see her cheating them both. He looked up at the sky, clear and frosty: a night for action, for steering small, for laughing and killing at the same time.The first night of 1943. And tomorrow they would sail into the new year like a prize-fighter going in for the finish. Nothing was going to stop them now.

Midday found them still drifting, still powerless. A succession of minor breakdowns involving in turn the fans and the steering-engine held up everything during the morning: at noon a defect in one of the oil pumps led to more delay. The suspended activity, the anti-climax after the first rush of feeling, was a severe test of patience: it was with difficulty that the Captain, walking the upper deck, managed to exhibit a normal confidence. Part of the morning was taken up with the burying of two more men who had died during the night, but for the remainder he had little to occupy him; and as the afternoon advanced and the light declined, a dull stupor, matching his own indolence, seemed to envelop the ship. Stricken with the curse of immobility, she accepted the dusk as if it were all that her languor deserved.

Then, as swiftly as that first torpedo strike, the good news came. Chief, presenting himself in the wardroom with a cheerful grin announced that his repairs were complete: he used the classic formula, "Ready to proceed, sir!" and he seemed to shed ten years in saying it. The Captain got up slowly, smiling in answer.

"Thank you, Chief. . . . A remarkable effort."

"We're all touching wood, sir." But he was almost boyish in his good humour.

"I want to start very gently. Twenty or thirty revs, not more. Will you put a reliable hand on the bulkhead?"

"I'll go myself, sir. The Chief E.R.A. can take charge in the engine-room."

"All right." The Captain raised his voice. "Pantry!"

The leading steward appeared.

"Ask Petty Officer Adams to come up to the bridge."

"Aye, aye, sir."

"I'll just ring 'Slow ahead' when I'm ready, Chief. We can do the rest by voice-pipe. If you hear anything at all from the bulkhead, stop engine straight away, of your own accord."

Within a minute or so he was on the bridge, the signalman by his side, Adams in the wheel-house below. Leaning across the faintly lit compass he called down the voice-pipe:

"How's her head down there?"

"South, eighty west, sir."

The two compasses were in agreement. "Right. . . . Our course is south-east, Adams. Bring her round very slowly when we begin to move."

"Aye, aye, sir." Adam's voice, like the signalman's hard breathing at his elbow, reflected the tension that was binding them all.

The Captain took a deep breath. "Slow ahead starboard."

"Slow ahead starboard, sir."

The telegraph rang. There was a pause, then a slight tremor, then the beginning of a smooth pulsation. Very slowly *Marlborough* began to move. A thin ripple of bow-wave stood out in the luminous twilight: then another. In the compass bowl the floating disc stirred, edging away to the right. The ship started her turn, a slow, barely perceptible turn, 125 degrees to port in a wide half-circle nearly a mile across.

Presently he called down the voice-pipe: "Steering all right?"

"Yes, sir. Five degrees of port wheel on."

The engine-room bell rang, and he bent to the voice-pipe, his throat constricted. "What is it?"

From the background of noise below an anonymous voice said: "Message from the engineer, sir. 'Nothing to report.' "

"Thank you."

A long pause, with nothing but smooth sliding movement. Then from Adams, suddenly: "Course – south-east, sir."

"Very good."

They were started. Forty-eight hours after the torpedoing: two days and two nights adrift. Course south-east.

The wind, now growing cold on his cheek, was like a caress.

That first night, those first fourteen hours of darkness on the bridge, had the intensity and the disquiet of personal dedication. It was as if he were taking hold of *Marlborough* – a sick, uncertain, but brave accomplice – and nursing her through the beginnings of a desperate convalescence. He rarely stirred from his chair, because he could see all he wanted from there – the sagging fo'c'sle, the still rigid bows – and he could hear and feel all the subtleties of her movement forward: but occasionally he stepped to the wing of the bridge and glanced aft, where their pale wake glittered and spread. Of all that his eyes could rest on, that was the most heartening. . . . Then back to his chair, and the stealthy

55

advance of the bows, and the perpetual humming under-current that came from the engine-room voice-pipe, as comforting as the steady beat of an aircraft engine in mid-ocean. He was not in the least tired: sustained by love and hope, he felt ready to lend to *Marlborough* all his reserves of endurance.

At midnight the Chief came up to join him. His report was good: the engine had settled down, the bulkhead seemed unaffected by their forward movement. They discussed the idea of increasing speed, and decided against it: the log showed a steady three knots, sufficient for his plans.

"There's no point in taking bigger chances," said the Captain finally. "She's settled down so well that it would be stupid to fool about with the revs. I think we'll leave things as they are."

"Suits me, sir. I'll be a lot easier, seeing how short-handed we are down there."

"You're working watch-and-watch, I suppose?"

"Got to, sir, with only two E.R.A.s I'd stand a watch myself, but there's all the auxiliary machinery to look after." He yawned and stretched. "How about you, sir? Shall I give you a spell?"

"No, I'm all right, thanks, Chief. You turn in now, and get some sleep." The Captain smiled. "I always seem to be saying that to you. I hope you're doing it."

Chief smiled back. "Trust me, sir. Good night."

Presently, up the voice-pipe, came Adams's voice: "All right to hand over, sir?"

"Who's taking the wheel?"

"Leading Seaman Tapper, sir."

"All right, Adams. What does the steering feel like now?"

"A bit lumpy, sir. It takes a lot to bring her round if she starts swinging off. But it's nothing out of the way, really."

"I don't want anyone except you or Tapper to take the wheel until daylight."

"Aye, aye, sir."

It meant a long trick at the wheel for both these two; but

56

inexpert steering might put too great a strain on the hull, and he wanted its endurance to be fully demonstrated before running any risks.

A moment later he heard the confirmatory "Course southeast – starboard engine slow ahead – Leading Seaman Tapper on the wheel," as Adams was relieved. Then the bridge settled down to its overall watchful tranquillity again.

Indeed, his only other visitor, save for Bridger with a two-hourly relay of cocoa, was the doctor, who came up to tell him that the midshipman was dead. It was news which he had been waiting for, news with no element of surprise in it; but coming at a time of tension and weariness, towards the dawn, when he was cold and stiff and his eyes felt rimmed with tiredness, it was profoundly depressing. The midshipman, as Captain's secretary, had spent a great deal of time with him: he was a cheerful, still irresponsible young man who had the makings of a first-class sailor. Now, at daylight, they would be burying him – and that only after alternate periods of agony and stupor, which had robbed death of every dignity. This, the latest and the most touching of the sacrifices that had been demanded of them, destroyed for the moment all the night's achievement.

Dawn restored it: a grey sunless dawn, only a lightening of the dull arch above them: but the new and blessed day for all that. As the gloom round them retreated and he was able to see, first the full outline of *Marlborough's* hull, then the shades of colour in the water, and then the horizon all round them, the triumph of the moment grew and warmed within him, dissolving all other feeling. By God, he thought, we can keep going for ever like this. . . . They were forty miles to the good already: there were only 260 more – three more nights, three more heartening dawns such as this: and *Marlborough*, creeping ahead over the smooth, paling sea, was as strong as ever. If they could hold on to that (he touched the wood of his chair) then they were home.

At eight o'clock, the change of the watch, he called Leading Seaman Tapper to the bridge, and told him to turn over the wheel to the regular quartermaster and to take over as officer of the watch. It was irregular (he smiled as he realized how irregular), but he had to get some rest and there was no one else available to take his place: Chief was owed many hours of sleep, the doctor had been up all night with the midshipman. Adams had been on the wheel since four o'clock. It simply could not be helped.

He lay down at the back of the bridge, drew the hood of his duffle coat over his face, and closed his eyes against the frosty light. It was such bliss to relax at last, to sink away from care, and he found himself grinning foolishly. Fourteen hours on the bridge: and God knows how many the night before. . . . He would have to watch that. Might get the doc. to fix him up. Leading Seaman Tapper – *Acting* Leading Seaman Tapper. . . . No, it couldn't be helped. In any case there was nothing to guard, nothing to watch for, nothing for them to fight with. Now, they had simply to endure.

CHAPTER 4

IT was at midday that the wind began to freshen, from the south.

The noise, slight as it was, woke the Captain. It began as no more than an occasional wave-slap against the bows, and a gentle lifting to the increased swell; but into his deep drugged sleep it stabbed like a sliver of ice. He lay still for a moment, getting the feel of the ship again, guessing at what had happened: by the way *Marlborough* was moving, the wind was slightly off the bow, and already blowing crisply. Then he stood up, shook off his blankets, and walked to the front of the bridge.

It was as he had thought: a fresh breeze, curling the wave-top, was now meeting them, about twenty degrees off the starboard bow. Of the two, that was the better side, as it kept the torpedoed area under shelter: but the angle was still bad, it could still impart to their progress a twisting movement which might become a severe strain. While he was considering it, Adams came up to relieve Tapper, and they all three stood in silence for a moment, watching the waves as they slapped and broke against *Marlborough's* lowered bows.

"You'd better go back, on the wheel, Adams," said the Captain presently. "If this gets any worse we'll have to turn directly into it, and slow down."

It did get worse, in the next hour he spent in his chair, and when the first wave, breaking right over the bows, splashed the fo'c'sle itself, he rang the bell to the engine-room. Chief himself answered.

"I'll have to take the revs off, Chief, I'm afraid," he said. "It's getting too lively altogether. What are they now?"

"Thirty-five, sir."

"Make that twenty. Have you got a hand on the bulk-head?"

"No, sir. I'll put one on."

"Right." He turned to the wheel-house voice-pipe. "Steer south, twenty-five east, Adams. And tell me if she's losing steerage-way. I want to keep the wind dead ahead."

"Aye, aye, sir."

The alteration, and the decrease in speed, served them well for an hour: then it suddenly seemed to lose its effect, and their movements became thoroughly strained and awkward. He decreased speed again, to fifteen revolutions – bare steerage-way – but still the awkwardness and the distress persisted: it became a steady thumping as each wave hit them, a recurrent lift-and-crunch which might have been specially designed to threaten their weakest point. It was now blowing steadily and strongly from the south: he listened to the wind rising with a murderous attention. At about half past three it backed suddenly to the south-east, and he followed it: it meant they were heading for home again – the sole good point in a situation rapidly deteriorating. He looked at the seas running swiftly past them, and felt the ones breaking at the bows, and he knew that all their advantage was ebbing away from them. This was how it had been when he had been ready to abandon ship, three nights ago; it was this that was going to destroy them.

Quick steps rang on the bridge ladder, and he turned. It was the Chief: in the failing light his face looked grey and defeated.

"That bulkhead can't take this, sir," he began immediately. "I've been in to have a look, and it's started working again – there's the same leak down that seam. We'll have to stop."

The Captain shook his head. "That's no good, Chief. If we stop in this sea, we'll just bang ourselves to bits." A big wave hit them as he spoke, breaking down on the bows, driving them under. *Marlborough* came up from it very slowly indeed. "We've got to keep head to wind, at all costs."

"Can we go any slower, sir?"

"No. She'll barely steer as it is."

Another wave took them fair and square on the fo'c'sle, sweeping along the upper deck as *Marlborough* sagged into the trough. The wind tugged at them. It was as if the death-bed scene were starting all over again.

The Chief looked swiftly at the Captain. "Could we go astern into it?"

"Probably pull the bows off, Chief."

"Better than this, sir. This is just murder."

"Yes. . . . All right. . . . She may not come round." He leant over to the voice-pipe. "Stop starboard."

"Stop starboard, sir." The telegraph clanged.

"Adams, I'm going astern, and up into the wind stern first. Put the wheel over hard a-starboard."

"Hard a-starboard, sir."

"Slow astern starboard."

The bell clanged again. "Starboard engine slow astern, wheel hard a-starboard, sir."

"Very good."

They waited. Those few minutes before *Marlborough* gathered stern-way were horrible. She seemed to be standing in the jaws of the wind and sea, mutely undergoing a wild torture. She came down upon one wave with so solid a crash that it seemed impossible that the whole bows should not be wrenched off: a second, with a cruelty and malice almost deliberate, hit them a treacherous slewing blow on the port side. Slowly *Marlborough* backed away, shaking and staggering as if from a mortal thrust. The compass faltered, and started very slowly to turn: then as the wind caught the bows she began to swing sharply. He called out: "Watch it, Adams! Meet her! Bring her head on to north-west," and his hands as he gripped the pedestal were as white as the compass-card. The last few moments, before *Marlborough* was safely balanced with her stern into the teeth of the wind, were like the sweating end of a nightmare.

61

Behind him the Chief sighed deeply. "Thank God for that. What revs do you want, sir?"

"We'll try twenty."

It was by now almost dark. *Marlborough* settled down to her awkward progress: both Adams and then Tapper wrestled steadily to keep her stern to the wind, while the waves mounted and steepened and broke solidly upon the quarter-deck. That whole night, which the Captain spent on the bridge, had a desperate quality of unrelieved distress. All the time the wind blew with great force from the south-east, all the time the seas ran against them as if powered by a living hate, and the vicious spray lashed the funnel and the bridge structure. At first light it began to snow: the driving clouds settled and lay thick all over them, crusting the upper deck in total icy whiteness. *Marlborough* might have been sailing backwards off a Christmas cake . . . but still, with unending, hopeless persistence, she butted her way southwards.

Five days later – one hundred and twenty-one hours – she was still doing it. The snow was gone, and the gale had eased to a stiff southerly breeze; but the sea was still running too high for them to risk turning their bows into it, and so they maintained, stern first, their ludicrous progress. The whole afterpart of the ship had been drenched with water ever since they turned; the wardroom had been made uninhabitable by a leaking skylight, the alleyway in which the men slept was six inches away with a frothy residue of spray. It was hardly to be wondered at, thought the Captain as he slopped through it on his way back to the bridge: poor old *Marlborough* hadn't been designed for this sort of thing.

He was very tired. He had hardly had two consecutive hours of sleep in the last five days; the strain had settled in his face like a tight and ugly mask. The doctor had done his best to relieve him, by taking an occasional spell on the bridge when the remaining four serious patients could be left: but even this seemed of no avail – his weariness, and the hours of concentration on *Marlborough's* foolish movements, pursued him like a hypnosis, twitching his eyelids when he sought sleep, making his scalp prickle and the brain inside flutter. Hope of rest was destroyed by a twanging tension such as sometimes made him want to scream aloud. When he sat down in his chair on that fifth night of sternway – the ninth since they were torpedoed – and hunched his stiff shoulders against the cold, he was conscious of nothing save an appalling lassitude. Even to stare and search ahead, in quest of those shore-lights that never showed themselves, was effort enough to make him feel sick in doing it.

He had no idea where they were. They had seen nothing – no lights at night, no aircraft, not a single smudge of smoke anywhere on the horizon. The sextant had been smashed by the shellfire, and there was no sun anyway to take sights by. Even at two knots, even at one and a half, they should have raised Butt of Lewis light by now, if their course were correct. That was the hellish, the insane part of it. Probably it wasn't correct: probably the torpedoing and the weight-shifting had put everything out, and the magnetic compasses were completely haywire. Probably they were heading straight out into the Atlantic instead of pointing for home. And Hell! he thought, this bloody cock-eyed way of steaming . . . you couldn't tell where the ship was going to. They might be anywhere. They might be going round in circles, digging their own grave.

Bridger, the admirable unassailable Bridger, appeared at his elbow. The cup of cocoa which seemed to be part of his right arm was once more tendered. While he drank it, Bridger stood in silence, looking out at the sea. Then he said:

"Easing off a bit, sir."

"Just a little, yes."

There was another pause: then Bridger added: "It's a lot drier aft, sir."

"Good." It was impossible not to respond to this effort at raising his spirits, or to be unaffected by it; and he said suddenly: "What do the hands think about all this?" It was the sort of question he had never before asked any rating except the Coxswain.

Bridger considered. It was entirely novel to him, too; what the lower deck thought of things, and what they said about them to their officers, were two different aspects of truth. At length:

"They're a bit sick of the corned beef, sir."

The Captain laughed, for the first time for many days. "Is that all?"

"Just about, sir. But we're having a sweepstake on when we get in."

For some reason the Captain felt like crying at that one. He said, after a moment:

"Has your number come up yet?"

"No, sir. Six more days to run."

There was much more that the Captain wanted to ask: did they really think *Marlborough* would get in: were they still confident in his judgment, after all these days and nights of blundering along: did they trust him absolutely? – questions he would never even have thought of, save in a light-headed hunger for reassurance. But suddenly Bridger said:

"They hope you're getting enough sleep sir!"

Then he sucked in his breath, as though discovered in some appalling breach of discipline, took the cup from the top of the compass and quickly left the bridge. Alone once more, the Captain smiled tautly at the most moving thing that had ever been said to him, and settled back in his chair to take up the watch again. He *wasn't* getting enough sleep, but the fact that the ship's company realized this, and wished him well over it, was as sustaining and comforting as a strong arm round his shoulders.

On the morning of the tenth day since they were torpedoed he had a conference with the Chief on the bridge. They had seen little of each other during the preceding time: five days of having the reversing gear in continuous action had proved an unaccustomed strain, and the Chief had been kept busy below, nursing the one remaining engine through its ordeal. Now, at nine o'clock, he had come up with some fresh news.

"Have you noticed the fo'c'sle, sir?"

"No, Chief, I hadn't." And yet another night on the bridge he felt no more and no less tired than usual: he seemed to be living in some nether hell of weariness which nothing could deepen. "What's happened to it?"

"The bows have started to bend upwards again." He pointed. "You can just about see it from here, sir. There's a kink in the deck, like folding a bit of paper."

"You mean the whole thing's being pulled off."

"Something like that, sir. It's a slow process, but if it gets any worse we'll lose the buoyancy of the fore-peak, and that may bring the screws out of the water again."

"What's the answer, technically?"

"Either slow down to nothing, or turn round and push them on again."

The Captain gestured irritably. "My God, it's like fooling around with a bundle of scrap-iron! 'Push the bows on again' – it sounds like some blasted lid off a tin!"

"Yes, sir." While Chief waited for the foolish spasm to spend itself, he wondered idly what the Captain *really* thought *Marlborough* should be like, after what she had gone through. "Bundle of scrap-iron" wasn't far wide of the mark: she could float, she could lollop along backwards, and that was about all. "Well, that's the choice, sir," he said presently. "I don't think we can carry on like this much longer."

The Captain got hold of himself again: at this late hour, he wasn't going to start dramatizing the situation. It was all this damned tiredness. . . . "We could just about turn round now," he said slowly, looking at the sea with its long rolling swell and occasional breaking wave-tops. "It was a lot worse than this before we turned last time."

"About how far have we got to go, sir?"

"I don't know, Chief." He did not make the mistake of admitting his ignorance in a totally normal voice, but he managed to imply that there was nothing to be gained either by a full discussion of it, or by surrendering to its hopeless implication. "If we were on our proper course we should

65

have raised Butt of Lewis a long time ago. Probably the compasses are faulty. I'm just going to keep on like this till we hit something."

Stopping, and turning the bows into the wind again, was an even slower process than it had been five days earlier: at times it seemed that *Marlborough*, lying lumpishly off the wind and butting those fragile bows against the run of the waves, *would not* come up to her course. The Captain dared not increase speed, in order to give the rudder more leverage; and so for a full half-hour they tumbled athwart the wave-troughs, gaining a point on the compass-card, sagging back again, wavering on and off the wind like a creaking weather cock no one trusts any longer. Down in the wheel-house, Leading Seaman Tapper leant against the wheel which he had put hard a-starboard, and waited, his eyes on the compass-card. If she wouldn't, she wouldn't: no good worrying, no good fiddling about. . . . All over the ship, during the past few days, that sort of thing had been growing: things either went right, or they didn't, and that was all there was to it. Between a deep weariness and a deeper fatalism, the whole crew accepted the situation, and were carried sluggishly along with it.

At the end of half an hour a lull allowed *Marlborough* to come round on her course. She settled down again slowly, as if she did not really believe in it, but knew she had no choice. South-east, it was, and one and a half-knots. It *must* bring them home. It had to.

It did not bring them home: it did not seem to bring them anywhere. They steamed all that day, and all the next, and all the next, and all the next: four more days and nights, to add to the fantastic total of that south-easterly passage. But *was* it a south-easterly passage? – for if so, they should by now have been right through Scotland, and out the other side: eleven days steaming, it added up to, and thirteen days since they had been torpedoed. It just didn't make sense.

The weather did not help. It did not deteriorate, it did not improve: the stiff breeze held all the time, the sloppy uneven sea came running at them for hour after hour and day after day. The ship took it all with a tough determination which could not disguise a steady, progressive breaking down. The bulkhead wavered and creaked, the water ran down the splitting seam, slopping about the deck, increased in weight till it began to drag the bows down to a fatal level. The noise mounted gradually to an appalling racket: clanging, groaning, knocking, protesting – the whole hull in pain, ill-treated as an old galled horse sweating against the collar, fit only for the knacker's yard but hardly strong enough to drag itself there. Gallant, ramshackle, on her last legs, *Marlborough* bumped and rolled southwards, at a pace which was itself a wretched trial of patience.

Above all, there was now a smell – a sweetish, sickish smell seeping up the ventilators from the fo'c'sle. It penetrated to every part of the ship, it hung in the wind, it followed them till there seemed to be nothing around them in the sea or the sky but the gross stink of the dead, those seventy-odd corpses which they carried with them as their obscene ballast. It could not be escaped anywhere in the ship. Every man on board lived with it, tried to shut it out with sleep, woke with it sweet and beastly in his nostrils. It became the unmentionable horror that attended them wherever they went.

They all hated it, but there was so much more to hate. The tiredness of overstrained men working four hours on and four hours off, for day after day and night after night, lay all over the ship, a tangible weight of weariness that affected every yard of their progress. The ship's company, whether watching on the upper deck or tending the boilers and the engine-room, moved in a tired dream barely distinguishable from sleep. A grotesque fatigue assailed them all: they stayed on watch till their eyes ran raw and their bodies seemed ready to crumple: they ate like men who could scarcely move their jaws against some dry and tasteless substance: they fell asleep where they dropped, wedged against ventilators, curled up like bundles of rags in odd corners of the deck. All of them were filthy, bearded, grimed with spray and smoke: there was no water to wash with, no change of clothes, nothing to hearten them but tea and hard biscuit and corned beef, for every meal of every day of the voyage. All over the ship one met them, or stumbled over them: wild-eyed, dirty, slightly mad. And all round them, and above and below, hung that smell of death, a thick enveloping curtain, the price of sea-power translated into squalid and disgusting currency.

And the Captain . . . he summed up, in his person, all that tiredness, all that stress and dirt, all that wild fatigue. He had had the least sleep of anyone on board, throughout the thirteen days: at the end of it he still held the whole thing in his grip, but it was a grip that had another quality besides strength – it had something cracked and desperate about it. His was the worry, and the responsibility, his the appalling doubts as to whether they were really going anywhere at all: he held on because there was no choice, because they could not give up, above all because this was *Marlborough*, his own ship, and he would not surrender her to God or man or the sea. Like a lover, light-headed and despairing, he hoped and strove and would not be foresworn.

The bridge was now his prison. . . . Wedged in his chair, chin on hand, a small thing was beginning to obsess him. On one of the instruments in front of him there was a splash of dried blood, overlooked when they cleaned up after the shell-burst. It had an odd shape, like a boot, like Italy: but the silly thing was that when he looked to one side that shape seemed to change, spinning round and round like a windmill, expanding and contracting as if the blood still lived and still moved to a pulse. He tried to catch it moving, but when he stared at it directly it became Italy again, a dirty, brownish smear that no one wanted. He roared out suddenly: "Signal-man!" and then: "For the Lord's sake clean that off – it's filthy!" and when the man, staring, set to work on the job, he watched him as if his sanity depended on it. Then he looked ahead again, scanning the horizon, the damned crystal-clear horizon. No change there: no shadow, no smudge of smoke, nothing. Where were they going to? Was there anything ahead but deep water? Was he leading *Marlborough*, and the wretched remnant of her ship's company, on a fantastic chase into the blue? And God Almighty! That smell from forrard. . . . It was like a curse, clamped down hard on their necks. Perhaps they were all going to perish of it in the end: perhaps the whole ship and her dead and dying crew, welded together in a solid mass of corruption, would one night dip soundlessly beneath the sea and touch the bottom a thousand fathoms below.

At 4 a.m. on the morning of January 14, Petty Officer Adams came up on to the bridge, to see the Captain before taking over the wheel. He had a pair of binoculars slung beneath the hood of his duffle coat, and from force of habit he raised them and swept slowly round the horizon, a barely distinguishable line of shadow on that black moonless night. He did this twice: then, on the verge of lowering his glasses, he checked suddenly and stared for a long minute ahead, blinking at the rawness, the watery eye-strain, which even this slight effort induced. Then, he said, in a compressed, almost croaking voice:

"There's a light dead ahead, sir."

The words fell into the silence of the bridge like a rock in a pool. They all whipped up their glasses and stared in turn – the Captain, the signalman, Bridger, with his cocoa-cup forgotten: all of them intent, tremendously alert, checking their breathing as if afraid of losing an instant's concentration. Then Adams said again:

"There it is, sir – only the loom of it, but you can see it sweeping across."

And the Captain, answering him, said very softly: "Yes." *It was* a light – the faintest lifting of the gloom in the sky, like a spectral fan opening and closing, like a whisper – but it *was* a light. For a moment, the Captain was childishly annoyed that he had not seen it first: and then a terrific and overpowering relief seemed to rise in his throat, choking him, pricking his eyes, flooding all over his body in a shaking spasm. The soreness which he had felt round his heart all through the last few days rose to an agonising twinge and then fell again, and then dropped his binoculars and leant against his chair. The wish to cry, at the end of the fourteen days' tension, was almost insupportable.

Round him the others reacted in their own way, contributing to a moment of release so extraordinary that no extravagance of movement or word could have been out of place. The cup which Bridger had placed on a ledge fell and shattered. The signalman was whistling an imitation of a bosun's pipe, a triumphant skirl of sound. Adams, unknowing, muttered: "Jesus Christ, Jesus Christ, Jesus Christ," over and over again, in a voice from which everything save a sober humility had disappeared. They were men in a moment of triumph and of weakness, as vulnerable as young children, as unstable, as near to ecstasy or to weeping in the same single breath. They were men in entrancement.

It *was* a light – and soon there were others: three altogether, winking and beckoning them towards the vast promise of the horizon. The Captain took a grip of himself, the tightest grip yet, and went into the chart-house to work them out; while all over the ship men, awakened by some extraordinary urgency which ran everywhere like a licking flame, leant over the rails, and stared and whispered and laughed at what they saw. Lights ahead – land – home – they'd made it after all. Some of them stared up at the bridge, seeing nothing but feeling that they were looking at the heart of the ship, the thing that had brought them home, the man who more than anyone had worked the miracle. And then they would go back to the lights again, and count the flashes, and start singing or cursing in ragged chorus. There was no one anywhere in the ship who did not share in this moment: the hands on the upper deck shouted the news down to the engine-room, the signalman on the bridge gave a breathless running commentary to the wheel-house. The release from ordeal moved them all to the same wild exultation.

Only the Captain, faced by the array of charts on the table, no longer shared the full measure of their relief. For he was now concentrating on something else, something he could not make out at all. They were lights all right – but what lights? The one that Adams had first seen was not Butt of Lewis: the other two did not seem to fit any part of the chart, either Lewis or the mainland round Cape Wrath, or the scattered islands centred on Scapa Flow and the Orkneys. He checked them again, he laid off the bearings on a piece of tracing-paper and then moved it here and there on the chart, hesitatingly, like a child with its first jig-saw puzzle. He even moved it up to Iceland, but the answer would not come – and it was an answer they *must* have before very long: they were running into something, closing an unknown coastline which might have any number of hazards – outlying rocks, dangerous overfalls, minefields barring any approach except by a single swept channel. Sucking his pencil, frowning at the harsh lamplight, he strove to find the answer: even at this last moment, delay might rob them of their triumph. But the answer would not come.

Presently he opened the chart-house door and came out again, ready to take fresh bearings and to make doubly certain of what the lights showed. Both the doctor and the Chief were now on the bridge, talking in low voices through which ran a strong note of satisfaction and assurance. The Chief turned as he heard the step, and then jerked his head at the lights.

"Finest sight I've seen in my life, sir."

The Captain smiled. "Same here, Chief."

"Is that Butt of Lewis, sir?" asked the doctor.

"No." He raised his glasses, checked the number of the flashes, and bent to the compass to take a fresh bearing. "No, Doc, I haven't worked out what it is yet."

"It's something solid, anyway."

"Enough for me," said the Chief. "All I want is the good old putty, anywhere between Cape Wrath and the Long-ships."

To himself the Captain thought: I wish I could guarantee that.

"Another light, sir!" exclaimed the signalman suddenly. "Port bow – about four-oh."

The Captain raised his glasses once more.

"There it is, sir," said the signalman again, before the Captain had found it. "It's a red one this time."

"Red?"

"Yes, sir. I got it clearly then."

Red . . . that rang a bell, by God! There was a red light at the end of Rathlin Island, off the north coast of Ireland: it was the only one he could remember, in fact. But Rathlin Island. He walked quickly into the chart-house, and moved the tracing-paper southwards. The jig-saw suddenly resolved itself. It *was* Rathlin: the light they had first seen was Inistrahull, the others were Inishowen and something else he could not check – probably an aircraft beacon. Rathlin Island – that meant that they had come all down the coast of Scotland, over two hundred miles farther than he had thought: it meant that they must have been steering at least fifteen degrees off their proper course. Those bloody compasses! But what did it matter now? Rathlin Island. They could put in at Londonderry and get patched up, and then go home. Northern Ireland instead of Butt of Lewis – that would look good in the Report. But what the hell *did* it matter? They had made their landfall.

He walked back to his chair, sat down, and said, in as level a voice as he had ever used:

"That's the north coast of Ireland. We'll be going to Derry."

It was a peerless morning: the clean, grey sky, flecked with pearly grey clouds, turned suddenly to gold as the sun climbed over the eastern horizon. There was now land ahead: a dark bluish coastline, with noble hills beyond. The Captain's stiff stubbly face warmed slowly to the sunshine: the ache across his shoulders and around his heart seemed to melt away, taking with it his desperate fatigue. Not much longer – and then sleep, and sleep, and sleep. . . . Bridger handed him the morning cup of cocoa, his face one enormous grin. But all he said was: "Cocoa, sir."

"Thanks. . . . We made it, Bridger."

"Yes, sir."

"Who won that sweepstake?"

"The Buffer, sir – I mean, Petty Officer Adams."

The Captain laughed aloud. "Bad luck!" For the ship's company that must be the one flaw in an otherwise perfect morning. There were a lot of the hands on the upper deck now, smiling and pointing. He felt bound to them as closely as one man can be to another. Later, he wanted to find some words that would give them an idea of that. And something about *Marlborough*, too, the ship he loved, the ship they had all striven for.

"Trawlers ahead, sir," said the signalman, breaking in on his thoughts. "Three of them. I think they're sweeping."

Back to civilization: to lights, harbours, dawn minesweepers, patrolling aircraft, a guarded fairway.

"Call them up, signalman."

But one of the trawlers was already flashing to them. The signalman acknowledged the message, and said: "From the trawler, sir: 'Can I help you?' "

"Make 'Thank you. Are you going into Londonderry?' "

A pause, while the lamps flickered. Then: "Reply 'Yes', sir!"

"Right. Make: 'Will you pass a message to the Port War Signal Station for me please?' "

Another pause. "Reply, 'Certainly,' sir."

The Captain drew a long breath, conscious deep within him of an enormous satisfaction. "Write this down, and then send it to them. 'To Flag Officer in Charge, Londonderry, v. *Marlborough*. H.M.S. *Marlborough* will enter harbour at 1300 today. Ship is severely damaged above and below waterline. Request pilot, tugs, dockyard assistance, and burial arrangements for one officer and seventy-four ratings.' Got that?"

73

"Yes, sir."

"Right. Send it off . . . Bridger!"

"Sir?"

"Ask the surgeon-lieutenant to relieve me for an hour. I'm going to have a shave. And wash. And change. And then eat."

Leave Cancelled

WHILE I was waiting for you in the foyer of that superb hotel, I started talking with the head porter. Once, during the time when we were getting engaged, you said to me:

"I think you talk to people – strangers – for a funny reason: not because you really want to, but as if you had to prove that you can make friends with anyone."

This was one of your more acute comments, sweetheart; there *is* some kind of back-handed conceit with prompts this habit of mine. But it really sprang originally from my being rather undersized and shy when I was younger, and having never quite emerged from the continuous ordeal which that entailed. It's a habit that pays dividends, at all events.

This head porter (who is quite a personage in London, by the way, so famous is the hotel he stands sentry for) had been attracting my attention for the last quarter of an hour by the competent way he had been dealing with the usual run of hotel problems – the old ladies caught in the swing door, the tarts who wanted to try their luck in the lounge, the drunk left over from lunch. He had an air of complete authority, the kind which is only challenged by the rash or the conceited.

I myself had been striding up and down, feeling sad and livid and nervous, all at once: as far as the porter was concerned, I did not need dealing with, but I knew he was fully equipped for the job if the necessity arose.

Bored with waiting, too nervous to settle down to anything else, I strolled over, on an impulse, and stopped in front of him, and said:

"Were you ever promised three week's leave, and then, on the first day of it, told it was all a mistake and they only meant twenty-four hours after all?"

He was a big man, and he looked down at me for a moment without answering. He had a good straight eye: on the impressive, straining chest the row of last-war medals confronted me. They stood for something, as they usually do, something right outside the master and man relationship. "Don't fool about with me," said the eye and the medals together, "I'm the head porter, you're an officer; but I know it all, I've lived it all, before you were born maybe, and no young squirts need apply."

But it happens that I have not got that kind of face or manner, and after a moment he relaxed and smiled, and said:

"Bad luck, sir. I've had a bit of that myself, but never that bad. Spoilt your arrangements, I expect."

"Written them off altogether, yes."

"Were you meeting your wife, sir?"

"Yes." There was sympathy in his eye: I needed sympathy, and I did not feel it was disloyalty to you, or showing off, to explain what it was all about. I added: "We were starting a delayed honeymoon, as a matter of fact. Now it'll be delayed indefinitely."

He shook his head and glanced sideways at a page-boy who was whistling, and then came back to me. A lot of men, up and down the social scale, would have been unable to stop themselves reacting to the word "honeymoon" in the usual way – that is, as if they saw the bed and the bride and the snigger of it, right in front of their dirty eye. But if he thought any of it, it didn't show in his face; which means that I had not, after all, betrayed you. I was glad.

He said: "I'm sorry to hear that, sir," and I felt that he *was* sorry. The touch of genuine feeling was all I had been wanting, and I relaxed a little and answered, looking round the crowd in the foyer:

"Thanks. . . . You're pretty busy these days, aren't you, one way and another?"

"Very busy, sir." He lowered his voice. "Don't know where they all come from, though, *or* where they get the money to do it. Having a good war, some of these people. Wish I'd had one like it myself, the last time."

I glanced back at his chest again. "The Military Medal says that you did not."

He shook his head: coming from a big man, the movement had an odd wistfulness, as if he realized that cunning will always outwit the good and simple. "I got that in the Salient, spring of nineteen-seventeen. Nobody's heard of the Salient nowadays. Some of them haven't heard of Dunkirk yet, either." He looked round the foyer, as I had done. "We have to watch a lot here that we don't like."

The conversation was subtly degenerating: I had my own views on the subject of "war-effort", but somehow I didn't want to join in the heresy hunt. It doesn't get you anywhere: that kind of nagging criticism never does. And I was too sad anyway. I hadn't told him the worst part, of course – I mean about marrying you two months ago, and our funny one-night honeymoon because of *your* leave getting sabotaged, and the battle course I had sweated through in the meantime, and how this meeting was to have made up for all of it, and now it wasn't because my regiment was going foreign.

Come to think of it, I hadn't told *you* the worst part either, yet. . . . That made me nervous again, the idea that in a few minutes you would be coming towards me, so happily, and I would have to stop you in your tracks. Indeed, the thought of what I would have to do to your happiness induced one of those ridiculous moments of panic, and all sorts of odd ideas – desertion, feigned illness, leaving you a note and running for it *now* – chased across my brain, one after another, like a splutter of matches in the dark. You were coming to me. You were meeting me with the same secret and loving excitement which had been mine up to three hours ago; and I had to make it falter and die, to change your expression utterly and destroy what I knew would be in your eyes when they met mine. If only I could –

The hall porter's voice recalled me to the fact that I was not yet in hell, but only hanging about on the verge of it.

My lad was at Dunkirk," he was saying, with a sort of subdued determination, "and at Sicily too, and sometimes I feel like standing here and shouting it out loud." (What on earth was he talking about?) "You'd think that people living in London and seeing a lot of uniforms all the time wouldn't forget the war so easy, but sometimes it seems the other way about. You can see them here night after night, chucking it about like dirty water – it'd do some of them a bit of good to get what you're getting, sir."

"Yes, I dare say it might." I recalled what he had been talking about, with an effort, and I acquiesced for the sake of not having to argue or become entangled in thoughts that did not concern you: I did not really agree. In fact I didn't agree at all. Once you start looking round to see whether the other fellow is matching your own effort, the machine automatically slows down and may come to a dead stop. People can't be taught their duty either by compulsion or by calling them names: the only way to teach anyone – man, woman, or dog – is by example. To hell with what the next man is doing; make your *own* effort, satisfy your *own* conscience, preserve your *own* integrity: if the others don't follow it can't be helped and can't be cured – least of all by striking attitudes, shouting "Slacker!" or coming to a stop and waiting, with an injured look, for them to catch up.

The idea made me impatient and I felt an extreme need to start pacing up and down again: and by good fortune the hall porter had to deal with a theatre-ticket inquiry at that moment, and I was free to become preoccupied with you once more. It was an odd thought that I should probably have been restless and nervous in whatever circumstances I had been waiting for you, even in the happiest anticipation: I'm not cast by nature as the confident, forceful lover, all poise and flaring nostrils, and you affect me (as you know, sweetheart, having helped me through it) rather in the manner of a small boy whose teacher affords him favours a trifle more grown-up than he is equipped to enjoy.

No, that's not quite it, is it? You give me assurance and

confidence when I am with you, by your own natural response, but this would only be the second act of intimacy (or whatever you call it in print) which we had shared, and the anticipation of it induced more sweat than sensuality. The privilege of your body is a royal favour: when you accord it I am, somehow, able to match the qualities of grace and fervour which the moment brings; but to wait for the accolade is an ordeal compounded of tension and shyness, and nothing much more.

The foyer round me was crowded and full of movement: people registering at the desk, people buying papers or theatre tickets, people paying their bills, people drinking, shedding top-coats, waiting for the lift, talking in groups or standing silent. Looking at them through the hall porter's sated eye, the impression *was* perhaps of a certain well-upholstered ease, a leisurely corner of the world insulated, by money, from the stress of war. If the atmosphere had been one of elegance, if the people had been good-looking or graceful, one might not have minded the contrast with remembered brutality; but most of the luxury products on view lacked distinction of any sort, if they were not actively unpleasing.

This was not the real London, of course: it was not even "upper-class" London, which has (to its unexpected honour) geared itself to the struggle with patience and distinction; it was some kind of gold-plated vacuum, unrelated to England or the war of human endeavour of any significant kind. Its inhabitants, by subtlety or ruthlessness, were able to cling to standards of luxury unattainable by the majority of their fellows, to escape the common war-time lot, to evade full citizenship; and they were the people who least deserved such a haven. For there *were* people who did deserve it, as a respite from other surroundings: soldiers sweating in some noisy hell, sailors at the extreme limit of strain and tiredness, airmen running on their nerves: it was not for them, they hadn't the price of admission, they were nowhere near winning it, and they would die before they ever got there – and that was the unfair part, the silly, raging shame, the fact which made one look round these permanent residents of Paradise and wonder what in hell one was fighting for.

I didn't like the place at all, except that it would bring me an unaccustomed comfort and the chance of concentrating on you in absolute warmth and security. It would aid our meeting at odd points: it meant good food and a tiled bathroom and smooth, clean sheets and a light by the bed. It meant not worrying about anything except the important things: it would set us free to enjoy each other.

It was, perhaps, not such a bad hotel after all. . . .

The time was three o'clock. I bought a newspaper, and read about an air-raid and a rude man in Hyde Park who had given a Miss Pauncefote, according to her sworn testimony, the biggest surprise of her life.

Then you came in.

2

You're lovely, of course: my eyes, most of my other senses, and the invisible male reaction to your presence, make that quite clear. You ought to love your mirror, if that is not a silly way of putting it: it shows you to be blonde, level-eyed, and rather grave, and that, combined with a slim, rounded, just-maturing figure, is a wholly loving combination. And then you have something else – a spark or a flame or the promise of warmth ᴗ some odd element which grips the inner imagination and turns every moment I spend with you into a prickling challenge to the best that is in me. You prompt, always, a desire of a kind more subtle than a sexual one: the desire to do my utmost to engage your attention, win your sympathy, and deserve your admiration. Straight masculine vanity has something to do with it, I suppose; but showing off has to be worth the trouble, and you make it so, you *are* worth every sort of effort – in talking, in mental adroitness, in playing the man – of which I am capable.

When I once told you this, you said: "It's nice to be spoiled.

But I'll try not to trade on it." So far as I can see, you never have.

It's difficult to say what is *really* behind that continuous effort to entertain you: it is not sexual ambition or the hope of any obvious reward; it is rather the absolute certainty that your standards are worth meeting and that to win your favour is a cast-iron triumph. I remember once reading a rather old-fashioned novel in which one of the manlier characters proclaimed that it was more exciting to hold the hand of a good woman than to shoot the works with a professional (I dare say it was worded more elegantly than this). To the best of my knowledge I have never done either, so I cannot return a verdict; but it is a fact, in the same tradition, that I would rather make you smile and seem happy, than to win the most loving welcome from any woman I know. (This you would no doubt answer by reminding me that I have been accorded the whole range of welcomes, from cheerful to passionate, by you in any case; to which remark I would probably return a self-conscious and meaningless grin.)

The working fact remains that to have you contented by one's side is quite exceptionally good advertisement for one's own entertainment value. The man must have something, you feel the spectators are saying. . . . Perhaps it is just vanity after all. But you *are* lovely, certainly.

You were lovely now, as you came towards me across the carpeted foyer. You walked with a young, swinging grace, as if each step were a cardinal statement of your happiness in being a woman. I shared that happiness. . . . It was a shock to realize that this was only the second time I had seen you out of that damned uniform (you were married in it, if you remember, and even your wedding night-dress seemed to have a grisly Service touch about it): a shock also to learn that you could after all dress with elegance and complete femininity, and that silk stockings of the proper shade might have been invented for just your shape of leg. Realizations of this sort have their place in the history of lechery, I suppose, and there was no doubt that to see you dressed as a woman should be, was a fairly sharp reminder that we were newly married and that tonight would end the two months' celibacy of two physically enraptured people. Would you like to pretend otherwise? I don't think so. Love is not lust-in-action, as we agree: but at the beginning, at the stage of physical discovery which is so sweet, it is never far from holding the foreground completely.

Seeing you in your smooth, honeymoonish red dress, I looked forward to the night-time, and for the moment it killed all the sadness that there was to be in our meeting.

I kissed your hand (our shy limit in public) and stared at you for a second or so. Then:

"Sweet," I said. "Hallo! You look lovely. Is that bag very heavy? It's got your new initials on. I'm afraid I have to go, quite soon."

Out of that odd, disjointed slice of nonsense you took what was important, and the shadow that flicked across your eyes seemed to traverse the limits of pain.

"How soon, darling?" you asked. "What's happened? Have they cancelled your leave?"

"Twenty-four hours," I said. "Till tomorrow morning. Then I'm off."

"Oh, God. . . ." You looked round the foyer. "Do people cry in this hotel? I expect not." Your eyes came back to mine. "I can't quite take it in, sweetheart. And you look so tired, too. How was the battle course?"

"A damned good imitation."

"And now this. . . . So soon. . . . Can we sit down somewhere?"

We found a quiet corner-settee in the bar, and when we were settled I gave you the full strength of it, as quietly and evenly as I could, while we looked at each other with that loving intentness which came so naturally. You kept silent while I was explaining what they had done to me: sitting there, with one leg bent under you, your lips slightly parted, your troubled eyes not leaving mine, you had an air of childish dismay which was entirely new. For you are very grown-up, really – more than I am, in fact – and I had never before seen you confronted by anything you could not deal with competently and concisely. Even the first time I kissed you (not exactly a cool occasion) you only said: "Was that as nice as you expected?" . . . So here, to see you undecided, unhappily confused by what I was saying, was in itself as deeply moving as anything in the story I had to tell. When I had finished, and fallen silent once more:

"It's for good, then, tomorrow?" you asked. "You won't be back in England for – for a long time?"

I nodded. "Yes, it's for good. I wish I could tell you more, sweet, but I can't."

"I know that."

"I'll just have to disappear some time tomorrow morning. There'll be a rather vague forwarding address, and that's the best I can do."

"How soon could I hear from you?"

"I don't even know that." All I did know was that it might be several weeks. "I've had three highballs already, by the way," I added. "You'd better catch up."

You nodded. "That might cure this immediate moment. It certainly needs something."

"It will help, anyway," I got up. "If I give the impression that I'm not as sad as you, put it down to that."

You smiled, not altogether successfully. "I know what you're feeling, sweet. I know all that you're feeling."

There was no waiter near by, so I strolled across to the bar to order the drinks; and then, resisting easily the allure of the glittering young thing who was sitting up at the nearest bar-stool combing her hair into the potato chips, I turned to watch you while I waited. You took out your mirror (as I knew you would) and tucked one strand of hair into place; but it was clear that you didn't really give a damn how you looked, and presently you dropped your hand and sat staring in front of you. I don't suppose you saw much there, either.

You were a picture of unmoving sadness at that moment: I wanted tremendously to help you, to take some of the weight myself, but out of my own weakness I could not see any obvious way. It was impossible to forget what this meeting was to have been – the start of three weeks' leisurely bliss – and what it had actually become, before we had even caught a glimpse of it. Our good-bye should have been far ahead, almost out of sight and hardly to be thought of, and now we were already starting to cross its threshold.

Yes, you were sad, as I was; and only when I was close to you again did your chin come up.

"I hope this drink is strong," you said, as you took the glass. "It has a lot of work to do."

It did do a lot of work: it, and the two that followed it and the plain fact of being together again. It wasn't really surprising: we had between us such a lot of things to cure depression – shared ideas, an easy and adult idiom, the certainty of love and fun and sensual pleasure. Our talk was jerky to begin with, as it often was before we had kissed each other and taken the edge off our shyness; but it improved gradually, it finally beat our circumstances and took on an agreeable fluency as well as a rising temperature. I must say that you looked quite entrancing as you sat there, your leg still bent under you, your skirt a generous way above your knee, your shining head now inclined towards me so that I could smell your hair, now lying back against the cushions as if to be at ease with me was all you had ever wished for. Now and again it was difficult not to lean over and kiss you. I don't know what the public reaction would have been, but it seemed that yours might have been favourable.

We returned, once only but importantly, to the fact of my departure.

"What sort of a honeymoon is this going to be, sweet?" you asked suddenly. "We have so little time to spend. How are we going to play it?"

"I'll tell you," I began, though at the moment of speaking I really had no idea of the answer. "We only have tonight true, but if we start thinking about that we'll never make anything of it at all. We'll just sit about, matching sad thoughts like – like rival military commentators, and wasting even the tiny amount of time we have together. The thing to do –" I searched for words, looking at the bottom of my glass, "is to try not to hurry. We know that parts of it are going to be swell, and it's lovely to be together again anyway. If we can hold on to that idea, treat it as one day among a lot of other days and not try to pack two hundred per cent into it, it should be all right." I smiled. "Chalk me up for one feeble understatement, will you? The next twenty-four hours will be not only all right, but the most perfect day of the lot so far."

"Then it's certainly going to be a winner. . . . You know, I was ready to be horribly depressed a little while ago, but now I'm not: not yet, anyway. You're a remarkable man, in your own particular way."

"Please don't commit yourself too far." We were staring at each other, as usual. In your eyes I saw nearly all that I wanted to see – laughter and love and happiness: the rest would have to wait, but you were already promising me that it was mine when I wished it.

"What's our room like?" you asked suddenly. "Have you been up yet?"

"Yes. It's very bridal, very bridal indeed. And also very expensive."

"How many beds?"

"Just the one."

"Ah . . ."

"Quite so." I smiled directly into your eyes, feeling very much your husband. "Perhaps I'm getting blasé, but it's odd to think that there was a time when we weren't married and I'd never slept with you."

You bit your lips suddenly, on the verge of laughter, and looking round me I became aware that I had spoken rather loudly, and that a fair number of people at neighbouring tables were in on the conversation. The reflective silence

85

which followed my last remark indicated that they had found it more interesting than their own.

You stood up, with a certain alacrity. "I'm going to unpack," you said. "Are you coming up?"

"Yes," I answered, glad to be let off so lightly. "Yes, I'll help you."

But I might have guessed that you would try to equalize the score, with perhaps a little to spare, and the return volley was not long delayed. As we walked between the tables towards the door you remarked, over your shoulder: "I must register at the desk before I go up," and added, in a high clear voice: "How do you spell your name?"

I am not easily embarrassed, but that was one time when I was.

3

In the bedroom I sat back and relaxed in a deep armchair, while you were busy unpacking and arranging things. There were mirrors all round us, and it was fun to watch your reflection moving about, to admire the way you walked, and to note, by the odd shyness in your face, that you knew you were being watched in circumstances that were still new and exciting to you. I expect my own face had something of that shyness too. We had kissed once, quickly, when the door closed behind us, and then you had moved out of my arms and not approached me again. Or had that movement, that withdrawal, been mutual? – a joint acknowledgement of the fact that we were very new to each other, and on edge because of it: that we were simply not used to being in a bedroom together, and did not quite know how to play it. Downstairs had been easy, smoothed out by the drinks and the crowds and the movement all round us: here, in this secure, anonymous isolated corner, with the silence and the thick carpet and the outsize quilted bed catching our eye the whole time, it would not have been normal for anyone save the most practised and familiar lovers.

86

We were many things together, but we were not that: that was something in the precious future.

From one point of view the room was just what we wanted – luxurious, private, impregnable. Indeed, it was almost too insistent on the point, it made things almost too easy. . . . Clearly it had been designed, with professional competence, for two people to "make love" in: I dare say it had been extensively used for that purpose: and perhaps it was *that* which grated – the idea of installing you, a virginal, barely awakened and adored you, in a place which had enclosed and accommodated scores of sophisticated lovers, and witnessed their embraces. Nothing could be more incongruous, nothing could be more sheerly distasteful, than to bring you into contact with that atmosphere of mass-produced, repetitive passion.

Don't let me picture you as the ignorant bride of fiction (and fact, for all I know), with a frown of disgust and a copy of *What Every Girl Should Know* concealed in your bouquet. You were never anything like that, thank God: your own brand of competent awareness, your candid acceptance of instinct, are as far from that tradition as they could be. But you came to me a virgin, after all (and how indignant you were when I asked you about it, the second time I met you: I had to spill my drink, simply to distract your attention): a virgin by cool choice, reserving with a charming determination your right of bestowal, but (when it came to the point) as shy and untutored as anyone could be.

For the moment, alone in this room, we seemed to have gone back to that stage. Perhaps we should have had one more drink. . . . I became aware that you were dawdling, doing nothing with a good deal of concentration: it was amusing, and moving, that you should pretend that you had not finished unpacking, solely in order to avoid coming nearer, but it had really gone far enough. At this rate the day would soon be running backwards instead of forwards. I sat up in my chair, and said:

"I'm here too. Remember me?"

Your face, startled at first, broke into a slow and loving smile, an acknowledgement of discovery and guilt. You stood still in the middle of the room, holding a hairbrush which you had twice carried from the dressing table to the bathroom and back again, and looked at me and answered:

"I think I'm shy, darling. Isn't it silly?"

I nodded. "Yes. Let's find a cure. Come over here and be shy in good company."

You walked over and sat down, first on the arm of my chair, then on my knee, then lying relaxed in my arms. We kissed and felt better, kissed again and knew that it was really all right after all, kissed a third time and began to drown. . . . You were rather breathless, and very warm and soft against me, and I wanted of course to undress you: it would only be the second time, and I knew you wanted it too. But for some reason the urge did not persist: I seemed to be having another idea at the same time, the idea that we ought really to delay this until the evening, that by hurrying we were trying to put too much into the day. I had said, earlier, that we should try to treat it as an ordinary, unhurried meeting: after all the urgent wish to have you close in my arms, I wanted us to prove, that this wasn't all there was between us, and to leave, when I went away, a whole range of memories of this twenty-four hours, instead of one specialized impression. . . . The feeling was so strong that I knew I had to act on it straight away: in a film or a book I would doubtless have suddenly turned cold and got up and stared out of the window, my shoulders twitching and God knows what besides. But since it was us, I leant a little away from you, and got my breath back, and then explained to you as simply as I could.

"Darling," I said, "can I say something rather odd?"

I felt you smile. "If I'm any good at guessing –" you began.

"No, it's the opposite. . . . I think I want to wait for this, though it may not seem like it, just at the moment. I know we've only got a few hours, but there's no need for us to hurry, is there? We've got everything else, besides sex. . . . We don't have to rush, just because it's the last time we'll be together. It needn't be that sort of day."

You were silent, and I lay back listening to your breathing and wondering if I had said it clumsily or brought you up too sharply. It was the sort of chance I had never taken before: where the strength of your urges was concerned I hardly knew anything about you. But it turned out that you had accepted the idea, in the way I had hoped, and to it, after a moment, you made your own contributions.

"I don't mind, sweet. If you want me in a — an obvious way, I won't worry. I won't feel that I'm being rated cheaply because of it. I can want you like that, too. In fact I do now."

"I know. But somehow — somehow the emphasis will be wrong. I don't really know how to put it without sounding complex and rather cold-blooded too, but I do want this day to be in the right order. And with just the normal amount of everything in it too. This is only the late afternoon, after all. I don't want us to try to break any records, just because we keep remembering that it's the last time I'll see you."

You laughed, for which I was glad. "Aren't men awful . . . I truly never thought of that, darling, though I suppose it *is* a consideration."

"It's a temptation, too." I kissed you. "Let's try it, some other time."

"All right. What now?"

I still wasn't sure. "Have I disappointed you?"

You shook your head. "Part of being married — one of the best parts — is being able to tell each other that sort of thing without the roof blowing off. How shall we spend the time, sweet? I've got some shopping to do, if you're feeling energetic enough for a walk."

I laughed in my turn. "That should cool the blood."

"Then we'd better apply it, here and now." For a moment you lay quiet in my arms, your beating heart seeming to be still playing the scene of a few moments ago, unable to leave what it really wanted; then you sat up and smoothed your hair. "I'll get ready, darling."

I stared up at you. "Don't fade out too completely, sweet. It *will* keep, won't it?"

You winked, and said: "That I can guarantee." The wink itself was a flawless tag-line, exactly what we wanted to close the scene and carry over to our exit.

4

War-time London is not gay, except for those running in rose-coloured blinkers. It is shabby and nostalgic: it needs cleaning, painting, doing over: much of it is laid waste, and the bare lots and tangled ruins of the old blitz days are never handsome, though they may beget a handsome sort of pride.

Pride is perhaps a London keynote nowadays – the excusable pride of endurance: and to walk slowly through a few London streets, as you and I did on that sunny afternoon, is to have that pride stirred and gently awakened again, without bombast but without shyness either. Odd things serve to do it, things that Londoners take for granted: a bare level space where a friend's house used to be: kids swimming in a firetank: a staircase still clinging to a flower-patterned wall and leading drunkenly nowhere: a foolish heart-warming sign over a wrecked shop – "YES, WE ARE BLASTED WELL OPEN!" . . . They are part of this fine city, whose recent history had probably been her finest.

I myself have a special feeling about London: I was born there: I have lived there all my life, and I cannot really live anywhere else. I was there for some of the worse blitzes, and on the night that the City was in flames. It might well have been the end of the world, that night: it was in any case a pretty good imitation of hell; but somehow we knew that it wasn't the end of London. That would take more than a German frenzy of destruction, however competently executed. And hell or not, I would rather have been there to share the ordeal, than have read about it afterwards and mourned the destruction at a distance. What one might call the St. Crispin's Day complex did not finish with Agincourt.

I think Londoners, by reason of that long-continued ordeal, have much to be proud of – collectively proud, that is, not just complacent and self-satisfied. Little people, fighting above ground or sweating it out in cellars, made London a big place in those days: individually, they drop back into littleness again, but the proud city that was in their charge remains – loved and laughed at, cried for and cherished.

I lost my own flat then – that was before I met you, when I was on leave after Dunkirk. It was one of the lesser blitzes, one that hardly made the headlines: but one building only needs one bomb for its disposal, and I returned from the country to find the house in the roadway and what was left of my clothes being collected into a heap by a tired and grimy air-raid warden. I had not known, till then, how private were some of my possessions. . . . I lost everything I had – furniture, books, pictures, gramophone records, letters – and I didn't give a damn. I thought I would mind tremendously, but that thought had been tied to a vanished tradition, and somehow it seemed the most natural thing in the world to start afresh, owning virtually nothing at all, while the country was under the threat of invasion, the Home Guard pretended valiantly that they were armed, and the massed air-raids began.

It was part of being an Englishman: the current price of nationality. A lot of people, myself included, think it is no price at all.

We went shopping at a leisurely pace. You wanted (of all things) a christening mug. I wanted a sponge: both of them were hard to come by and both, when we found them, ridiculously expensive. (I really don't know who buys small shrivelled sponges at two pounds sixteen shillings and six-pence a time: only bloody fools like me, probably.) But it was fun to be your escort, and to watch you while you talked to people and tried to charm them into producing what they manifestly had not got: fun also to feel that I was the proprietor of an exceptionally lovely person whom a lot of people were staring at. I know you don't dislike my feeling like that about you, or I would not mention such a quintessence of masculine conceit. But it is a fact that when I am with you I have that sense of proprietorship very strongly all the time: it seems to me to be one of the more precious facets of marriage, that loving awareness that you belong to me absolutely, and are content to do so.

There was no doubt, by the way, that people stared at you: indeed, there seemed at times to be nothing but eyes all round us, admiring or speculative or purely covetous. I suppose you are used to it by now, as all beautiful women must be, and that it needs no effort of composure to meet or ignore these glances, and that the sort of physical shyness which make a young girl, for instance, fold her arms across her bosom when she is standing among strangers, is in the dim past, as far as you are concerned. But it still must be odd to know that you are watched and commented on for nearly all your waking hours; it must be difficult also not to develop a tough or defensive manner, both unattractive, in order to counter it.

I remember once, when I said something about it to you, you answered:

"That's only a tiny part of being a woman. You have to take it in your stride: sometimes it makes you furious, sometimes it's a lovely tonic, and you'd feel furious if it *didn't* happen. It's been going on for so many thousands of years anyway that we must have a sort of inherited talent for dealing with it. . . . But there are other things a hundred times more worrying, which seem to have been gradually pushed on to women: things like preserving self-control not only in yourself but in the person who may be trying to break it down. It's unfair, really, that we should be expected to have enough self-control for two, and that chastity should be *our* responsibility, but it almost always is: given opportunity and a plain choice, few men will help you. . . ."

"That's a low estimate."

"But isn't it true, sweet? Most men, if the opportunity is given them, will have at least one try, just to prove they're grown-up. . . . It's something we have to be competent about, anyway – dealing with all comers, from the lamb to the wolf, and never hurting the one or flattering the other. And even that only touches the fringe of it: there's something else far more important in womanhood – the fact of being, at the back of it all, the most vital element in nature, the matrix of life. That's what never quite leaves you, if you are really aware of being a woman: the fact that you carry the touch-stone of the whole design in your own body. It's complex – and completely fascinating. I wouldn't be a man for any money you like."

On this bright afternoon, while we walked about and people looked at you, I remembered that conversation and decided, once again, that you really knew far more of what it was all about than I did. . . .

No one looked at me, because I was a soldier.

A soldier. . . . Airmen have the glamour, sailors make people smile: soldiers excite no reaction at all, save (sometimes) impatience or a faint derision. We know about it, and accept it as a natural outcome of recent history, but I think it is unfair. It sprang, inevitably from Dunkirk, and Singapore and Norway and Crete – all the places where British soldiers, matching flesh against steel, proved their humanity by ceasing a futile resistance. Does that sound like whining? Probably, coming from a soldier, it does; and yet the excuse is put forward to clear, not the Army, but the whole country that lies behind it, and that is where the unfairness comes in. To my mind, we – the soldiers – were made the scapegoats for the scored feelings of all Great Britain: the effect of those failures – the retreats, the surrenders, the basic flops – was so mortally felt by the British people that they tried to salve their pride in laughter, at the expense of the men who were immediately involved.

Defeat on the battlefield, instead of being entered as a

debit in the *national* ledger, was dismissed as a purely Service fiasco, only to be expected from pongoes with falsetto words of command and curly moustaches.

That may sound over-subtle, but I think it is true. When people see a soldier they are reminded of their own short-comings and failures, of errors of policy and lack of foresight: they would like to concentrate their attack on these, but the soldier is the handier target, and so they get him in their sights and start sniping. In some quarters, slow to react or unable to read headlines, that sniping has never ceased.

We accept it, as I say. . . . But the next time you see a sol-dier, and feel like shrugging your shoulders and muttering, "Dunkirk harrier!" or any other neat epithet, just remember that the weapons you gave him, to fight at Dunkirk and a lot of other places, were *your* blunder and *your* disgrace.

All of which is a long way from that day of ours, and I suspect that it is only jealousy of your monopoly of the public regard which makes me mention it. . . . When we had done our shopping it was time for tea: the effect of the whisky was ebbing rapidly, leaving behind it that residue of dry-mouthed yawns, which only an armchair and a soft drink can cure. These we found, in an unlikely-looking hotel where I had never been before, full of holy calm and the more captious sort of old lady: we sat in the lounge, feeling young and preoccupied with each other and tremendously superior to our surroundings. It seemed to us, for that short interlude, that we were the only people in the room who had ever been properly alive – the usual denial, by the young, that the old can ever have enjoyed themselves or found life exciting and hopeful and concentrated. We looked round us – I knew you were doing it too – and wondered arrogantly why, after leading such wasted lives, these people could behave with such curious assurance. Good heavens, we must be the only couple with hangovers who ever had stepped inside the door. . . . Without doubt, we ourselves would be regarded with the same good-natured contempt by the next generation: and without doubt we in our turn would be roused to laughter

or a fuming impatience by young people who knew everything for the first time in history. . . . That is a war which will
never end, and both sides, slugging away manfully, extract
the maximum of entertainment from it.

As soon as we were on our way again, and strolling
towards the hotel:

"What shall I give you as a going-away present?" you
asked me. "I've quite a lot of money. What would you like,
out of the whole of London?"

"Nothing."

"I want to give you something."

"You're doing that all the time."

"Something to take away with you, so that you can look at
it and remember today. Do you want anything to wear?
Something to keep you warm?"

I laughed. "You'll get no information from me that way.
I'm not saying whether I'll need to be kept warm or cool – or
even whether I'll be wearing clothes at all."

"Difficult. . . . When will I know, darling?"

"What?"

"Where you are, and how far away?"

"I don't know, sweet. Not very soon, I'm afraid. You
mustn't worry if there's a bit of a gap before any letters
arrive." That was the most I could say of a journey which I
knew was going to take me half across the world and away
from you for a minimum of two years. It was that desolate
prospect which I did not know how to keep from coming
between us, or rather from so affecting my manner and spirit
that it would destroy the day altogether. This was our first
real parting, and without being able to practise on something
less ruthless and final I did not know how to deal with it. I
wanted tremendously to share the whole thing with you,
telling you all I knew and feared, as well as the credit side of
it – the fact that the job was exceptionally worthwhile and
might pay a notable dividend that would have been a relief
of an obvious sort; but the blanket of absolute secrecy which
had been placed over the near future made it impossible.

I knew then that I would have to feel the crux of our parting quite privately, and somehow conceal the fact that the assignment I was going on meant extreme hazard in scarcely tolerable surroundings, and my conviction that the majority of my regiment would be slaughtered in the process.

Of course, I knew also that by the morning you would have guessed most of it, though you might not tell me so and might not even refer to it again. Even at this stage of our marriage, we were too close to each other for you not to divine so strong a feeling in me. The thing would be like a sword lying between us all the time. . . . And I am a bad actor, where the hiding of emotion is concerned. None worse, in fact.

But that was still over the horizon. . . . Your present to me turned out to be a pair of fur-lined bedroom slippers – or rather boots – of such elegance and splendour that they obviously had no idea there was a war on.

5

The play we had chosen to see, and for which the same hall porter had somehow managed to get us two perfect seats, was Congreve's *Love for Love*. I sometimes wonder by what astonishing stroke of luck it happened that this admirable play, performed by a distinguished cast headed by John Gielgud, should have been available for us on just the night we needed it most. It was exactly what we wanted: a play of love, witty, lecherous, and delightful, which dealt with formal and civilized amours in a world which enjoyed them for their own sake and was neither jealous nor censorious of the diversions of others. We needed and welcomed it for so many reasons, diverse and cogent; for the wit it lavished on us, for its inherent promise that the springs of the mind and the heart would never be choked, for the plain sensual excitement which it induced, it is above all a play to be watched by lovers who can laugh together with tenderness and passion, who can mock their own fervour and still be consumed by it. It was, therefore, a play for us.

Do you remember that scene where the wife and her lover (I am far from text-books, and my memory for names is bad) talk softly together while the husband nods in his armchair, and then, after bundling him out of the way by the most transparent of stratagems, they take up a candle apiece and tiptoe off to bed? For some odd reason that seemed to be us, and we lived their exchanges vividly as we watched them: the man seeking her answer with a vigilant eagerness, the woman gently delaying him, the pair of them somehow agreed, even as they fenced, that the night before them was to be joyfully and tenderly shared. While they were playing that scene you held my hand tightly: when they tiptoed from the darkened stage you sighed: when the curtain came down you turned towards me with such candid desire in your eyes that I could have taken you in my arms there and then.

"Oh, darling!" you said. "This is lovely. This is just what we wanted."

"Yes."

"How good they were together! They were telling each other all the time that it was all right, even when they seemed to be denying it. That is what love should be like."

"Of course, you and I are a little more respectable."

"Are we? Not in feeling, surely. I don't care whether it's a lover or a husband –"

"I'm a husband," I interrupted.

"But in a way it *is* like that for us, isn't it?" You were gravely serious now, though in your face lingered the loving concentration of a moment ago: the people moving round us as they relaxed for the interval were still not in our world at all. "We have the same sort of secret agreement, that certainty, all the time, that whatever we are saying or doing we shall be together and happy, a little later on, at the end of the day. That's the best of marriage – of our sort of marriage, anyway: we can argue, we can be emotionally apart, but we know that in the end it will all be resolved and we will be close to each other again."

"That's behind everything we do, now," I agreed. "There's

97

always that certainty, and we always have it to look forward to, even at the most unlikely times, even if we're arguing like wild cats about the future of the universe."

"Even then . . ." You smiled. "All the books say it is bad to feel sure of each other, and especially bad to admit it, and all the books are wrong. Someone should rewrite them. It's feeling sure – sure of a welcome, sure of love, sure of fun – that makes it so lovely."

"It should be less exciting."

"*Is* it?"

"No. More. But that might be –"

"What?"

"That could be just the honeymoon, couldn't it?"

"Is that what you feel?"

Uncertain, I looked up at the balconies and the arching roof overhead, blurred with cigarette smoke. "Darling, I don't know enough about it. Neither of us does, at this stage. It's lovely now, because we don't need any – any outside stimulus. We're new to each other: we both like to be sure of something that we find so sweet."

After a moment you said: "How far are you looking ahead?"

I took your hand again and squeezed it tightly. "Darling, I don't *know* anything about it. I'm only guessing, and it may be bad guesswork."

"But you are optimistic?"

I nodded. "Yes, I am. In fact I couldn't be more so, and I really don't know why I started arguing about it. I married you because –" I stopped, and smiled, and corrected myself: "I mean I asked you to marry me because you were the only person I had ever met who seemed to promise not to grow less precious as time went by. And if you think that sounds too cold-blooded and calculating, there are a lot of other reasons, some of which can be put politely, others not."

You smiled in turn, and looked round slowly at the packed rows of people, and back again to me.

98

"You have my permission to become unprintable, if you feel like it."

A woman sitting in front of us turned round at that, and gave me a long, challenging stare, which I bore as best I could. It was clear that two acts of the play had not conditioned her either to Congreve's language, or to his line of thought. I decided to stick to generalities.

"I'll go into that later," I said. "But –"

You giggled suddenly, and when I realized why, I found myself blushing – something I had not done for a good many years. That was the first time I realized that you had what might be called a masculine side to your mind. It hadn't occurred to me before. (But perhaps I have been wrong about women all the time.) I decided that I liked it: that is, as long as it was exhibited only to me.

That "only to me" reservation is a preposterous viewpoint, of course: a viewpoint so thoroughly male and illogical that it will not bear examination; but I think it is pretty well universal among people who surmount a certain dead-level of toughness and vulgarity. Almost all men enjoy sex jokes, provided they have a smattering of wit or incongruity to eke them out: they enjoy telling them (perhaps in a sterilized version) to women they know well; but they do *not* like women to take the lead in that respect. To most men, in fact nothing is more embarrassing than for a woman to volunteer an indecent joke, as a matter of casual conversation, or to show herself ready to initiate that kind of session. Her ability to express herself, if necessary, as coarsely and succinctly as a man, is occasionally attractive: it can, at the right moment of exhilaration, be amusing; but she should await his lead all the time. It is rather like a man's club, which admits women to an annexe, and enjoys having them there, but which steadfastly refuses them full membership. Granted, again, that it is illogical and unfair: but it is true, and it does hold good, and any transgression stands out as a *gauche* and irretrievable blunder, unlikely to be forgotten.

That didn't refer to us, of course – another illogicality, this time home-made. If you had a coarse, or rather a sexually candid, side of your mind, that was fine, and you could go ahead and display it to me any time; I knew that you would keep it for me, as a secret only to be confided to someone you trusted utterly. It was, of course, exciting in a subtle way: above all, it was part of being in love and being, whenever we chose, one person instead of two.

We were one person now, as the house-lights darkened again, and our hands sought each other's, and the players returned to offer us more riches, more delight.

6

For people like us there was only one thing to do after the curtain fell on that admirable play, and that was to have a drink at the Café Royal.

The Café Royal. . . . You know how I feel about that place! I think you have come to share the feeling. For me, it is London – London in a certain mood of talkative exhilaration, London as a focus of intelligence, London as a refuge for people in love. You have laughed at me before for what you think is an out-of-character "foreign" streak in my make-up – as if I would look more natural to you if I walked up the Rue Royale exhibiting check plus fours and a smouldering briar; but certainly, long before I met you, Paris had given me an ineradicable liking for the life which centres round the café table.

It is hard to define, that life, and it invites the charge of triviality, even of blatant idleness, when it is abused or misinterpreted; but, broadly, it propounds the idea that one can work hard and effectively, and still think that the best way of passing the time, the best introduction to or solace for that hard work, is to sit at a table at the Dome or the Rotonde and reorganize the universe to one's own exact taste. It is not waste of time, it is time itself come to full flower, time as an educator and a warm comfort. From it, I myself can draw every kind of feeling and every variety of entertainment. I like talking, I like drinking, I like watching people, listening to them, falling silent, quarrelling about essentials, and agreeing on trivialities. All those things are part of living, the blessed leaven that makes the whole thing tolerable. All those things you can find over a café table, stimulated by alcohol, sweetened (if you are lucky) by the knowledge that at your side is love in its most companionable form, love awaiting its natural tide and not wasting the intervals in boredom, Pekinese dogs, or chocolate creams.

I shall always think that men and women, when they are not in bed, should have their elbows on a marble-topped table, their eyes occupied sometimes with each other, sometimes with the passing scene, their voices mingling unhurriedly, and their hearts as close as the two wine glasses that stand between them. And if that is an escapist picture, let us all escape, and find it. It is preferable to almost every other twentieth-century method of employing the mind and the body, and it has ambition, greed, and the cruelty of man to man beaten into a cocked hat.

The Café Royal has always been a trifle more respectable than either of the two Rive Gauche institutions I have mentioned, but still it has a lot of the same tradition, it had the right idea. . . . The war has changed it, put the prices up, given it a touch of formality it never had in the late nineteen-thirties, when hair was worn at the alert and uniforms were practically the mark of the beast; of its former habitués, most are in the Services and many must be dead; but it can still give a welcome of a particular sort to those who need it. That welcome we found ready for us, when we strolled in arm-in-arm from the darkened street: of all the endearing oddments, nothing had changed – the plush seats, the crowding mirrors, the intent, articulate people, the tall glasses of lager beer – they were all there for our reassurance, forming the background of our choice or the half-hour's relaxed contentment we had come in search of.

Except for the friendly waiters and a man who had been an advertising copy-writer before the war and was now some kind of arbiter of destiny at the Ministry of Information, there was no one there we knew: happily isolated, we took time out from everything, enjoying a kind of suspended animation which we could only afford if we did not think of the swiftly passing moments. At the back of my mind I knew that time was already running, running, running against us; but better not to count the hours, when they were so few and so dear. . . . Memories of the play returned to us, like messages from an odd spirit-world which thoroughly approved of all we were doing: it was impossible not to feel much in love, when the mood of the evening had been pointed out to us with such wit and such elegant authority.

At one point you referred to this, interrupting some choice and authoritarian comments of mine in a way which showed that you were not attending as closely as you might have been. I did not mind.

"Darling," you began.

"M'm?" I was sitting close beside you: your leg was touching mine, by no accidental contact, and the sleeve of your red dress made a vivid contrast with my drab khaki uniform. I was utterly content: for all the brush of the crowds round us we might have been on a desert island together. .

"Seeing *Love for Love*, and enjoying it so much – has it made a difference to what we feel for each other?"

"Do you mean in the long run?"

"No; just this evening – in fact, just this moment. Watching it so attentively – *living* it, in fact – was exciting in an obvious way, wasn't it, apart from the more subtle enjoyment we had from it?"

"Yes, it was." I turned towards you. "I think it affected us both in the same way – a sort of prompting of desire. Does that worry you?"

"Not really. It just seems to be an odd sort of message to get from the seventeenth century. Was it meant to have that sort of effect, do you suppose?"

"Possibly. It must have been written to attract the customers in the first place, and that brand of excitement was just

102

as saleable then as it is today. But in any case it was an accurate account of lover-like tactics in those days, and so it was bound to affect us like that."

You frowned. "I feel that somehow we ought to be beyond the range of that."

"More cold-blooded?"

"No – more self-sufficient. We don't need it, do we? We ought to be – we ought to want each other just as strongly, no matter how we've passed the evening or what sort of things we've seen. All that kind of outside stimulus – a lush tune, a lot to drink, a thin-ice novel – shouldn't really be so potent – in fact it shouldn't make an atom of difference one way or another, to people who are closely in love."

"But, sweet, we can't live in a vacuum. These things are bound to have an effect. And we *would* be wanting each other now, this moment, whether we'd seen the play or not. Isn't that true? You know what's happening to us just now. My leg touching yours is exciting, isn't it?"

"Very."

"Well?"

"But I'd rather you didn't get the same excitement from anything else. You do, don't you? It isn't a private affair at all. A picture of one of those little sweater-girls would do just as well as my leg."

"Up to a point, yes."

"What point?"

"A picture is – just a picture."

"And the best kind of love is three-dimensional, with central-heating, huh? That's a little hard on my morale, you know – taking up where the pin-up girls leave off. It makes it seem rather a detached sort of operation. And in any case you mightn't be touching my leg if we hadn't seen that play."

I decided that this had gone far enough. "As God is my witness," I said in a loud voice, "I swear I should be touching your leg now, even if we'd spent the evening in two cold baths a hundred yards apart. In fact, if there weren't so many people round me I should be –" I stopped, deciding that this also had gone far enough, even for the Café Royal.

You laughed. "No – really?" Then you put your hand on my thigh, in a way I found hard to bear with composure. "All right, I believe you, without any further evidence. It's just that I didn't want to feel that Congreve had helped too much. After all, we *are* on our honeymoon."

I stood up and pushed back the table. "Not right here, we're not. But follow me."

"Where are you taking me now?"

"Famous last words. . . . We still have a substantial dinner to eat, precious."

"Sorry," you said. "I misunderstood you. . . . I hope the whole thing isn't bluff on your part."

You looked sweeter than life itself as you walked with me to the door.

As soon as we had crossed the threshold, groping our way a foot at a time into a pitch-black Regent Street, the air-raid sirens sounded.

I began to tremble, I always do: it's been like that ever since Dunkirk: nothing can cure it. My company was thirty hours on the beach before it was taken off, standing in water much of the time and enduring a continuous slaughter by bombing, which drove a number of men mad and, as far as I was concerned, ensured that an air-raid warning transformed me automatically into a helpless and spiritless wreck. The first note of the siren was like an injection of cowardice, which reached the heart instantly. . . . Oddly enough it always got better when the raid itself was on and the bombs began to fall; but the subsequent waiting put me into a sweat of fear, which I had absolutely no means of controlling. It was as final as a leprosy: as final, as indecent, and as incurable. You knew all about it, of course, because I had told you – and anyway you had once or twice been with me when it happened, and it isn't a thing I can disguise.

It isn't a thing you can help me with, either; it just had to be sweated out, endured as a spasm of cancerous pain must be endured when there are no drugs to hand. I have never seen my face during the process (and thank God it was dark at the moment): I have heard the rattle of glass against my teeth and gripped my two hands together in a furious effort to stop them trembling, but I have never seen my face, and I never want to.

You squeezed my arm tightly. "Hold on, dearest. I'm still with you."

"Yes, darling, yes."

I went on trembling. All around us was an unseen, foreboding activity: the darkened street was full of voices – voices thoughtful or foolish or maddeningly confident. Quickening footsteps, police whistles, ambulance bells, flashes of gun-fire in the far-off sky – all the horrible accompaniment of the waiting period was there, pressing round me, getting the better of my nerves, making the skin of my scalp prickle and run with sweat. Even with your arm tightly held in mine, I felt quite alone: sweet and loving though you were, close though our two hearts and bodies, this other thing was going to be enough to destroy our time together. Even if it stopped now, this instant, we were already the losers, out of our precious day. . . . Another girl might have been disappointed that she could not distract my attention, might even have made an issue of it: but not you, not you. You knew the right answer and there is love and there is fear, and the two cannot always cancel out.

Picking up my thoughts: "If this keeps on," you said, "we shall just have to try to concentrate. They mustn't take our time away from us like this."

"Oh, Lord, sweet, I'm sorry." My lips were so dry, and trembling so much, that I could hardly articulate. "Sweet, you should get yourself a man. . . ." That was how it always affected me: I felt that I wanted to abandon everything, even you, and go away and hide or cut my throat.

You pressed even closer to my side. "I have the man I chose. What do you imagine I want – a block of heroic asbestos? If you weren't the sort of man who can't be afraid, you wouldn't be sensitive and understanding as a lover. It all goes together. . . . And what do you think I'm here for? What do you think these two arms—" You suddenly swung round, in the darkness, and put your face against mine. "Oh, darling, I love you so much, whether you're laughing or whether you're afraid."

Someone, forging along in the darkness, bumped against us as we blocked the pavement, and said, "Break it up, for God's sake!" in an irritable voice. We *did* laugh at that, both of us, and then there was the sound of distant aircraft, and an almighty bomb-explosion on the south bank of the river, and I knew I would be better in a minute and would slowly come out again on the other side. I might be a few pounds lighter, but I'd still be sane. I gripped your shoulder with that slight downward pressure which privately means a lot to us, both as a signal and as an effective kind of embrace, and I said:

"Not long now. They've started properly. You know it's only the waiting."

"I know."

We began to walk once more, pacing slowly arm-in-arm towards the hotel: there were the same bustle and the same menacing sounds all round us, but now there were other things too – the continuous pin-point sparkle of ack-ack shells, the solid thud of bombs, the criss-cross sound of aircraft engines. It was no terror in the blood now, it was just an air-raid, after all. . . . The fresh air cooled my scalp again, the trembling died away: you felt me easing off, but subtly aware that I might now be feeling ashamed of myself, you forbore to comment on the fact. Instead you looked up at the southern sky, now glowing with a pretty pattern of murder, and you said:

"It's down at the docks again. The third time this week. Those poor people . . ."

Though aware that your pity was really for me, I did not mind.

7

Dinner. . . . There was one bad moment just before we went into the hotel, a sudden realization that time *was* slipping by and that our single evening, lovingly partitioned into successive episodes, was now well on its course. I had an especial fear that the rest of the time might be all like this, until the end, and that this preoccupation (which you had remarked before) with "last things" – last meal together, last drink, last kiss, last naked embrace – might hold sway from now onwards, and give the evening a grisly and morbid tone from which it would never recover. Once we settled down to that train of thought, peace of mind would vanish for ever – we might contrive a smile, but our eyes would never leave the clock.

I guessed that you felt this pressing of time, in some measure: I myself had it in full strength; indeed, for one fleeting second-rate moment it overtopped everything else, making all that we had done so far that day seem childish and worthless compared with what we *should* have been doing. It seemed inconceivably foolish that on the very last occasion when I would have the use of your body, your sensual and active co-operation in love, we were throwing away the chance of exploiting it. Why, in God's name, had we "wasted time" in the theatre, when we might have been together in bed? *Were* we married, or weren't we? What was I, after all? – a eunuch? A bloodless fish? A little boy? Why hadn't we dived in straight away? Two heads on a pillow was the life, not two spaced seats in the fourth row of the stalls. . . .

That foolish moment did not last long: sense and taste asserted themselves, the knowledge that you were not thinking or feeling on these lines at all, that what we shared was not simply the sexual interplay of two bodies, but a more precious exhilaration altogether – a thought coupled with the rueful acknowledgement, somewhere in the background of my mind, that I was now thirty-five, not nineteen, and that however long one spent in bed, the number of times one could "make love", with any degree of intensity or effectiveness, was strictly finite. Boastful day-dreaming was all very well; performance was what counted. . . . At that and the foolish picture of frustration it brought with it, I laughed out loud; and when you asked me why (and refused to be side-tracked). I told you as politely as I could – which was not, in point of fact, particularly polite.

"Women don't really think like that," you answered slowly. We were nearing the hotel now, moving through the darkness towards the warmth and promise of shelter. The gun-fire and the noise of bombs was receding again, as the "run" part of the tip-and-run raid got under way. "They haven't that masculine idea, that every minute available for love-making must be used to the utmost, even – even if it entails a physical effort. That's what men feel, isn't it?"

I nodded. "Most of them, I suppose. There's always an inclination that way. If they've made love several times, and there's still, say, an hour to go before the time of parting, there's always the thought that it shouldn't be wasted, and they will make a tremendous effort of concentration and fervour, sometimes quite artificial to begin with, in order to achieve what they want."

"Artificial?"

"Oh, yes. It's in a good cause, you see, and the ending is the same anyway, however it started. Vanity has something to do with it, I suppose – the most personal and potent of all masculine vanities. And there's another idea behind it, the idea that they should do their very best to give the woman the utmost pleasure she is capable of experiencing. It's not all selfish, or showing off: not selfish at all, sometimes. Women are – greedy in the same way, aren't they?"

"Not to that extent, no: not to the point of stimulating or inducing desire."

"They do that sometimes."

"Maybe. But they really do prefer it to be a natural happening, without an effort, without consciously thinking, 'If

I can somehow manufacture the initial urge, *which I don't at the moment feel*, the rest will follow.' "

"But the other thing, darling: the idea of not wasting time, when time is short."

"Do you think we've been wasting time?"

"I had a stray thought. . . . It's tied up with what you yourself want, too. Now, at the honeymoon stage, you *are* almost always ready for it, aren't you."

"Yes, sweet, in a way. If you wanted to go to bed at an odd time of the day, of course I'd come with you; and when we got there I'd enjoy it as much as you would. If you wanted to make love in a funny place – such as here and now" – and you suddenly leant the length of your body, from breast to thigh, against mine, so that the words "here and now" took on a quick, startling lasciviousness – "then I should be ready. But somehow – it isn't something I should volunteer, out of its turn: I should always wait for you. It's so much more natural that way."

I bent to kiss you. "If you lean against me like that, dearest, you won't have long to wait."

After a pause: "You know, I like you to want me. It's such a lovely compliment: it's like a white gardenia in your hair – something you can look at in the mirror and say: 'That means he adores me.' "

"And beyond the compliment?"

"Beyond the compliment," you paused again, "is the natural reaction of being wanted, the desire that matches your own. It's here, sweet: it always will be, strong and lasting and very ready. If you really think we've wasted the day so far, then I agree. And if you can't wait, neither can I."

"I can wait."

"Sure?"

"Yes, certain. I said it was only a stray thought. Whatever we do is lovely. It always is. It doesn't have to be in bed."

You squeezed my arm again, gently. "We haven't wasted any time at all, have we? Time *is* slipping by, I know: but it's going just the way we want it to go."

Except that it was going tremendously, ruinously fast, I agreed with all my heart.

Dinner. . . . Our hotel had an international reputation, faithfully mirrored in the prices, for superb food. I am not rich, but tonight the fact was irrelevant – almost frivolously so: where I was going to money would have less significance and less effective value than a handful of poker chips, and a certain Parthian extravagance seemed excusable in the circumstances. At any rate we made that a memorable meal, as far as the Minister of Food and his curiously Spartan taste would allow: cold consommé, lobster Newburg, a cheese soufflé, which was cooked at the table-side with immense ceremony and considerable fire-risk: and a bottle of champagne so fabulously expensive that after drinking it one felt one had probably contracted a mouthful of gold teeth. Around us were many other couples and parties enjoying themselves in the same uncaring fashion: innocently young R.A.F. fighter-pilots, enraptured lovelies, American soldiers so good-looking and so clearly irresistible that hearts must have been cracking like chipped ice all around them. It was a familiar wartime scene, the scene one carried back into the dirt and drabness of combat. It wasn't *exactly* what one wanted, true – it had too much of the Cinderella story about it; but it was the current brand of civilization, a reasonable substitute for sanity.

"You know, some women *can* enjoy the war," you said, looking round you pensively and then back to me. "I don't mean that in any cruel sense but obviously if your heart is not tied, if you're not married or engaged to a man who has to leave you and go off into danger, you can have a lovely time nowadays. Everything is there for you, everything you dreamed about as a débutante, or read in the shiny magazines fun, love, laughter, without any strings to them." You nodded your head towards a beautiful girl, with a bright flower in her hair, who was looking over the rim of her glass as she drank

110

to her two escorts, both American army flyers. "That one, for instance."

"I noticed her."

"I noticed *you*. . . . She's sweet and lovely, and damned lucky. She must be having the time of her life: unlimited dates, unlimited admiration, glamour and excitement without a break as much as she likes. And the uniforms give it the final kick, somehow. If she sleeps with men it doesn't really signify: it's part of her war effort – she can do a ninety-six-hour week on it and people will only stand and cheer. And when the party's over and it's time to say goodbye, there is her heart, intact and ready for the next one."

"Would you want to be like that?"

"One can't help feeling a little envious."

"But *would* you, really?"

"I don't know, sweet. I thought I'd grown out of it. But I sometimes wish – oh, that you and I could be in love with each other in normal times, without the separation and the heartache. Or even that I wasn't so much in love with you. It's a bad war for wives, dearest."

"I know, I know. But you're not at all that sort of girl, are you?"

"What sort?"

"Oh – trivial and decorative and impermanent."

"I *am* decorative."

I lifted our bottle from its silver ice-bucket. "Have some more champagne – it'll give you self-confidence. . . . You're not decorative as a career," I went on. "Your career is different. There are two roles for women to play, not only in war but all the way through: they can be an aid and comfort and an ally for someone, or they can be the opposite – the destroyer of peace, the itch in the blood. You *could* be the second: you have that disturbing element in you – I don't know what it is, but it is potent, something I must have."

"I give it you."

"Yes – and all the rest besides. For me you are the first kind of woman, the person I have to have in the background,

111

to make any sense out of this war. But giving it to me is no blessing for you; it only means that you have taken on a continual doubt and anxiety. Women like you might have been especially invented, just to suffer in war-time. The other sort always have the best time, and are free to make the most of it. War brings them to full flower."

"To full flower," you repeated. "Darling, that's true of some men, isn't it? Not just the natural adventurers, but lots of ordinary people too. Particularly the ones that had rotten jobs, or no jobs at all, in peace-time."

I nodded. "That's the hell of it. Millions of young men – kids, most of them – are getting their first real taste of real living in this war: before it happened they were either in a job they loathed, or else propping up a street corner in some dirty derelict mining town in South Wales. It's a pretty poor advertisement for the twentieth century, but it's true; and how they'll feel when it's all over and they have to go back to the old life, I don't really know."

"That's going to be true for everyone."

"To a certain extent. It depends what you were doing before the war. It's all right for me: I didn't need the war to rescue me from poverty or dull surroundings. I didn't need the war to give me a good life. I had the hell of a good life – not much money, but plenty of work and plenty of travel – before all this started. I think I'll be able to go back to it again, unless they invent something to take the place of roads and bridges and tunnels. But these kids – war has given them, for the first time, a bit of colour and movement and lots of new friends. The change has been a godsend to them. The change back will be extraordinarily tricky. It might be very dangerous, if all there is to offer them is a duplicate of their pre-war misery. That kind of discontent is the perfect breeding-ground for Fascism."

"But surely that is so discredited –"

"Oh, it'll have another name – the United Freedom Party, probably. But it will be the same dreary brand of politics – regimentation, toe the line or lose your job, join the party or

112

else, stick your head out and we'll split it open for you, no individuals need apply. There are going to be thousands of young men who will welcome that sort of thing, simply as a refuge from thinking, a relief from boredom."

"What's the alternative?"

"I don't know, sweet. That's the awful part. I *feel* it, but I don't know. And while people like me are hanging about and guessing at a solution, the first silver-tongued bastard who comes along is going to sweep the field – and leave it a hundred times dirtier than it ever was before. I can see the whole thing happening, almost over the week-end."

You smiled directly into my eyes. "How about some more champagne for *you*?"

For a moment I was irritated by the flippancy of the remark, then I realized why you had made it and I relaxed. You were right, of course – not only was this the wrong evening to peer into the dubious mist ahead, but it was also the wrong mood to do it in. If one lost hope now, when the strength and the weapons were still untried, what prospect was there of making sense out of the future? None but the brave would be able to fashion that future: none but the brave would deserve it.

"It's all right, sweet," I answered. "When that week-end does come round, you and I will have something to say about it, too."

We danced. I am not a good dancer, thank God, but it was pleasant to have an arm round you as we circled the room, and to supply the solid anchor for your own undeniable grace. They played an old tune of ours, "It Could Happen to You"; and holding you close, feeling your hair brushing my cheek, your hand in mine, and your body moving in frank unison with my own, it seemed that there *was* nothing that hadn't happened to us, in the realm of love and happiness. We were married, we were one: we had to part within a few hours, but we would carry with us something of this closeness, some glow of instinct which would be a reminder,

113

deep down in that inner core of belief and feeling, and no other person would do for either of us. It was beyond sex, though sex was one of its strong fibres; it was the reason for living, translated into a language so personal and idiomatic, so exclusively and secretly ours, that it could be neither learnt by anyone else, nor ever forgotten by us.

Back at our table again, there came an odd interruption in the pattern of our evening.

We had noticed earlier on a man sitting by himself at the nearest table to ours, a morose-looking naval officer, who had attracted our attention by his solitude, his ferocious concentration on his own company, and the nervous tension which made him fidget, play with the cutlery, ruin a handsome poulet en casserole – do anything, in fact, but enjoy himself as he might have done. He was also rather drunk, in an unspectacular way; a state which he now advertised by gesturing at nothing with his arm, knocking over his glass, and sprinkling the hem of your dress with some hard-won brandy.

You were angelic – almost too angelic, I thought – when he apologized: this may or may not have been what prompted him to turn in his chair and introduce himself formally. But perhaps it was only boredom. . . .

"Monsarrat." He slurred over the name, and tried again. "Monsarrat. . . . It's a difficult name, and I'm a bit pickled, anyway. Monsarrat – got it?"

"Yes, I've got it," I reassured him. "Don't you write books about the Navy?"

He looked pleased, and didn't try to disguise it, which I rather liked.

"Yes. You ought to read them." He nodded solemnly "They're very, very good. *Have* you read them?"

"Good God, no!"

"Spoken like a man. . . ." He looked at his watch. "Have a brandy before I go?"

I glanced across at you, and you nodded. "Thanks – we'd

like to. What are you celebrating – the end of leave, or the beginning?"

"The end. God! It's always the end of leave – nothing but saying good-bye and running for bloody trains." He caught a passing waiter's eye. "Waiter! Nine brandies, please. . . . The service is very slow here," he explained. "You have to take precautions. . . . Nothing but saying good-bye, and catching bloody trains. . . . Sorry," he said to you. "Just a rough sailor. Sad, also."

I was beginning to decide that he was rather a bore after all, but you gave him another chance.

"Who do you have to say good-bye to?" you asked him.

"Wife, child. This is where I produce my photograph." He brought out a snapshot of a pretty girl and a rather gangsterish-looking infant, sitting out-of-doors in the sun. "The kid was angry about something when that was taken. I forget what, but it rather hits you in the eye, doesn't it?"

"He looks sweet," you said.

"Takes after father," said the naval officer.

"Is he talking yet?"

"Just a few simple phrases – 'Religion is the opium of the people' – 'You have nothing to lose but your chains' – oddments like that. . . . I don't see much of him," he went on: "not half enough, in fact – I seem to be missing the most interesting part, and saying good-bye is always a bit trying. But it's quite a routine, by now. I have to leave the house about seven in the evening, so we bath him and put him to bed, and then I catch my train. Happens at the end of every leave: bath, train journey, dinner by myself in London, another train down to the ship. Sad. Here's the brandy. God bless you both, and thanks for listening. Depressing, isn't it?"

"Very," I answered. "Let's all be depressed together."

"I thought you looked pretty cheerful. Married?"

"Yes."

"Good thing to be," he said with authority, as if he had been originally responsible for the whole idea. "On balance, that is: the partings are hell, but it's the only thing to have in the background, these days. But of course it's worse for the girl – different and worse."

"How different?" we asked.

"Well . . ." He considered, frowning at his brandy as if it had suddenly started arguing. "Take my own case. I have an interesting job, a perfect job – command of an escort ship that does a lot of hard work, one way and another. As soon as I leave home I have that to concentrate on: and it has everything, it takes the place of everything. It gives me enough excitement, danger, interest, variety, and hard work, to fill every hour of every day. I simply haven't got time to sit around and mope. But what has she got, when I leave? A complete let-down: a house that is not her own, work that is only drudgery, business with rations and coupons and queues that is enough to drive her right round the bend. There's no glamour or significance to it, nothing to persuade her that it is really worthwhile."

"But it *is* worthwhile, isn't it?" you asked.

"Hell, yes, a hundred times. This country – any country – would come to a dead stop tomorrow, if the women who make and run homes threw their hands in. *Their* job is half of England, half the world. But it must be impossible to see that, when the results are so negative."

"Doesn't the child make a difference?"

"So she says. A vital difference, in fact – although it increases the drudgery about a hundred per cent, I reckon. But I've always felt that women have the worst of war. I dare say they have the worst of peace, too," he added thoughtfully, "but that's part of a larger question."

You smiled. "Much larger."

"Are you on leave too?" he asked.

"Yes. Off tomorrow."

"This is our honeymoon," you said suddenly.

"Now why did you tell him that?" I asked, surprised.

"I thought it would cheer him up."

"Oh, it does, it does," said the naval officer. He looked at his wrist-watch. "Shouldn't you be in – I mean, have another brandy!"

"Your very good health," you said composedly.

"Likewise." He drank, and set down his glass – one of an imposing clump of empties. "I couldn't be a soldier to save my life," he said, going off at a tangent. "Sticking bayonets into total strangers, storming the beaches under shot and shell. . . . Not for me."

"I think you have a rather romantic conception of soldiering," I said.

"Not for me," he repeated. "And as for flying . . . If I couldn't be in the Navy I think I'd rather do nothing at all, even if it meant some bloody-minded old faggot dishing me out with a white feather every hour of the day."

"It's not so bad as all that," I insisted.

"Well, anyone who can stand it has all my admiration."

"What's your own job like, anyway? That's probably something I couldn't do to save *my* life. I should be seasick anyway, apart from not liking rum and torpedoes and surprises like that."

"Oh, my job's fine, particularly now that I've got my own command. All in all, I suppose it's been more boring than dangerous: nothing but convoy after convoy, for month after month – I've been in escort ships ever since I joined the Navy. But it's had its moments, certainly: we've all dodged a lot of funny things in our time – torpedoes, bullets, blitzes. The Atlantic and the East Coast were pretty bad in the old days. It used to give me the creeps sometimes – it still does, now and then. Ships blowing up and burning, night after night, or sinking without a trace, almost before you could turn round. I remember –" he paused, and then shook his head.

"Go on," I said.

"It was just a chance thought. I don't know why it came back. But I once had to go on board a merchant ship that had just been bombed, to see if they could get her going again – otherwise we were going to sink her with gun-fire.

117

She'd had one smack on the bridge. Stopped everything. I tell you, when I got on deck and began to walk forrard towards the mess, the horrible mess I knew was there, I felt like turning round and diving overboard again."

He took a drink of brandy. "And it *was* a mess, all right. There was only one of them left alive – half alive – the rest of them were smeared all round the bulkhead in glorious Technicolour." Suddenly he gestured, in a fashion at once affected and compelling. "*That's* why I don't want to die. I have a kind of aesthetic objection to looking like that – or like one of the exhibits we sometimes pull out of the water, bedraggled, swollen, half eaten by fish, or pecked over by sea-gulls. There's something about a skull bleached by sun and sea-water –" he stopped dead again, and then looked towards you. "Sorry," he said gently. "Damned sorry. And you on your honeymoon."

"That's all right," you answered. "Doesn't it do you good to talk about it? I expect you wrote those books for much the same reason."

He smiled at me. "She's clever," he said. "Hang on to her."

"Until tomorrow, I will."

"Of course – you're pulling out, too. That's not much of a honeymoon, is it? What went wrong?"

I explained about the cancelled leave and the disappointment generally, and added: "There's a story there for you, if you want to write one. A good-bye story. Nothing special to it, but it must have happened to so many people. They might like to read about it."

"Wish I could," he answered. "But I've no time for anything but scribbles. Wait till after the war."

"Are you going on writing then?"

"I hope so. Actually I want to write for the theatre, if I can break into it. I've got one grand idea for a play that I was working on just before the war began: the heroine starts as a patient in a lunatic asylum, falls in love with one of the doctors, and gropes her way to sanity by way of sex. Not a dry eye in the house!"

"No audience, by the sound of it. . . . What about films?"

He shook his head. "Don't like them. Don't like the *people* in them – narcissic young men and glorified harlots. They seem to be the stock types nowadays – they, and what they call the character type, who's always some old snide Irishman with a face like a shrivelled walnut and a brain to match. Still, I prefer him any day to the young female eyeful with a nine-inch smile and her hips swinging from ear to ear. Or Errol Flynn impersonating a hero and brandishing his weapon all over the place. They give me the horrors."

I laughed. "You seem to be subject to the horrors. . . . Well, I hope it's going to be the sort of world where you *can* write plays, in reasonable peace."

"I shall make it so!" He banged the table with his fist, and added, unnecessarily: "This brandy is really very good indeed. . . . That's what we're put here for," he went on, "not to see what sort of a world it turns out to be, but to mould the things ourselves. All these indications of a servile state to come –" He gestured. "There's plenty of talk about the post-war world, but from what an angle! It's all of what 'they' are going to do to us: how many jobs, how big a pension or a dole 'they' are going to allow us to have. Preposterous! People who sit about like mice, waiting for things to happen to them, deserve nothing and will probably get just that. The world is *ours*, not 'theirs': ours to make, ours to take hold of, ours to fashion. Listen, chum," he said, nearly falling out of his chair, "I'm not going to hang about while somebody else decides what sort of a life I'm going to live. By God –!"

"Commander – the neighbours!" you said.

He looked round. "Oh – sorry. . . ." He waited until some of the surrounding interest and, indeed, indignation had subsided, and then continued: "But you see the point, don't you? If you don't make a success of your own life, if you don't make an individual effort, 'they' won't do it for you. In fact, just the opposite: they'll simply spit on their hands, take one good grip, and have your guts for garters."

"It sounds like the jungle."

"Ain't it so?"

"But do you really want to be a success, on those terms?"

He smiled. "I can't make up my mind. But on the whole ... Success is disappointing, failure is seedy; on the whole it is better to be successful."

"Why 'disappointing'?"

"Don't you think it's true? Whenever I get something, I always want the next thing ahead. When I first joined the Navy, my greatest ambition was to be First Lieutenant of a corvette. When I got the job, the Captain was on my neck all the time, and I wanted a command so that I'd be free of pin-pricks. Now I *have* a command, and of course there's the operational staff to cope with, and it's like being pecked to death by a flock of birds with brass beaks."

"Aren't you rather beyond the reach of that sort of thing?"

He laughed out loud. "Good heavens, no! In fact I'm standing right in the line of fire all the time. By God, I remember when my ship gave the wrong recognition signals and the Admiral had me up about it. 'Monsarrat,' he said, 'I'm afraid you're in the rattle.' 'What, again, sir?' I said. 'Yes, my boy,' he said, 'again. . . .' You'll understand that I'm glamorizing the interview a bit, because actually as soon as I got inside the room, blood, hair, and toe-nails began to fly, and I nearly lost my half-stripe. But that's another story." He looked at his watch suddenly, in a swift, nervous movement. "Hell! Time's up! I must go and plough the ocean. What's happening to you tomorrow? Are you going – um – abroad?"

"Yes."

"Odd if I convoyed you. . . . Well" – he held out his hand – "thanks for the session; it's been a lot of fun. Have a good – no, that's a silly remark. God bless you both." He smiled again, and was gone.

He left behind him one of those natural reflective silences wherein a leave-taker is privately summed up by the people he says good-bye to. It is not necessarily critical, but the

120

space has to be filled. You broke the silence first, in a way I hadn't been expecting.

"Oh, darling," you said, "will you be like that, when you leave me?"

"Like what?"

"Sad and nervous and jumpy. He was hardly drunk at all, you know: just immensely depressed at saying good-bye and having to go off to sea again. Will it be like that for you?"

"No," I answered after a pause, "it won't be like that for me. There's probably something in sea-going, some special kind of loneliness and separation, which he had met before and can foresee each time. We are going to be different." (I didn't believe any of this, but it sounded plausible.) "In fact, we *are* different, already – we're spending all of the time together, right up to the last, instead of my having to be by myself, and missing you. And in any case, have you forgotten that we are on our honeymoon, and that upstairs is a room not only much more expensive than any you have yet slept in, but with a supremely comfortable bed and a man to go with it."

You smiled. "No. I haven't forgotten. But tell me some more about it."

I told you some more.

"Darling," you said, "you have a nice way of putting things, though it might not suit everyone." You picked up your glass, your loving eyes holding mine in a warm glow. "Your arms, my defence, my arms your recompense," you murmured, and drank. Then you pushed back your chair. "Let's go up," you said, happily. "I'm in good form."

8

There should be asterisks here, I suppose, and if I wanted to cheapen the thing I should put a lot of them in, and start again with: "The waiter knocked on the bedroom door, and brought in the breakfast tray." That is called "leaving it to the imagination" – of all things, the foremost current indecency. But somehow I don't think our love-making was of the asterisk order, was it? Love-making is never unmentionable, though some versions of it may be brutal or foolish; and the love-making of two people who, adoring each other, are about to part and wish to say good-bye with their bodies as well as with all the rest, is not the kind that needs to be censored.

Besides, I want you to remember it, all of it, as I do. This is what our good-bye was like. Please remember that, as long as you can.

The room, with the curtains drawn and the bedside lamp glowing and falling softly on the turned-back sheet and on your insubstantial chiffon night-dress which lay waiting for you, was even more suited to our private delight than it had seemed during the early afternoon; now it had something more than comfort, it had a personal welcome for both of us, promising that whatever we did there would be aided by a dream-like and sensuous luxury. . . . While you were having your bath I sprawled in an armchair and finished my cigar (you called out to me: "How very masculine that is!" To which I replied: "And it's not the most masculine thing about me, either. . . .") then I started to undress. The fur boots you had given me caught my eye, and I put them on: they looked exceptionally handsome and they gave to my naked body an oddly rakish air, a touch of Cavalier irresponsibility, which was exactly what I was feeling at the moment. They had something, those boots: they were good boots to go to bed in.

Again you called out from the bathroom:

"I'm getting lonely in here. You're very quiet. What are you doing?"

"Walking up and down in my fur boots," I said. "I look like Charles the First dictating a letter."

I could almost *hear* you putting your head on one side. "That's rather hard to imagine," you answered at length. "Come in and show me."

You were like a jewel in that bathroom, a creamy, glowing

122

focus of all the warmth and light in the world. The opaque, faintly scented water hid your legs, lapped round your middle, left sweetly outlined your breast and shoulders. Your hair was pinned up on top of your head, like a little girl's. You were smiling up at me. I had forgotten you were so lovely.

My own body, toughened, scarred in two places, knocked about, felt awkward and intrusive by comparison, and something seemed to have rendered it unfit to be close to yours: the dirt and stress and pain of the last few years had somehow disqualified it from sharing your tenderness. But:

"You have a nice figure," you said.

"I have *very* nice boots."

"Yes, indeed."

"You have a nice figure, too." I looked down at your nineteen-year-old body, with its clear skin and its fresh perfection of line; and then I looked at myself in the full-length mirror. Something I saw there crystallized that sense of unfitness, and I said suddenly:

"Oh, God, I wish I'd met you about fifteen years ago. I'm too old for you."

You stared. "You're not too old at all!"

"But if I were twenty instead of thirty-five –"

"What difference would that make?"

"All the difference in the world. *That's* the age to be in love, not –" I gestured impatiently. "I'm not sure what it is I want to give you, but it has something to do with being young and graceful and sunburnt: more of a lover and less of a husband, perhaps. You deserve someone who can look as fresh and vital as you're looking at this moment."

"Don't you feel like a lover?"

I smiled. "Surely. And that, at my age, is almost improper. And I think I could have been a more attractive and virile one at twenty. Now I'm almost past it – the wild, to-hell-with-it part anyway."

"Oh, yes, you're past it all right." You held out a hand. "Help me up," you said, and as I pulled you, you rose suddenly upright, a warm, dripping figure, naked and flawlessly lovely. Then you put a wet hand on my chest, surrounded by a little haze of perfumed steam. "If you are past it now, sweet," you said, "it's just as well I didn't meet you when you were at the top of your form. And don't shake your head like that, because you know quite well what I'm talking about. . . . Now hurry up, and have your bath, and let's have no more nonsense. Past it, indeed! . . ." You wrapped the towel close around you, and trailed away into the bedroom, grumbling charmingly and leaving tiny wet footmarks, while I winked to my reflection in the mirror. The idea I had brought up had seemed important for a moment, when I compared our two bodies: now it didn't matter a damn. I felt as much past it as Casanova at fifteen.

I had only been in the bath a moment or two when you called out:

"Darling."

"Yes?"

"How long will you be gone?"

I knew what she meant, but I said: "About ten minutes. Have patience."

"How long really, sweet?"

"I don't know."

"What would be the most?"

"About – about two years." That was likely to be the least, as far as I could gather, but it was secret anyway, even if I had been able to bring myself to tell you the whole truth. "Why do you ask, darling?"

"I was thinking." A pause. Then: "Children."

"Oh . . . I'd been thinking about that, too."

"What do you think?"

I splashed about with my hands in the water, wondering exactly how to put it. "It's so much *your* affair, darling. You know I'd love one, but that's only *my* point of view; I don't have any of the worry or the hell – it's your responsibility, it's your body that has to be used."

"It is yours."

124

"Is it, darling? Well . . . I thought we'd probably have one later on, after a year or so, but now that I'll be gone for so long, and you'll be alone, it seems rather a good idea. In fact it's far more than just that. But *only* if you're absolutely certain about it yourself."

Through the open doorway your voice came low and gentle, confirming our accord:

"That's what I thought too. Ordinarily I'd want you to enjoy me for quite a long time, and I'd want you, too, for myself – that's part of what we got married for, isn't it, and it's never seemed to me a selfish point of view – but if you're going to be away anyway . . ."

"Yes, darling."

"So we'll just –"

"Yes."

It was an odd conversation to conduct between two rooms, out of sight of one another, but perhaps this was the best way of settling it – not because of shyness, but because the subject had so much emotional content, such potential sadness at this moment, that a detached approach was the only way through it. Face to face with me, watching my eyes, you would have been reminded that this might be the last chance you would ever have of conceiving a child by me: that mutilation might prevent another, that you could be widowed months before it was born. . . . Of course I wanted one, as close to your image as possible; but your inclination in the matter was paramount. It was such a very easy wish for me to have: the bill for it was all yours, and you would be alone all the time you were paying for it.

I got out of the bath and started to dry myself. Your low voice called again:

"That's settled, then. Of course, we're only guessing: it may not work."

I felt I was being insulted, none too subtly. "Work? Of course it will work. Who do you think I am?"

"Just a man, sweet, just a man."

"If you know a better method –"

"Oh, I think it's come to stay. . . . Why do you feel so sure? If you say anything like 'Years of practice', I shall lock that door."

"Wait till I'm on the right side of it. . . . When we agree that I am to give you a child, precious, I think we will make a success of it."

You laughed softly, almost to yourself. "We'll see about that when the time comes."

"The time is here," I said and walked through into the bedroom. You had been brushing your hair before the mirror: when I came in you rose suddenly, and we looked at each other. Then the few paces between us melted away. Your eyes were indescribably gentle and loving as I took you in my arms: your body felt as softly compliant as the nightdress which graced it. Presently, with my free hand, I pressed downwards on your breast and shoulder, as if drawing myself up to you: then I kissed your soft mouth and held you against me, until an adorably familiar movement told me that simply holding you was no longer enough for either of us.

Asterisks now? I still don't think so. Do you remember what a strange night, confused and lovely, we made of it? It seemed to contain everything, that night – everything in the physical realm, everything in the emotional: dissolving all the earlier shyness and hesitation, we seemed to traverse the limits of every sort of feeling, from the spurring of a candid sensuality to the secrets of a floating dream-world where we travelled together, clinging to each other in a sort of light-headed, astonished ecstasy. It was our last night together, and it became memorable, by a natural process. We did not set out to make it so: it happened. We were lucky of course; but it was really astonishing what two heads on a pillow can concoct.

If that is not too strong a word. These things are not planned or worked for – they simply take place, without effort or forethought, between two people in love: they express,

126

subtly, a simple and endearing fact. I don't mean the dreary "variations", the mechanical jiggery-pokery which seeks to turn love into a gymnasium exercise. Those things are for the bored or the perverted. But there are, genuinely, so very many different sorts of love-making – friendly, emotional, purely sensual, laughing: it is the change of mood which makes for the variety, and which can carry you urgently or swiftly or unexpectedly through a lovely countryside, some parts of which are as familiar as instinct can make them, and others unsuspected until by chance you lead each other to them.

You and I were lucky, sweet – lucky and yet deserving. We earned that night and the delight it gave us by being completely in love, in the most unselfish way possible – that is, with the idea of doing the least for ourselves, and the most for each other, that lay in our power. On those terms love is glorified beyond any physical expression of it. It becomes an ecstatic mutual service, a competition in tenderness and exhilaration in which neither can be the loser.

Thus were we lucky. . . . There was the first time – inevitably wild, since we had not seen or touched each other for over two months – when we each took such frank delight in our power to excite and to give release to the other: when, drunk with your magic, I was laughing and shaking you gently and making you glow and move with me, and sigh and lose all control for the last few moments, and then cry and whisper, "How can I let you go?" and then smile again and say, "How lovely that was!" After it we were close and loving and contented, with all the wildness and the jitters gone, the way it was after we had given each other everything we could of love and shared sensual excitement and fun. And even as we lay a little apart in our relief, we were both thinking: this is love, we have all this, and in a short while we can, if we want to, have it again. . . . That was something else we could do to each other – leave the recollection, even at such a moment, that the future could match the past.

There was, a little later, that odd half world of which I

have spoken, visited by us as we lay clipped together in entrancement: a secret world, swinging between heaven and earth, wherein we seemed to float on an ecstatic timeless sea, where only at the very end did our bodies give bodily evidence of their desire: where you wept bitterly, half for the nervous relief, half with the sadness of parting, and I matched your tears with my own. You did not mind, did you? Or think less of me for those tears? They were not masculine, by any standard, but then men should not always be masculine: men should sometimes cry, for only thus can they honour the women who give them everything in a moment of lavish tenderness.

When we entered and shared that world together we had the same bodies and were the same people who, a little while before, had been lost in another and wholly different ecstasy. We were the same people, but the things we did together, and to each other, were as different as any two human activities could be. I do not know what that proves, unless it be the scope of humanity: but we *were* lucky to be able to embrace together the twin worlds of the senses and the spirit, and to carry each other so easily and inevitably from the first to the second and, as we soon showed each other, back again.

For a little later we were physically enraptured once more. . . . I remember that, suddenly aware of a fresh urgency in me, you lay back looking distractingly lovely and available, and yet somehow afraid of what I was about to do to you: afraid that some movement I might make, or fervour I might reach, would be so overwhelming to your senses that you could not guarantee a sane response: that you might die upon a moment of communicated lust. . . . I leant away from you, enjoying your loveliness and your confusion in equal, unrelenting measure; and then as I bent forward and down again the picture diminished, and the changing focus, on the verge of blurring to nothing, took in only your loving, startled eyes and your delighted breasts.

Sweet, you were so lovely. . . . You don't mind my occasional frankness, do you? It's part of us, isn't it? – to be

articulate about our love-making, to mention the fact that a
certain movement, a certain kind of caress, gives us pleasure
or exhilaration. Remember how you suddenly remarked, out
of nowhere: "Very glad to have you aboard, sir!" and I said:
"Dear me, what *do* they teach you in the Wrens?" and you
answered – no, it's unprintable after all, but you probably
do remember. . . . That is how we should talk, to match what
our bodies did: our love-making was never furtive or embarrassed, a pair of groping hands in the darkness and an
awkward silence in the morning: if we liked something we
told each other, with laughter or tenderness or further desire.
That is how it should be, surely – a fully shared blessing, the
communion of two people who, discovering love, are jointly
gripped by its intricacy and its power to move.

YOU: "That was love."
ME: "It was everything."
"We're lucky."
"Yes."
"Are other people as good?"
"I've an idea that they are, yes."
"Everyone?"
"No. People with imagination and some kind of close tie,
and, I suppose, good bodies. But that's probably more
common than you'd think."
"It's disappointing, in a way, I want us to be special. I
don't want any other woman in the world to feel just what
I'm feeling now, or any other man to have the same pleasure
in a woman as you had then."
"I'm contented enough not to feel jealous. . . . If other
people can approach that standard, or even catch a glimpse
of it, good luck to them."
"Good luck to them. . . . Darling, it won't always be like
that, will it?"
"No."
"What will happen to it?"
"It will fade."

"Ah. . . ."

"It must. Very slowly, perhaps, but it must. Time will – will take the edge off it. We'll probably never want each other quite so sharply as we do now, or have the same kind of overwhelming desire, or the same shattering relief. It can't do anything but grow less."

"That's sad."

"Ah, no. We'll have something else to put in its place, some other brand of exhilaration. In fact, probably we won't even miss it. Somehow it will deepen as it grows quieter: we'll still want each other and enjoy each other, but it'll be more with the heart than with the body."

"But you'll *want* me less?"

"Physically? Yes."

"Because you'll have had me a lot of times?"

"Yes."

"It's difficult not to feel that there's something horrible in that idea."

"But it'll be the same on both sides, sweetheart – and as long as we acknowledge it, and don't pretend to each other, what does it matter?"

"Suppose one of us gets tired before the other?"

"There's no comforting answer to that one."

"What *is* the answer?"

"Hell."

"For both."

"Yes, for both. There's nothing but misery in it. The loser will feel unwanted and left behind, and will be horribly hurt by it: and the winner – if one can call it that – the winner will feel guilty, and ashamed of his lack of desire, and then angry because he is made to feel ashamed when it is something he cannot possibly help."

"You said 'He'."

"I meant 'he or she'. You know that. It can happen to either side."

"Yes. . . . You were right, there is no comforting answer. . . . Is it true, from the masculine angle, that when you've had

130

a woman once, or twice, or a dozen times, you don't really want her any more?"

"Yes."

"Darling –"

"What?"

"Say something more about it. Make it sound less – less brutal."

"Sweet, I tried to give you an entirely accurate answer. When you've enjoyed something, after wanting it for a long time, you never wanted it in exactly the same way, do you? As a matter of fact, it simply isn't there any more: what you wanted had disappeared, has been spent. After all, there was only one – one virginal you, wasn't there?"

"And now you don't want me?"

"Now I want all the other you's – the later, lovelier ones. But I don't want the girl I started the honeymoon with, because she doesn't exist any more."

"That's a quibble."

"Yes, it is rather, isn't it? . . . But it really isn't a 'brutal' idea – or rather, it's only brutal if you think of marriage as a series of sexual exercises linked by daylight. That's not the sort of relationship we have in mind."

"No. But I still don't want to feel that there's a night coming you won't really care whether you sleep with me or not."

"Somewhere in the future there *is* a night like that. Darling, I can say to myself, when I have you in my arms: 'I'll never grow tired of this.' I can whisper it to you at the same time. But it'll be a lie. In the sense that I'll become less interested in enjoying your body, and more intent on simply binding up my life with yours, I *will* grow tired of it. So will you, in the same way. And when we've reached that stage, when we've explored sex thoroughly, and found out what gives us comfort, and what suits us after a bottle of wine, and what we feel like when the spring comes and we wake up with the sun on the pillow – then we'll start being married."

"What is this, then?"

"Our honeymoon."

"Darling, I think I shall like being married to you, after all."

"At present I like the honeymoon best."

"Me, too."

"And I'm not tired of you."

"No."

"In fact I may have made a mistake when I said that some day I would be."

"It seems possible."

"I must have been mixing you up with someone not quite so lovely and smooth and warm."

"An obvious error."

"I won't make it again."

"I don't intend to. . . . Darling, you must get some sleep, mustn't you?"

"Presently, yes."

"I mean presently."

We slept very little, of course: it was one of those nights when sleep is jealously grudged, for the ruthless way it blanks out the time together. Time lost at such a moment is the saddest of all: sleep, lonely sleep, can wait till later, but now every waking minute must be hoarded before it slips away. Occasionally we would doze off, but one or the other would soon stir, impelled to consciousness by this sub-conscious desire to lose nothing of our time together, and once more we would talk or kiss or lie in close contentment.

We talked a lot, that night: even if we had not been so new to each other, so eager to explore, we were aware all the time that the things we said now would have to last us for years to come. . . . Some of what we said was happily unre-cordable, some of it about our child, some of it about the future and our hopes in it. We talked, perhaps, most about that, because it had the most promise surrounding it. The past, before we met, seemed uninspired, the present was constrained and fleeting: only tomorrow, the world's tomorrow, held the springs of happiness and a warm and hopeful significance.

True, the springs were still secret, the significance a trifle cloudy: one had to peer about a bit to divine the hope – and still more to justify it. . . . I didn't really agree with what the sailor at dinner had said – that is, the idea of carving out one's own life from surrounding circumstances and the opposition of ambitious or greedy people: I am not that sort of man, partly from diffidence, partly from the conviction that such personal striving makes for a desolate world.

I had remarked that such a self-seeking civilization would be like the jungle, and he had agreed, without seeming to find anything out of the way in the idea; and his plan for the future – a future patterned on the uneasy past – certainly wasn't going to sweeten that jungle or make it any more tolerable for its minor inhabitants.

I had high hopes for that future, as I told you, but they sprang more from the humility of man (what that sailor would probably label his servile nature) than from the force of arrogant self-determination.

Christ taught humility and neighbourly co-operation; but I would have thought of them anyway. . . . It has always seemed to me that one should maintain a formal pattern of good conduct, not because of any supernatural compulsion, but simply because it is more *efficient*. Dishonesty and self-seeking do violence to this pattern of co-operation: they may be more profitable to the individual, but they distort his surroundings so much that in the end those surroundings become intolerable for nine-tenths of his fellow-men.

Reason will tell you this: reason will confirm that a pattern – a co-ordinated, smooth-working picture – is vital, if life is to have any dignity or significance at all. The wish to "behave" does not need the fear of punishment or the hope of heaven hereafter to give it validity: it springs from common sense, the sense of community, the constant awareness that if you conduct yourself decently and unselfishly you aid the betterment of your surroundings, while if you conduct

133

yourself like an ape with an acquisitive nose and itching fingers, you are fashioning, for man to live in, an ape's horrific world.

The sailor at dinner might say: First establish your impregnable place in society, then use it well: otherwise a tougher customer than you will get there first, and use it badly. That is all right if you are immunized against power, if you are confident of being incorruptible in a corrupt milieu. I have never yet met, or even observed at long range, such a man: the man who can preserve, against the tide of success, the ethics of humility, or who can be trusted with total authority when he has won it against opposition.

No. If power corrupts, fight corruption – not in others, but in yourself. Collect nothing you do not need: compete with all men, in the most rewarding of all forms of competition – service. Such conduct will produce its own design: a unique and formidable pattern, fit for the greatest as well as the humblest nation on earth.

This was not all we talked about in bed, but it was part of it. . . . I have always believed that such a discussion, involving the higher thought in somewhat dubious surroundings, is a superior way of passing the time: Sacred and Profane Love within the confines of a spring mattress. And if you exhaust a subject or run out of adjectives, no awkward pause ensues.

Behind it all, of course, colouring our exchanges and giving them an unreal and speculative quality, was the question of whether we would ever share a future together, no matter in what form it was cast.

"If I am killed," I began at one point, towards morning, when the hands of the clock seemed to be racing, and through the thick plush curtains there edged a shaft of grey, unwelcome light, "if I am killed –"

I felt you stiffen in my arms and then, as suddenly, relax again.

"It's all right," you said. "I *can* talk about it now, here, as long as I can feel you close to me, though later I may remem-

134

ber and be sad about it. . . . If you are killed, what do you want me to do?"

"Remember me – be sad for a long time – then remember me again, and be happy. If you have a child, I shall be there, in him. If you are alone –" I paused, feeling that I was helping you not at all and should never have started talking about it. To embark on the subject, and then to fail, was immeasurably worse than silence. Sweet, we have only a short memory to share, but it has been lovely. It will last a long time: when it begins to fade, don't be sad about it or think you are being unfaithful to me. That won't be true at all, and I would never want you to have that feeling.

You were lying with your head pillowed in the crook of my arm. Now you turned, burying your face in my shoulder so that I could hardly hear what you were saying, and spreading the bright fan of your hair across my chest. I loved you very much for your closeness to me.

"I hope I have a child," you murmured. "I wish one knew straightaway. . . . If I am left alone, I don't expect to be very brave about it for a long time afterwards. There'll be no quick flourish: I know just the sort of ache I shall have for you. I know just the sort of tears. . . . But later on . . . Darling," you said, with a sudden touching humility, "I'm only nineteen. You won't forget that, will you?"

In the half-light I nodded, pressing you close to me, understanding all that you were thinking but could not put into bleak words. "I know. I know. You are only nineteen, and life can't ever be over then, however bitter it may be at the time. Do you think I would want you to turn your back on it, because of the happiness we gave each other?"

"You wouldn't be disappointed if –"

"I should be disappointed if a person as sweet and lovely as you went to waste, after I was gone. . . . Sweet," I said, very slowly, "I think that's all I want to say – about – the – idea – of – you – marrying – again. . . ."

I felt your lips forming to a kiss on my shoulder. "Same here," you murmured. "Tired, darling?"

"I am only human," I answered, after consideration.

"May I say that you have proved it? How much of the night is left?"

"Technically, none."

"So it's good morning. . . ."

"Yes. A very, very good morning, sweet."

"And thank you for a lovely night."

"It's me that should be saying that."

"All I did was just lie here."

"You have a short memory." I felt your eyes closing, and I shut my own. "That's about the only thing you didn't do," I murmured, "but I'm not complaining. . . . Remind me in the morning to tell you how lovely you were."

"Morning now."

"Not yet, precious, not yet."

"All right – not yet."

So, for a space, we slept together.

9

I kept waking up, or perhaps I was never fully asleep; but somehow I was aware of the passing of all this time, dreamlike and uncontrolled.

For us it was the division between the past and the future, between our day of meeting and our day of good-bye; the hours now made up the dark, neutral ground between, and we crossed them swiftly. You slept uneasily – or did I dream that I watched you? Sometimes you whispered to yourself, and once you threw an arm across my chest as if you would anchor me and time together, and somehow stay the sun. Your body felt hot, and when I touched your forehead it had a slight, fevered dampness, which seemed childlike and pathetic.

The grey minutes were ticking away: it was difficult not to call after each one, for the solemn and inexorable procession was now paying us no attention at all. Lying there, we were discounted, indifferently ignored: we had had our lovely day and night, and they were being borne away, as a street is swept clean of flowers after a village festival, whether one would have it remain in fancy dress a little longer, or not.

Somehow, some remote, invincible authority, gives an order, and the party is over. There is no argument, because it has been tried before and it is never any good.

Here the authority was the hated clock, and most remote and invincible of them all, and as between sleeping and waking the successive chimes of London advanced the day towards us, I thought (or dreamt that I thought) that I would never listen to a church bell again without a nervous and sweating anxiety that you would soon be taken from me.

When sleep did come it was a fearful and shadowy business, attended by flocks of demons striving murderously to claw us apart.

10

We had wished each other good morning, but of course it was not a good morning: it was a terrible one.

When I finally woke up and opened my eyes I found that you were watching me, and that I had surprised you in a look of such compassionate tenderness that I pitied you for the thoughts you must be having. But I did not ask you what they were. . . . Instead I smiled and said: "Do I look very old?"

You shook your head. "You look like a baby, sweet."

"A rather knowing infant. . . . What time is it?"

"Nearly nine."

"Oh. . . ." I rolled over and reached for the telephone. "Breakfast now?"

"Yes, please."

Somehow we both knew that there was to be no more love-making: that neither of us wanted it or could have summoned up any sort of fervour or impulse. There was between us now, a faint weariness of the spirit, as well as our bodies reaction to the night's expense of energy: it was the beginning of good-bye, and we both knew it through and through, from the moment of waking. An old and foolish dance tune popped into my head – "But in the Morning, No?" That seemed to cover it.

When I had ordered the most attractive breakfast permitted by the regulations I turned back and took you in my arms, without saying anything. There was an obvious change even in the feel of you: you seemed colder, more detached, keeping tight command of yourself because you had to. I felt the same way myself. The whole room was beginning to shout, "Time's up!" with the most dreadful clarity and persistence, and we had nothing to keep it at bay except a disregarding tenderness for each other. And if what I felt now was anything to go by, that was not going to be enough.

Presently I said: "Lovely night, sweet."

"Yes."

"I love you."

"I love you."

There didn't seem to be anything more to add. Already I was beginning to feel dead inside. We lay there quietly until breakfast was brought in.

This was the breakfast we were going to have enjoyed so much – the flourishing signature to the start of our honeymoon. Now it was everything but that: it was our last meal together, it was the end of our shared life, for as far as the mind could see. It had grapefruit and an omelet and toast and marmalade and really excellent coffee: but it also had "Finish" on the menu, and it was unadulterated hell throughout.

At one point you said:

"What time do you have to go?"

"About noon."

"Station?"

"Not straightaway. Report to H.Q. first."

"I think I'll go back home today. I've nothing to do in London."

I nodded. "Yes, that's the best idea, darling." I thought for a minute, while the bedroom echoed. "Nothing to do in London" as if it were some dreary kind of curse. Then I added: "Why not catch the eleven o'clock? Then you won't have to hang about afterwards."

You looked at me and said: "Yes, I will. Don't come to the station, though. I'll just go off in a taxi."

"All right."

Then you began to cry. You had a piece of toast half-way to your mouth, and you suddenly looked at it and then your mouth crumpled and you dissolved into pitiful tears. Momentarily I was almost panic-stricken, with no notion what to do: there you sat, so shaken by your sobbing that you could control none of your movements, so helpless in your distress that had you not been relaxed against the pillow you might well have fallen. It seemed that your heart was already broken. . . . I put my arm round you and held you close, until the first shaking storm of your grief had passed; then, when you were no longer out of control but rather crying like a little girl lost among strangers who she does not trust, I said gently:

"Don't, sweet. Please don't. I don't think I can bear it if you cry."

You were wordless, and your tears still fell, as if reproaching me for being able to talk at all, when we were in such a wilderness.

"You've been so good up to now," I said. "Much better than me, really – you've been able to make me forget it all, while you must have been remembering yourself. . . . This *is* nearly the end, I know, but somehow we've got to deal with it, as we've dealt with everything else so far."

Quieter now, you laid your wet cheek against mine. A tear which splashed on to my forearm made a little pathway for itself and then gradually dried to nothing. It was the last one to fall. . . . I could feel your eyelashes blinking, and the muscles of your throat swallowing and swallowing. You were really very brave and good.

139

"It was what you said last night," you whispered presently. "I'm so sorry, dearest. . . . I suddenly remembered what you said about not coming back."

"I'll come back."

"It's such a long time. I won't know what's happening. You'll be fighting – there'll be all sort of dangers – you won't hang back, you'll be in front – you know you will – why do you have to be an officer. . . .?"

"That doesn't make any difference."

"It might do. Promise me –"

I interrupted you. "Anyway I haven't the feeling I'm going to be killed." Out of sight, I touched the wood of the bedside table. "Darling, I've side-stepped nearly every sort of missile in this war: the luck will hold." I knew this was bad talk, but somehow I did feel it, very strongly. "You'll see – I'll be back almost before you've missed me, covered with medals and a matted beard."

You smiled at that (as well you might) but you said: "It'll be so lonely."

"Lonely?" I took you by the shoulders and shook you gently. "Do you think you will be alone?" I asked. "You have a husband. . . . Only the good-bye is sad, precious – the rest is so strong, and has such hope buried deep inside it, that it can never fail us. Isn't that true? When I am gone I don't take everything with me. The best part stays with both of us all the time: it's the part we've built together and live on now, the part we'll have in the future. And in a little while I shall come back, and we can share it all again."

"And you'll take care of yourself?"

I nodded. "I shall take care of myself. For you, for me, for the child you may have *there*," and I touched you lightly, bending over to kiss you at the same time. There was salt on your lips, the last trace of the tears. For a while we held each other closely, while I stroked your breast and played with you. Between us there was a small prickling of sex, which helped to smooth out and resolve the difficult moment but was not strong enough to arouse either of us fully. Presently it died, and you sat up and said: "I must have my bath, darling, and pack," and then you got up and left me alone.

I watched you as you put on your wrap and straightened your hair before the mirror. The room was very silent all round us: even the clock, the hostile witness, was noiseless.

It was not the worst moment of all, but it was getting on towards it.

You came out of the bathroom and stood by the bed and looked down at me, and asked gently:

"Shall I get dressed?"

It was sweet of you to ask: I knew that you were tired and quite sexless at that moment, and yet you thought only of me and a possible last-moment of hunger in me. But it wouldn't have been any good.

"Yes," I said. "I'm sorry. . . . Yes, do."

You shook your head. "You know it would be the same for me, too."

I wanted to watch you dressing, which you do very gracefully, but it would have had nothing in it but sadness now, so I went off to shave and have my shower. Ordinarily, looking at myself in the mirror, I would have joked about the respective shadows under our eyes – yours had a faint violet stain, which it was very touching to have induced – but now, once again, there was no fun in having sweetly wearied each other: it was only sad, only destroyingly pathetic. I felt somehow that we were not doing well: this was not the sequel which the night deserved, however abrupt its ending; but I didn't know of any cure which wouldn't take more spirit than I had left.

Your crying had had something to do with it: you had only expressed, in your own tender way, what both of us were feeling, and it now felt as if the language you had been using was really mine as well.

But when I came back from the bathroom I found that you were now taking hold of the thing yourself – a better hold than mine: for my entrance coincided with that of a waiter bearing two champagne cocktails. If he was startled by the sight of a naked man in fur boots stalking into the bedroom, he didn't show it and never spilt a drop.

When he had gone: "Clever girl," I said, smiling at you.

"It was just an idea."

"The best today."

And so it turned out. The drinks cured nothing, of course, but (as had happened at the beginning of our meeting) they carried us past a corner that had a cutting edge to it. They even tided over the most wretched item of all, the packing, which had about it a feeling that something dear and precious was being throttled inch by inch. To see all the things you had looked so lovely in – the night-dress, the blue wrap, the flower-patterned mules – disappearing one by one for the last time was something hardly to be endured.

We were dressed, and it was time to go.

In your street clothes you suddenly looked grown-up – competent, individual, and also very attractive. I looked at you, realized all that I was leaving, and wondered how we were going to manage the next few moments, and the ordeal which was now demandingly upon us.

You put your arms around me, "Well, sweet?" you said.

I nodded. "I'm afraid so."

"You look good in your uniform."

"I don't feel very much like a soldier."

But holding you close like that, I *was* strengthened. You're such a lovely child, and to have you in one's arms is always a potent reminder of manhood. You felt as you had felt last night – warm, and straight-legged and undeniably mine; and the fact that you felt sad also, and that your under-lip was inclined to droop and your head lay on my shoulder as if it wanted to rest there for ever, all these were a summons to action and responsibility. They had to be met, and met they would be.

I put up my hand on your bright hair. "Take care of yourself, darling," I said.

"I will."

"And have a baby if you can."

You nodded, and I kissed you.

"*My* baby, I mean."

That made you smile, and you raised your eyes until they held mine. I hoped that I could match the love and tenderness I saw in them.

"It will be yours. . . . Be careful, won't you? Don't forget I love you. . . . Kiss, sweet."

We kissed, very gently, and afterwards your arms dropped and there was a little space between us. That space was never closed. Once more you let your eyes go up to meet mine: then your glance went round the room, saying its good-bye, and then, mutely valorous, you turned away from me and walked towards the door.

I followed. Presently the door clicked behind us, and our short lease was ended.

The door had a number on it which I have remembered. It was easily memorized – number 365. Number of days in the year. No connexion with us. We hadn't had a year. In fact we'd hardly had a day.

11

There remained a little time to spare before you need leave for the station, and rather than hang about doing nothing, we walked down the hill to Savoy Gardens.

It was odd to be outside in the cold, fresh air, after the continuous warmth of the hotel: somehow it signalized a lot of things which had already taken place – the good-byè, the transition from yesterday, the brief honeymoon's ending. Indeed, what we found there had, for us, a ludicrous novelty. There was faint sunshine, and children conferring round a statue, and old men feeding sparrows with bread which they might well have been needing themselves: there was the river through the railings, and a policeman speaking unsmilingly into a telephone, and a man selling peanuts and postcards of Cleopatra's Needle: in fact there was, in full and sudden measure, the thing we had been forgetting about – the routine unalterable outside world.

143

It was almost impossible to believe that it had been going on all the time.

We strolled along very slowly, arm in arm (to hell with the regulations on a day like this, I thought): you and I in love. I forgot what we talked about, but I don't expect it had much either of wit or continuity. I know that *my* mind, at least, was darting about, in a disjointed effort to cover all the ground: the sweetness of last night, the light touch of your hand in mine, the parting just ahead, the intensive and demanding world I would be stepping into, in a couple of hours time. I could not help looking forward to that: preoccupied as I was with you, my mind kept stealing glances at the future and the mixture of ordeal and exhilaration which lay there for me. There were still plenty of problems lying in wait. If my company could only stay as good as they were now: if Sergeant Hanson had filled in those returns properly: if those new fuses weren't all they were cracked up to be . . . All that had to be dealt with, as well as our farewell: all were worth squaring up properly, once I had settled down again. But what was that settling down going to be like, if the farewell was like this?

The farewell was here, anyway. We walked back up the hill, not speaking any more; inside the hotel lobby I retrieved your suitcase and we waited while a taxi came. The same head porter was standing near by, but after a glance in our direction he turned away and did not watch us any more. He must have seen many people like us, and we must have been easily recognizable.

We had said it all already, but we said it again, as if sharing something dear and original with each other.

"Take care of yourself."

"Please be careful."

"I love you, sweet."

You kissed me, and got in, and drove away.

"Good-bye," I said. "My love. My love."

Then I was *really* alone.

12

The room when I returned to it had the emptiness of a private hell. I leant with my back against the door, and looked around, and thought: "It happened here with you, and now you aren't here any more and I have to leave myself in a few moments." Then I sat down on the tumbled bed and ate two portions of marmalade and the piece of toast you hadn't been able to deal with, and wrote you (as I had promised) a note before leaving for good. There wouldn't be time for me to get one from you, but that was something which couldn't be helped.

Up the air-shaft which was all the view we had had (or needed) came the strains, from someone's damned radio, of "I'll Be Seeing You . . ." Of your physical presence in the room, nothing now remained, except a trace of lipstick on the pillow, and an untouched cup of coffee. Of your real presence, nothing was lacking: the loveliness, the fun, the close accord, the sadness, and the adoration – all were there, all round me, as strong as ever.

All the other things we shared were there, too. Remember them, sweet: remember them well, for we still have them waiting for us. I repeat to you now what I said when you cried: only the good-bye is sad – the rest is still ours. I shall not see you again during this war: that means years; but there is between us a flame that is going to burn, sometimes feebly, sometimes with an aching fierceness, until we can join hands again and marvel at its strength. You know that we have it: remember it, remember me, stay close.

We made each other so happy that now we cannot help being sad. But it is still there: and for my part there is no desolation which fighting and work and hope of you cannot cure. I have a tremendous job to do, before I can come back to you: so have countless others, before they can meet again the people they love. We are a strong company, because we believe in that job and because we have people like you to return to, when the thing is finished with.

Finishing it is wholly worthwhile, of itself (you know what I feel about that): but having you in the background takes me past those parts of fighting which are *never* worthwhile – the induced hatred, the brutal intent, the necessary, humourless treachery, the dabbling in blood for fun. There cannot be effective war without them – and that, by God, is no recommendation.

But when I do come back I shall be all yours: sharing if I can the best that is in me, taking from you the strength and guts and urge that alone can make sense out of my life.

It was the hardest of all to leave the room, darling: I walked round and round it, remembering you, I kissed the pillow, touched the towel you had used, stared at a cigarette with lipstick on it. The images crowded into my mind were bound to be sensual ones, for there, all round me at the last, were you and the joy I had of you, only a little while ago. Remember, sweet? Please remember – but remember much more. Remember how at the end it was not sensual love any more, it was nothing but tenderness, nothing but our two hearts pulling at each other.

That moment of parting. . . . I carry it with me now, like a charm – or like the white flower in your hair. It is not lonely: it has for company that other confused moment in our dream-world of that night, when we *could not* leave each other, when you cried as I did, when I said: "The time is racing like your heart," and touched your breasts with tears.

Heavy Rescue

1 · SEPTEMBER

GODDEN joined the end of the short queue leading into a room labelled, "Officer-in-Charge."

He didn't feel much out of place, in spite of the new surroundings and the way people were walking from room to room in a great hurry; many of the men in the queue looked much the same as he did – middle-aged, grey, dusty – though there *were* one or two in funny-looking clothes, and a sort of artist chap with a beard, and a couple of kids of twenty or so who should have been along at the recruiting office instead of here. But it was nothing out of the way, and certainly not as exciting as he'd expected when he suddenly made up his mind on the pavement outside. It was like queueing up at the Labour, and God knows he was used to that . . . "Air Raid Precautions – Volunteers Enrol Here," the notice had said; and he had straightway known what he wanted to do, and understood why he had been wandering about on that sunny September morning, feeling lost, feeling on the verge of something terrific, something to match the beginning of a war, and Chamberlain's speech, and that first startling siren. "Air Raid Precautions – Volunteers Enrol Here" – that might make sense of a lot of things, whatever it turned out to be. Digging trenches, maybe, or filling sandbags. But anything to get started: that was how he felt.

The queue moved on: talking, scraping its feet on the rough stone passage, trying to be normal and unconcerned.

When it was Godden's turn he found himself standing in front of a table, with a young chap, a clerk by the look of him, seated at it shuffling through a lot of papers. There were other people in the room: a girl talking on the telephone, a

Red Cross sergeant, two men at another table writing away without looking up at anything. Whatever was going on, it looked like the real thing; it looked as if a little bit of the war was getting under way here. That was what he had been wanting.

The clerk took his name and address and then looked up, pencil poised over a form. "Well, what's it to be?" he said.

"What is there?" asked Godden after a pause, to see if the clerk made any suggestions.

The man looked up at him, sharply: took in his tough, broad body, his shabby clothes, his oddly gentle face: decided he wasn't the smart sort after all, and, relaxing said:

"First Aid Party. Stretcher Bearer. Rescue Party. . . . Can you drive a car?"

"No," said Godden.

"What's your job? When were you working last?"

"February." He no longer felt ashamed of that question.

The clerk pursed his lips. "What at?"

"Roadwork – labouring."

"All right. What about Heavy Rescue then?"

Godden nodded. He liked the sound of it, though he didn't know what it meant. "That'll do fine."

The clerk wrote something on a card, and handed it across. "Take this to the Paddington depot – that's at Praed Street School. They'll fix you up. . . . Next!"

Clutching the card, Godden walked out into the sun again.

Praed Street School was just what one would have expected from that desolate section of London: a tall, gaunt arid building, dusty and echoing, full now of a throng of people wandering to and fro through the classrooms, or milling round the improvised canteen at one end of the hall. Already there was a painted sign over the entrance, "Rescue and Stretcher Party Depot No. 1" and a sentry, self-conscious in a steel helmet and greenish-yellow gas-proof overalls, standing on the top step. When he saw Godden he asked: "Got your card, mate?" and when he had turned it over he said, with a jerk of his thumb: "First on the left, inside. They'll tell you what to do."

Once more Godden joined a queue, and waited. This time, armed with the card, he felt more sure of himself: he already had some sort of status. In one room of the building someone had evidently found a piano and was banging out the "Beer Barrel Polka". Godden found himself humming it cheerfully. This was more like it. He was one of a crowd now. More like the last war. Not on his own any more.

This time the man behind the table was a Borough Council official, precise and briskly spoken. He wanted to know a lot of things: the sort of work Godden had been doing, how long he had been unemployed, whether his cards were in order, whether he had been ill recently. To all the answers he listened with his head cocked on one side, as though to catch some undertone of falsehood; but at the end he seemed satisfied, without enthusiasm, that Godden could do the work involved, and he entered his name and address on a permanent register, and took his insurance cards.

Then he said: "Which is it to be – day or night work?"

"How do you mean?" asked Godden.

The man looked up impatiently. "You can work from eight till eight daytime, or eight till eight during the night. Two shifts – do you understand? The pay is the same. Which do you want?"

Godden thought. It was one of those decisions he had not had to face for over twenty years. Hitherto, there had been only one cast-iron rule – do exactly as you are told, conform to our routine, or take your cards and get out. To have a choice – any choice, however small – seemed to increase his stature a hundred-fold. Day work or night work. It didn't make much odds really: Edie would grumble and nag about it, anyway, whichever he did. But air-raids came at night, didn't they? And that was what he wanted to help in – the bombing which was going to start straight away, so the papers said; that very night, as likely as not. That was what he had been thinking about all day, since Chamberlain's

149

speech, and it was what everyone seemed to be certain of: this was it, this was the proper start, tonight they'd be over in clouds, same as Poland, with mustard gas probably, and hundreds of people killed straight off. That was why he was standing here. He wanted to help when it happened.

"Make it nights," he said.

"Very well." The man made another note against his name and sat back. "You'll start tonight. I'll put you down in one of the heavy squads: you'll see it on the noticeboard later. Take a look round now, if you want to, and come back here sharp at eight o'clock."

Godden walked out, feeling suddenly elated. "One of the heavy squads" – he like the sound of that. It meant something, something solid and comradely. It was a job at last, and a lot more than a job. Once again it was like a bit of the last war, the best bit. And the pay was good, too: three pounds a week, less insurance.

It was the most he had earned since 1929.

The time by the clock in the big main hall was two in the afternoon. Godden would have liked a cup of tea and a bit of cake, since he had missed his dinner (there'd be trouble about that from Edie, when he got home); but he hadn't any money on him. Someone in the queue had said something about "meal tickets", but he didn't like to ask about that yet. He rummaged in his pocket and drew out the half cigarette he'd stowed away earlier. When it was lit he started to look about him.

Already there was a lot going on, a lot of people making a start at this new job. In the main hall, empty of furniture except for the piles of children's desks stacked at one end, and some clothes-racks along the wall, were about a hundred men; talking in groups, sorting through the kit issued to them, trying some of it on – gumboots, and steel helmets, and bulky, odd-coloured overalls. Stretchers were being brought in and piled in rows: five in a pile, for each of the ten stretcher-party squads, whose kit was neatly laid out in

150

one corner. A St. John Ambulance corporal, a little wizened man with a lined, humorous face, was demonstrating a leg-splint to a small circle. Godden wondered if he'd have to learn that job himself. He hoped not: it looked a bit too fancy. He walked through into another room: the mess-hall, with scrubbed trestle tables, and a few men settled down to cups of tea. Nothing there for him, yet awhile. . . . He wished he could find something to do. Even though he wasn't due to start until eight, he didn't want to leave. This was different from an ordinary job.

Outside, in the yard, there was a line of six rescue-party lorries, labelled "heavy" and "light" and piled with wooden shores, sawn planks, blocks and tackles, axes, crowbars, hurricane lamps. Men were climbing over them or looking at them from the ground, men like himself, used to this sort of gear. On an impulse he picked up an axe and swung it: caught the eye of a young chap perched on the roof of a lorry, and put it down again, feeling foolish. But it *had* felt good, all the same.

Suddenly, startlingly, he heard his name called, from inside. "Godden!" said a strong voice. And then, again: "Godden! Anyone know what he looks like?"

He walked through into the main hall, feeling something he had not felt for years: a separate person, a unit of a team, wanted for some special job. No one had really *wanted* him before, for as long as he could remember. Now he was on somebody's list, a name they were calling out, a person they were looking for.

There was a big man standing in the middle of the hall, with a piece of paper in his hand.

"You Godden?" he asked as Godden approached.

"Yes."

"I didn't know if you'd gone yet." The big man looked at him, sizing him up: he was a good head taller than Godden, tough and unsmiling, in a washed-out khaki shirt. "You're in my squad – number three."

"All right," said Godden.

151

"I thought I'd get you sorted out, those that are here. This is Isaacs." The Jew standing at his elbow nodded and smiled, not moving the fag-end of the cigarette from one corner of his mouth. "Know anything about this job?"

"Enough, I reckon."

"There's eight of us in a squad. Here's the list." Godden looked at it, saw that the big man's name was Watson, saw also, with tremendous satisfaction, his own name half-way down the list, next to Isaacs. He read it through as if it were a star football team: "Squad Three: Watson (Leader), Horrocks, Wilensky, Godden, Isaacs, C. Peters, B. Peters, Platt." He was right in the middle of the thing now: it was official. . . . "We go out with the stretcher-bearers when there's a raid," Watson went on, "and help them to get people out – shoring up, or breaking through a wall."

Godden said nothing. It sounded the sort of thing he wanted to do, above all else, but he was wary of showing anything of that feeling.

"I'm driving," said Isaacs suddenly.

"Then I hope you're good at it," said Watson.

"Used to have a lorry of my own. Bust it up. Hit the kerb and overturned."

Watson stared at him, still unsmiling. "Are you trying to cheer us up?"

"No," said Isaacs. "I was telling you why I'm a driver."

Godden said, nodding at the list: "Are there any more of them here?"

"No," said Watson. "They must have signed on early, and gone home." He yawned and stretched. "All right – eight o'clock then. We'll get sorted out when we're all here."

"Think they'll come to-night?" asked Godden. "Jerry, I mean."

"Bloody fools if they don't. Stands to reason. Take us by surprise, that's what they want to do. We'll have to watch out." He yawned again. "Well, see you later."

He left them.

"Big bastard," said Isaacs, without heat.

"What's the matter with him?" asked Godden.

"Chucking his weight about already. I know *his* sort. 'You're in my squad.' Bloody sergeant-major, that's what he is."

"But he's the squad-leader."

"Blasted little Hitler," said Isaacs. "What a war. . . . Well, I'm off. No overtime on this job for *me*."

Godden let him start off and then left the building himself. He didn't feel like that about Watson, or about the war or overtime or anything. But he wasn't going to argue. He was still feeling his way.

He walked slowly home, thinking of the step he had taken and recalling what he had seen of the depot. He had liked it a lot. Of course, it was grand to be in work again, on any terms, after the months and years of mucking about, of slammed doors and barred factories: after the curt answers and the shabby tactics of the Labour Exchange. But more than that: here was something about the job itself: it was the sort of thing a chap like him *ought* to be doing in war-time. Twenty-five years ago he would have been along at the re-cruiting office by now – in fact, that was exactly where he had been, twenty-five years ago; now he was past that sort of thing, but he wasn't past giving a hand in whatever job they could use him. And this job, rescue work in air-raids, and the atmosphere down at the depot on the first day of it, seemed to be part of the same worthwhile story. It recalled the war years very strongly, and the feeling they had all had then. There was the same sort of comradeship, the same sort of team feeling: he might have been Corporal Godden again – Corporal Godden, D.C.M., of the East Surreys, with a Lewis gun section to take care of and a definite responsibility to discharge.

He had never spoken at all about that Distinguished Con-duct Medal, except to say, the first time he was home on leave: "It wasn't much: I must have been a bit mad, I reckon." In winning it he had charged a German machine-gun

153

pit, shouting obscene and forgotten blasphemies: he had killed four men with the bayonet and strangled a fifth with his bare hands. He was twenty-eight at the time, lean and good-looking, and just married to Edie: now he was fifty, not much good for anything, unemployed since February and for long stretches before that: on and off the scrap-heap for twenty years and more.

Something had gone wrong in between. What was it? What had changed him from Corporal Godden, lining up for his medal at Buckingham Palace with Edie, pretty and breathless, looking on in ecstasy, into "old Godden" (if anyone took the trouble to call him anything), steadily getting poorer and shabbier, never in a job worth counting on from one week to another, and now not much better than a street-corner loafer. What had changed Edie herself, who had been so slim and shy and lovely, into the shrill discontented woman she now was? What had changed the pretty little baby, laughing all the time and twining minute fingers round his own, into Edna – fifteen years old, snuffly and whining, rude and slangy, slamming doors and giggling in corners, laughing at him when she dared, but for the most part going her own pert peroxide way?

Had it been his own fault? Edie for example. . . . That had gone wrong almost from the beginning, as soon as he was demobbed, with time on his hands and a bit of money to spend. When the money was gone everything else seemed to be gone with it, and that had somehow given the tone to most of the things between the wars. He had tried to settle into jobs, but the jobs themselves seemed to melt into nothing, before he had time to look round. He had tried to make Edie happy, but that again had disappeared, as soon as he was out of work and there was no money coming in.

Of course, she nagged a bit. In fact she nagged nearly all the time now, in a high, shrill voice that he'd got into the way of not hearing at all: about the money: about clothes for Edna: about her brother, who was a clerk in the city and doing so well. "Why aren't you more like Walter?" she had said, not once, but scores of times; and when, goaded, he had once answered: "There's no one like Walter – and a bloody good job too!" she had talked and nagged and screamed of nothing else for weeks afterwards.

She talked like that in front of the child, too. Godden had objected at first; but that was a long time ago. . . . Now, of course, Edna was taking the hint from her mother, and was as rude, silly, and uncaring as she liked. He was just beginning, after a series of flaming scenes in which Edie had joined, to shut his ears to that, too. Perhaps everyone's kids grew up the same way. Not much he could do about it anyway, without everlasting rows, and he was sick to death of those.

So Godden's thoughts wandered, as he turned into his own street, the dirty cul-de-sac off the Harrow Road, where they shared a seven-roomed house with two other families. What he *didn't* think about, the thing he never gave a thought to because it had never yet crossed his mind, was why he felt as he did about the Army, and England, and joining up straight away, and helping people in air-raids. No one had helped *him* for more than twenty years. His wife alternately laughed, sneered or raged at him, his daughter was growing up in the same dreary image. The place he lived in was the same "home fit for heroes" he had finally found in 1919 – a damp and crowded little hell with, now, the cracked decay of 1939 and the drains of 1850.

The England which had welcomed his services, with a beaming smile in the Great War, was now baring its gums and getting ready to accept them again – but what it had done for him in the meantime was like some sordid confidence trick with a rotten-cored apple. And yet here he was, on the first day of another war, taking another bite of that same apple, "joining up" without a thought, without hesitation, without really believing that he had any other course.

Not quite "without thought", perhaps; but almost. Vaguely he realized that it wasn't much of a world off the Harrow Road, that it was wrong that Edie should have to go out office cleaning in order to make up the rent and that Edna (as she had pointed out on one vile, unforgotten occasion) got more money as a "starter" at Madame Marie's than he himself now drew from public assistance. But he didn't connect this with anything more complex than the circle of his own family: he didn't think of it as the fault of any system or group or organization. What he did think, from reading the newspapers, looking at cinema posters, and listening to Edie, was that there must be something wrong with himself.

The delight of professional patriots, the despair of social historians, and the irrational pride of England, Godden went down the basement steps to the corner of the house where they lived.

"Rescue work? You're daft!" Edie Godden banged down the plate with the over-cooked, dried up kipper on it, and put her hands on her hips again. "Why don't you get yourself a proper job for once? What's rescue work? Who could *you* rescue? I'd like to know!"

"It's air-raid precautions," answered Godden for the fifth or sixth time. He had known it would be like this, but it was impossible to explain why he had missed dinner, and why he would have to go out again after tea, without going into details of the job. He had thought she might be pleased about the money, but she wasn't.

"Are you one of those wardens?"

"No," said Godden. "We go out when there's a raid, and give a hand, like." (Shoring up and breaking through walls, Watson the squad-leader had said, but he wasn't going to say anything about that to Edie. It would only start her off.)

"What sort of a hand could you give in an air-raid?"

Godden, munching dry flaky fish and trying to wash it down with tea, didn't answer for a moment. Then he said: "They'll tell us all to-night."

Edie Godden sniffed. "They'll have to tell you a lot before it makes any sense. What do you want to get yourself mixed up in that lot for? Walter's firm is going to make uniforms, he says. There's thousands in it. Why don't you get yourself a job like that?"

Once again Godden paused before answering. All he knew was that he didn't want that sort of job at all. It wasn't what you ought to do in war-time, not if you could help people other ways. Air-raids were more important. For weeks now, he had had a picture of what an air-raid might be like, and the number of people who might be needing help when it came. He'd seen a film once (the cinema in the Harrow Road put them on in the mornings, for the unemployed, threepence a time) with an air-raid in it. Bombing in China, or something; a kid stretched out on the ground with its clothes torn and blood-stained, and a woman with her hair hanging down acting crazy over it, waving her hands and crying. Godden hadn't liked that picture, or the things it meant: he had wanted to pick up the child, take care of the woman, give her a cup of tea or something, tell her it would be all right.

He felt like that about all sorts of people – about everyone, in fact, who had a run of bad luck or needed a hand. There were plenty of those in the Harrow Road . . . his reverie was interrupted by Edie.

"Hurry up with that plate," she said. "I've got to do some proper work, if you haven't."

"It's a government job," said Godden. "Because of the air-raids."

"Government! You'll be saying you're in Parliament next. Another excuse for hanging about doing nothing, more like."

Edna came in, from the bedroom she shared with her mother. (Godden slept on a camp-bed in the kitchen where he was now eating.) Edna was dressed to go out, in a brown coat with a piece of fur round the collar, yellowish silk stockings, and a shining black handbag. Under the gaslight her hair had a thin metallic glint. Godden saw that she had been making up again – there had been a row about it a couple

157

of days earlier: the childish mouth stood out in a straight wet gash, the red patches on the sallow cheeks were like fever marks. His daughter, fifteen years old, and looking like a Praed Street tart already.

"You going out?" he asked, rather sharply.

"Pictures," said Edna. Even in that single word she achieved the whining tone she had now permanently adopted. It sounded like a sulky complaint. He wondered what sort of a place this Madame Marie's could be, if they put up with that sort of thing from a kid.

"It's the first night of the war. You ought to stay at home with your mother, instead of gadding about looking like a—"

"Like a what?" said Edie sharply.

"Nothing," said Godden.

"You leave the child alone. Why shouldn't she have a bit of fun? She pays for it, doesn't she? I don't see you doing much staying at home, either. Dad's got a job," she added to Edna. "Rescue work in air-raids, he says."

"Sounds soppy to me," said Edna. She looked at herself in the mirror over the mantelpiece, and pushed up her hair at the back. "Rescuing what, may I ask?" she said, and giggled rapturously at her wit.

Godden said nothing.

"I'm going out myself, anyway," said Edie, "so there's no cause to go after Edna just because she wants a bit of fun."

"You and Edna ought to go away, really," said Godden. He had finished his tea, and wanted a cigarette, but the packet was crumpled and empty. The yellow gas-light, bubbling and purring, made the kitchen a cosy place to relax in: it might have been a nice little home. "Away from London, I mean," he added.

"Where to?" asked Edie.

"Out in the country somewhere. There's places. It says so in the papers. Evacuation scheme, that's what it is."

"Lot of nonsense," said his wife. "That's just for the kids."

"Grown-ups too. Everyone. I saw it in the papers. In case there's big raids."

"Catch me going off to the country!" said Edna. "No shops or anything. Give me the creeps."

"You'll do what you're told," said Godden.

"Leave the child alone, can't you?" Edie broke in. "Anyone would think you'd bought the place, with your rescue work and your three pounds a week."

"Three pounds!" exclaimed Edna, in a high affected voice. "Wonders will never cease. Well, I must be going. Good-bye, soaks – I mean folks!" She giggled again, patting her hair.

"Enjoy yourself, love," said Edie fondly.

"You know *me*," said Edna. The door rattled behind her as she went up the basement steps.

There was silence in the kitchen after she had gone. Godden knew he ought to speak to Edie about the child, who was getting worse every day, but it would mean another row straight away, and he didn't want to start that tonight. It was a special night for him – the war, a new job, a place in the same old team again. . . . He kept silent until Edie, after tidying up at the sink had put on her hat and was ready to go out. Then he said, in an effort to be friendly:

"Not working, Sundays, are you?"

"I'm going round to Mrs. Lambert's," said Edie briefly. There was no answering friendliness in her voice. "What about in the morning? What time do you finish at this job of yours?"

"Eight," said Godden. "Back here about half-past."

"I can't cook you breakfast then. I've got to start early tomorrow, and Edna's got quite enough to do getting ready for her work."

"I'll do it myself, then."

"And there's no need to be a martyr, either."

Godden said nothing.

"Don't mess up the stove while you're at it," Edie went on. "I've enough cleaning to do as it is."

She put her hat straight before the mirror, buttoned her coat, and left the house.

Godden sat on, thinking of the coming night's work,

wondering what time the raids would start. In a way, he was looking forward to the air-raids. It was a chance to do something at last.

For the first time for many years, he put on his medal ribbons before he set out for the depot.

It was good to walk out of the house, not pointlessly as so often in the past, but on his way to work.

Just before eight o'clock that night, "Rescue and Stretcher Party Depot No. 1" was a very full and noisy place. The day-shift, rather a scrappy, disorganized collection of that first Sunday afternoon, were turning in their equipment and preparing to leave: the incoming night-shift, after signing-on in the Control Room, were waiting about until they had a bit of elbow-room to organize themselves. At the moment they were all mixed up together in one moving, aimless throng – rescue parties, stretcher parties, drivers, first-aid instructors, with a sprinkling of Red Cross and St. John uniforms here and there; but already, as they waited and watched the day-workers leave, there was a subtle tension in the air.

It was that prime tension of the war, the edge of something unknown but inevitable. September the third had been quiet so far, but they were now embarking on its crucial hours – the night shift; and from now on, as the crowds in the main hall thinned, leaving only themselves to take the weight, theirs was the true ordeal and the true danger.

So far the others had only been playing at it, filling in the time; but the real thing might break loose at any moment – the newspapers and the radio, with their brutal news from Poland, underlined this continually – and they themselves were left, the Stoic garrison, to live out the coming night.

Presently, as they waited, a tall man, in a well-cut dark suit, stood up on a chair and called for silence. The crowd in the main hall, who had been waiting for something of the sort stilled expectantly; and the man began to speak, with a brisk confidence which they recognized and welcomed.

"I just want to tell you," he began, "a few things about the job you're taking on, and the sort of work you can expect.

This depot is part of the Borough organization for dealing with air-raids. I don't know when they'll come – tonight quite possibly – but we've got to be ready for them in any case. In the next few weeks we'll have plenty of training. I hope: in the meantime we'll have to do the best we can." He let his eyes go round the room. "We're very glad to have so many volunteers: it's been a splendid response, and a great credit to Paddington. You will probably find this place a bit crowded and uncomfortable until things shake down: but we hope to organize a proper meal-system in the canteen, and beds and mattresses for those squads which aren't at immediate readiness.

"If there's an air-raid you'll all be going out together as soon as an incident is reported in this district, whether the raid is still on or not. There's a steel helmet for every man on the job, by the way, and we should have enough service gas-masks for everyone by next week. The stretcher parties will deal with the casualties lying about the streets, in the first place; and the light and heavy rescue parties will get to work releasing people who may be trapped in houses, so that the stretcher-bearers can deal with them too. As soon as we can arrange it, there'll be a full programme of First-aid training, with an examination, for all stretcher-bearers; and we may have to ask the Rescue Parties to take elementary training too. But that's looking into the future a bit. For tonight I just want to be sure that you're ready to move out if you're called on.

"You've all been organized into squads, as you know: stretcher-bearers and rescue parties alike. Make sure you know your squad-leader and squad number. There'll be sentries provided by these squads, to look after the lorries and to watch the doors. Squad-leaders will fix the rotas for this themselves: they'll also be responsible that their squads are ready to go out at short notice, any hour of the night. The warning-system should give you plenty of time, as we'll get a confidential warning before the sirens go. But," he smiled, "accidents do happen, and you've got to be ready to move quickly if necessary. Cars and lorries should be warmed up every hour, just to make sure they're in working order. That's about all, I think," he concluded. "If there's anything you want explaining, go along to the Control Room and see the officer in charge. I hope there'll be nothing happening to-night, but if there is, the best of luck, and I'm sure you'll all do a good job!"

Unconsciously, Godden had been standing stiffly to attention all the time that the man spoke to them. The words and the manner of delivering them, had recalled very strongly the long-past war years, with their sense of some supreme effort soon to come, and the stimulation of being trusted by authority at a moment of crisis. So often had Godden's platoon commander spoken to his men, when there was a job – a patrol or a raid – to be undertaken, and their comradeship in danger was nearing its testing-time. So often had Godden tensely listened, striving to feel he was worthy of the trust, and would not let his part of the undertaking down. So, now, the link with that past and all it had stood for made itself felt, pulling him into the team again, giving this job its final worthwhile feeling.

Air-raids tonight, the man had said. Very well – let there *be* air-raids. . . . In that room they were all ready, and would not fail each other, or the man who had trusted them and wished them luck.

Across the room Godden saw the squad-leader, Watson, talking to a small group of men who stood round him, and he made his way towards him through the throng. Watson, who was explaining something to Isaacs, broke off as he approached, and said cheerfully:

"Here's the missing link now. That makes up the squad."

Godden smiled without saying anything, and then looked round the group of men. There were seven of them, well-assorted: Watson and Isaacs (who was looking rather disgruntled, as if the speech had offended his principles in some way) seemed like old friends compared with the rest. There was a foreign-looking chap – that would be Wilensky, thought Godden, recalling the name on the list and immediately labelling with it a man with a big, curved nose and a halo of greying hair, who had the self-contained, inward look of a foreigner feeling his way in entirely novel surroundings. Next came two young fellows so alike that they must be the two with the same name – C. Peters and B. Peters – brothers, most likely. That left the tall, thin man in the faded boiler-suit who must be Platt, because the last one, nearest to Godden now, was – yes, by God, it *was* old George Horrocks, his pal from years back that he hadn't seen since just after the war! Godden had specially noticed the name on the list, but it was a common one and he hadn't really connected it with old George. And now here he was – or what was left of him. For it was clear, at a glance, that the same thing had happened to Horrocks as had happened to Godden: they had both stepped down, today, from the same dingy scrap-heap where, on and off, they had both spent the arid, desolate years between the wars.

Godden felt sad about that for a moment, because Horrocks had been, in the old days, a rolling, jolly sort of man, the unpromotable buffoon of the company but the kind of buffoon who can turn serious in a tight corner and do his bit as well as any long-faced "dependable" type: now he was not much more than a tramp, by the look of him – frayed flannel trousers, the pocket-linings of his coat hanging down in tatters, the greasy old cap on the back of his head framing a grey, lined, stubbly face. "Godden and Horrocks – the Old Firm" – that was what they used to be called, in those companionable days in Flanders; and that was what they still looked like, only in a shabby futile sort of way – a pair of old dead-beats with nothing to choose between them, now resuming partnership at the bottom of the scale.

Godden held out his hand. The others, except Watson who was working something out on the squad-list, were watching their meeting with the slightly envious interest of people who are for the moment, without anyone to talk to.

"Why, George, fancy meeting you!"

Horrocks smiled broadly for a single moment, as if within his dulled face someone had flicked a lamp on and them off again. He said: "Bill Godden!" in a rough, pleased voice, and shook hands. Then he resumed the featureless expression, the obvious desire to escape notice, which now seemed to be normal with him.

"What got you into this, George?" asked Godden, sure that Horrocks would produce some surprising reason which would make them both laugh.

After a pause, Horrocks said: "It's a job."

Just that, nothing more. No jokes about it, no pretence (as in the old days) that because the two of them had taken on this odd job, there was something cheerfully shady about it which would put the firm of Godden and Horrocks in a cheerfully privileged position. Horrocks, clearly, was past all that sort of thing: now he either worked and ate, or did neither, and the intervening shades of experience had disappeared in an overall grey acceptance of fortune. He had been defeated too long.

Watson now interrupted the exchange by saying:

"Let's get this sentry duty settled before we do anything else."

They gathered round him as he stood there with the squad-list in his hand. All over the big hall there were similar groups clustered round their leaders, settling the first outlines of their new job.

"We've got to cover four hours," Watson went on, "from midnight to four o'clock. We're working on a rota with the other squads, and the time we cover will change every night. There's seven of you to do it –"

"Eight," broke in Isaacs suddenly. "Eight in a squad."

"I'm not doing sentry duty myself," said Watson shortly, after a pause.

There was a silence in the group, and then Isaacs said:
"Why not?"

"Because I'm the squad-leader – that's why not."

164

Godden and the others thought this was a sufficient answer: Isaacs clearly did not.

"There's nothing in the rules," he began belligerently.

Watson frowned. "What rules?"

"The rules that chap was talking about. He didn't say anything about squad-leaders not doing sentry, did he? Seems to me –"

"Awkward bastard, aren't you?" Watson interrupted him, almost genially. "I'm not doing sentry because I'm the squad-leader, and I'll be in the control room when the squad's on duty, ready for when there's a report of a raid, and anyway I don't want any bloody argument about it from you."

The others were watching them. They were not backing up Isaacs in the least, but they wanted to see how Watson justified his position as leader. So far he seemed all right.

"I wasn't arguing about it," said Isaacs, trying another tack. "I'm entitled to know the rules, aren't I? This isn't Germany, you know. We don't want any dictatorship here."

"For Christ's sake get on with it," broke in one of the Peters' brothers. "I want a cup of tea."

"I'm only standing up for all your rights," complained Isaacs.

"You wait till you're asked."

"All right, all right," broke in Watson. "Let's start again." He read out the list of names, and the time of sentry-duty for each man – thirty-five minutes apiece. Then he went on: "The lorries are what we've got to look after – to see that they're not meddled with, and that the lamp on the corner is kept alight. If there's a warning the sentry will wait until the driver – that's Isaacs," he added, with a trace of a smile, "until Isaacs comes out, and then join up with his squad, ready to go. Is that clear?"

One or two of them said, "Yes". And then the Pole, who had been watching them all warily without speaking, said suddenly:

"We will have arms?"

"Arms?" echoed Watson, rather puzzled.

165

"Arms," repeated Wilensky. "The sentry, to guard the cars."

"No," said Watson. "There's no call for that."

"There could be sabotage," said Wilensky laboriously. "In Poland it is reported that some of the fire-engines were sabotaged."

"Nothing like that here, mate," said the other Peters brother. "This is England, you know." But he said it kindly, without any edge: echoing in his tone what they felt towards Wilensky now that they knew he was Polish, because of what was happening at that moment to Warsaw.

It was growing darker outside: the beginning of the crucial night. Number Three Squad drew its meal tickets (to the value of "One Shilling") and settled down in a corner of the mess-hall with tea and sausages and chips. An old woman and a night-club singer, a young man famous at a different social level for the polish and obscenity of his repertoire, were running the volunteer canteen: the woman cooked the food on a stove as battered and cranky as herself, the young man served up the plates with a bright allusive prattle which might have been a riot at the Four Hundred or the Coco-nut Grove but it was nearly incomprehensible here. He had been christened Cuthbert by the rescue parties, many of whom thought he was a lunatic. But the food was all right; and free, too.

Horrocks, warming a little to the meal and the cheerful atmosphere, was volunteering to Godden something of what had happened to him since they last met.

"I had a bit of a shop, to start with," he said. He talked in a very quiet voice, out of the side of his mouth, as if what he was saying could land him in trouble if it were overheard. "Sweets and tobacco – over in Camden Town. But it didn't go."

"Independent operator, eh?" said Godden, grinning.

Horrocks said: "That's it," without taking in the point of the remark. In the old days, "independent operator" had

166

been their term for the sort of one-man scrounging which could, at the risk of a stiff sentence for looting, sweeten life in the back areas of the Western Front. It was clear that Horrocks had forgotten almost everything that was cheerful about the past: the history and feeling of his defeat had swamped all the unessentials of life.

"Then I got taken on in a shop – same line, tobacco and cigarettes – but they started putting in girls instead of men, so I was out again. I tried for a factory job, but they wanted girls again after a bit – kids, most of them, fifteen bob a week, instead of paying men's wages." He said this without bitterness: these were things which "they" decided, and there was nothing to be done but go somewhere else. "Then I got a porter's job – block of flats in Hampstead: that was all right for a bit, but there was a mistake over a parcel being delivered to the wrong flat, and I got the sack. I was working at Smithfield Market for a time, on and off, till a little while ago. And then this came along."

He stopped, and took a sip of his tea. It was hard to realize that this meagre recital had covered twenty years of his life, that this had been, for him, the sum of the brave post-war world they had talked about so cheerfully in Flanders. . . . Godden traced with his finger the circle of a wet stain on the rough deal table. Horrocks's story, with one or two changes, might have passed for his own, but obviously Horrocks had come out of it very differently. He wasn't bitter about it, neither was he still hopeful: he was just dead. And this present job – obviously they felt differently about that, too. Horrocks had come into it with none of Godden's memories and feelings of the last war: he hadn't "joined up" because there was work to be done and people to be helped in air-raids, he had just taken it on because it was the only thing that offered.

"How's the wife?" asked Horrocks after a pause.

"All right," said Godden.

"You had a picture of her. I remember. Used to pass it round."

"Yes," said Godden.

He got up and went over to the canteen hatch to replenish his cup of tea.

"Here you are, ducks," said the night-club singer. "Cheers but does not inebriate, *I* always say. If you don't like our goods, put 'em where Cleopatra put the asp."

"What?" said Godden.

"No offence where none intended, I'm sure." The young man, whose style after six hours of this sort of thing was getting rather ragged, hitched his shoulders impatiently. "What's the Savoy Grill got that we haven't got here, except a few tablecloths and Carroll Gibbons? Knock three times and say that Joe sent you."

"Ah," said Godden, and retreated with his cup of tea. The young man reminded him of an officer they had once had. Not a good officer.

"Can't make that chap out," he remarked when he got back to the table. "He goes on and on, and you can't get any sense out of it."

"Slumming, that's all he's doing," said Isaacs viciously. "Coming down here and pretending he's one of the workers. We don't want his sort here."

"He's working hard enough," said Watson. "How would you like to sling cups of tea and plates of food around for six or seven hours on end?"

"A bid for sympathy, that's all it is. You always see a lot of that, at times like these."

"What good would that do him? What the hell are you talking about?"

"Never mind," said Isaacs mysteriously. "There'll come a day when we'll know who's on our side, and it won't be fancy young bastards like him."

"What side is that?" asked Watson curtly.

"Backside, I should say," broke in one of the Peters brothers, the one who had clashed with Isaacs before. "You talk like one of those daft chaps in the Park." He rapped on

168

the table in front of him. "If you want to kick up a row, for Christ's sake go and do it somewhere else."

"I wasn't kicking up a row."

"It was a bloody good imitation then."

"Now then," said Watson with determination. "This is a rescue squad, not the bleeding House of Commons. Let's give it a rest."

In the silence that followed (for already they all recognized Watson's clear authority) the Pole, Wilensky, took out a ponderous silver watch and looked at it.

"Eleven o'clock," he said. He was frowning deeply. "If they come, they come soon. We should be ready."

Godden thought: he's about the only one who's got the right idea. He and Watson, that is. Maybe it'll be better when the raids start. But we've got plenty to do before we get this lot straightened out.

Towards midnight the depot was showing signs of settling down for the night. The old woman in the canteen had gone home, though the night-club singer dozed on in a kitchen chair, his young-old face revealing in repose a strained, unsure anxiety. In the deserted mess-hall two men, stretcher-bearers, finished their long card game in yawning silence, amid the dirty teacups and half-eaten pies and plates smeared with congealing gravy. But the big main hall was still alive. One end of it, brilliantly lit, was crowded with wakeful figures: there were the stretcher-bearers who were due to go out first if a call came: there were the two rescue squads who were also first on the duty list: there was the stretcher-bearer officer-in-charge sitting at a table checking names and numbers: there were two or three men playing the fool with some forgotten gym equipment, getting in everyone's way and being loudly cursed from all over the hall.

But among them all, as they waited for the time to pass, there was an obvious tension, revealed here and there in an ear cocked to catch a sound from outside the building, or in those who kept strolling to the open doorway and peering up at the night sky; and this tension, receding into the shadows, seemed to affect the other, darkened end of the room. Here the men who would not be on duty until later were trying to get some sleep. There were no beds, that first night, and very few blankets: the men lay uncomfortably on their backs or slouched against an angle of the wall, staring round them at the unfamiliar room or up at the shadows of the lofty roof; pulling at cigarettes, which glowed suddenly in the darkness, muttering and tossing in the effort to find a comfortable position on the bare planked floor. Their kit lay ready to hand beside them – steel helmets, rubber boots and overalls, torches, first-aid bags, all the grim, workman-like gear they might be needing within the next few minutes; they were waiting for it to happen, as the ready squads under the lamplight were waiting: there was no relaxation in this muttering, twitching throng of men, who coughed in the close, frowsty air sealed up by the black-out, or mumbled to those lying beside them, or cursed the noise at the other end of the room.

This was not like any other night, it was not given for sleep and rest; nor were they simply men lying there sleepless – they were guardians, selected to bridge the darkness and the first dubious span between peace and war.

Godden had tried to sleep for the last hour before he was due to stand his sentry-duty, but sleep would not come. From the roomful of men, alert or uneasily dozing, he had caught the prevailing tension, and he recognized it, his memories of the other war crowding in to prompt him, as the restlessness of men on the eve of action. There was no cure for that. . . . After a time he abandoned the attempt to settle down, and joined a small group among those at the other end of the room. They were listening to one of the stretcher-bearers, a gaunt young man in corduroy trousers, an open-necked khaki shirt, and a heavy green overcoat, who was propounding what was clearly an unpopular argument.

"If we were all pacifist," said the young man, "there'd be

170

no war." He was addressing himself especially to a tough-looking rescue man with a white scarf knotted tightly round his throat. "That must be true, surely."

"Someone would always start it," said the rescue worker. "Stands to reason, you'd be attacked."

"But if we were all pacifists," insisted the young man, "all over the world, I mean."

"But we're not," said several voices at once.

"I said *if* we *were*. We've got to persuade people, that's all, so that everyone refuses to fight, all over the world. Then there'd be no war, would there?"

"How are you going to persuade them?"

"By setting an example. By not fighting. By not resisting anything they do."

The rescue man laughed scornfully. "Bloody fine chance we'd have if we tried that."

"It's worth trying."

"What are you doing here, then? You ought to be at home, letting them drop bombs anywhere they like, if that's the way you feel about it."

"I want to help if there's a raid," said the young man sulkily.

"Setting a bad example, that's what you are. Fighting the naughty bombs. That's resisting, isn't it? You'll get the sack if you don't look out."

Godden, unaware that he was listening to one of the most crucial of the current dilemmas, was somehow drawn to the young man, in spite of the stand he was taking. He must be a conchie, of course, but that wasn't always the disgrace that the papers made out.

Godden still didn't know, after all these years, quite what to think about conchies. There'd been some good ones in the last war – Red Cross chaps and stretcher-bearers – as well as some proper bastards, who were just out to dodge the column. It depended what it was that turned them away.

He was interrupted now – they were all interrupted – by

the officer-in-charge, who bounced out of the Control Room, blew a whistle, and shouted: "First four stretcher-bearer squads! Get in the cars and stand by!"

The whole room woke up with a jerk. Stretcher-bearers started to fling on their equipment, tripping over each other as they made for the door, arguing hotly about the helmets and satchels they had snatched up in the rush. The men in the darkened part of the room stood up to watch them, and began scrambling into their own equipment, so as to be ready in case their call came. Squad-leaders were shouting to their squads, to hurry them up: the storekeeper dropped a pile of steel helmets with a reverberating crash: there was a volley of curses as five men, racing for the doorway, arrived at the same moment and jammed in the entrance; and from outside, topping everything, came the roar of engines as the cars were started up.

"It's a test," said the officer-in-charge rather lamely, taken aback by the uproar he had let loose.

"Christ, why didn't you say so?" exclaimed the rescue man with the knotted scarf. He took a deep breath, and expelled it abruptly. "Good as a dose of salts, that was! I thought the bastards were overhead already."

Godden, who had followed the last of the stretcher-bearers out, had stood on the pavement edge and watched the cars roar away on their time-test, the tail lights streaming up the road and out of sight, like sparks before the wind. The quick alarm had excited him, he wanted to miss nothing of its savour.

When the cars were finally out of sight he walked back to the line of lorries parked in the mews courtyard at the back of the building: as he came into the circle of light shed by the hurricane lamp, Platt, who had the first sentry duty, stepped forward to meet him.

"How's the time?" asked Platt. The old boiler-suit he was wearing gave him a scarecrow air, and the shadow he cast against the opposite building was as tall and thin as a piece of scaffolding.

"About half-past twelve," Godden answered. "I'll take over now, if you like. Anything doing?"

"No. Only those crazy bastards in the stretcher-cars. You'd think they were going to a fire."

"Good practice for them."

"Good practice for the undertaker, if they hit something." Platt sounded cold, and rather depressed. "Any tea going inside?"

"Canteen's still open. I should wake Cuthbert up and ask him."

"Probably get a damn' silly answer."

Godden laughed. "Shouldn't wonder." He looked up at the sky, framed between the buildings on either side. It was clear and peaceful. "Do you think they'll come tonight?"

"Sure to," said Platt. "Knock-out blow, that's what they'll try, if they've any sense. Same as Poland. Look at the mess they made there."

"We'll be better prepared, though."

"We'll need to be." He stretched and yawned: under one of his armpits a ragged seam gaped for a moment, like an echoing mouth. "Well, I'm going to get some sleep, before the fun starts."

"You'll be lucky if you do," said Godden. "It's a proper circus in there."

"They'll have to get it organized. Beds or something. Like that chap said."

"It's only the first night. You've got to remember that."

Left to himself, Godden walked down the line of lorries, and back again to the lamp. Sentry duty again – after all these years. . . . He felt a strange mixture of feelings inside him: excitement after the rush of the cars going out, pride in this small job, the first bit of responsibility he had been given for many years, doubt of what the rest of the night might hold for them. If the bombs started coming down, as it seemed they must, how would it turn out: how would he and the rest of them inside deal with it? How would Edie and Edna face it – they must be back home by now, maybe sleeping, maybe wakeful and waiting for the sirens to go. It was odd to be on guard like this, watching over the lorries, and this corner of London, and Edie and everybody else. It made him feel like a man again: in fact he *was* a man again, and this job was as good as anything in the old days, and maybe he hadn't changed so much after all. . . . Walking up and down in the darkness, Godden shed the dreary past, feeling deep inside every part of him the return of a forgotten confidence.

A scream of brakes from the main road brought him back to the immediate present. It was the stretcher-cars returning, or rather the first of them, far, outstripping the other and rounding the final corner in a wicked side-slip that made the tyres squeal. When it drew up at the door the stretcher-squad tumbled out, exclaiming loudly about the trip in tones which blended relief, blasphemy, and admiration in nice proportions. They were followed by the driver, slamming the car-door behind him with a triumphant crash. It was the young man who, a little earlier, had been seeking converts to pacifism.

"Have you broken the record?" asked Godden

"Just about." The young man had an air of exultation which had been missing earlier: indeed, he somehow gave the impression that this was the first time he had been really excited and pleased about anything since he left school. . . . "Three and a half minutes from Paddington Hospital to here. It shook up some of the squad a bit. One of them tried riding on the running-board, at the start, but he changed his mind half-way."

"Don't blame him," said Godden. He liked the young man better in this present mood – sure of himself, intent on a swift and finished job. "Anything doing up at the hospital?"

"No – it was just a speed test." He grinned. "And we won. . . . Well, I must get some sleep, before the real fun starts."

He disappeared into the depot. Presently the three other cars made their appearance, more cautiously, and the helmeted stretcher-bearers inside got out and went down into the main hall again, lugging their haversacks and blankets. Silence returned to the mews, and Godden resumed his slow-pacing. He was due to be relieved very soon, but he was wide awake and in no mood to settle down for the night. This job had already given him the liveliest time (except for the war) that he could remember: in the past few hours he had seen more new faces, spoken to more people, and had more variety and excitement than had come his way for years. Impossible to settle down or relax now that the climax and the point of it might be close at hand. Like the young pacifist, like many of the others – perhaps even the majority – he felt, for the first time, that he wasn't just wasting his efforts, playing out his existence, or making futile gestures against the deadening tide of history. What he was doing had some sense in it at last.

As he came to the end of his beat and turned, the sirens sounded.

Listening to the rise and fall of that eerie wail, Godden could hardly believe that this was it. . . . From inside the depot came unmistakable sounds of activity – trampling feet, the blast of a whistle, confused voices, a man shouting above the noise: "Switch the light on!" Gleams and shafts of lights appeared here and there in the street, as people, forgetting their undrawn curtains, switched on bedroom lamps or opened front doors to peer out: a small knot of house-holders, gathering at the street corner, glanced up at the sky and then looked towards the depot, as if expecting some immediate counter-action.

Then suddenly, everything seemed quiet: the sirens slid down the scale to silence, noise receded from the main hall, the voices died within, leaving only a waiting tension. God-den, cocking his head on one side and listening for the sound of planes, became one with all the rest of the city, alert and attentive.

After a few minutes, Isaacs, the squad driver, appeared, slightly out of breath, buttoning up his coat as he ran: he was followed by seven or eight other men, some of whom climbed into the stretcher-cars while others made for the rescue lorries. Isaacs stopped when he saw Godden.

"We've got to start up the engines," he said. In the dim light his beaky face looked almost parrot-like, and the helmet perched on top of it gave him a foolish and repellent air, like the traditional bulldog-in-the-sailor's-cap of the Sunday papers. "Give us a hand with this choke, will you?"

"What's happened?" asked Godden, puzzled. "Where's the rest of the squad?"

"They've changed the plans," answered Isaacs, and snorted derisively. "Trust them. . . ! No one's to come outside until the squads are called for. We're all sitting down in the shelter. Here, hold on to this while I swing her, and drop it if I give a shout."

"What about me?" asked Godden.

"You stay here, I suppose. They will want a sentry – that is, if anyone in this racket knows what he does want, instead of chopping and changing every half-minute."

"It's the first night. You can't expect much."

"Sounds like a honeymoon," said Isaacs sneeringly. "I know what I expected *my* first night – *and* got it!"

The lorry next to them started up with a roar, as did their own a moment later. The noise filled the whole mews, echoing from side to side, and during the short time that the engines were left running, the tension seemed to be superseded by a purposeful activity. This uproar, these acrid exhaust fumes, had the feeling and the direct quality of war. Then, when the engines were switched off and the drivers returned one by one to the depot, the silence and the waiting began again.

Godden filled it by talking: to remain silently in the dark mews was to be too much alone. He talked to the stretcher-bearer sentry on the main doorway, he talked to an old couple who came out on their front doorstep and asked him what the sirens meant, he talked to Horrocks, who had arrived to relieve him on sentry-go. What he said – what they all said – had no significance at all: they were none of them attending to the answers they received, or even to the sound of their own voices: they were waiting for something quite different, and thinking solely and privately of that.

Above all, the old grey-haired couple – the man snuffling in the cold air, the woman shivering and clasping her hands – seemed especially distracted by this waiting period, and unable to meet it with any normal reaction; and their few remarks were so disjointed and inconsequential that it was difficult to answer them without drawing attention to their nervousness. Godden, observing the state they were in, thought suddenly, in an odd moment of awareness: these are the sort of people we've got to help, on this job. . . .

But not this time. The All Clear brought the scene and the tension to a close, on a heartening note which made them all foolishly optimistic again. Jerry must have been scared off after all. . . . The old woman, turning to go back into the house, said:

"Was that an air-raid, then?"

"No," said Godden. "It was a warning."

"Oh. . . ." Clearly she understood hardly anything about it. "Do you think there were any bombs?"

"No," said Godden again. He waved a hand vaguely towards the south. "We must have driven them off before they got here."

The old woman shook her head and, abandoning the mystery, stumbled back into the house.

After handing over to Horrocks, Godden went down to the control room, a small shored-up office with a big wall-map of the borough, where Watson was talking to the officer-in-charge and to an intent telephone operator. They all looked up when he entered, and Watson asked:

"O.K. outside?"

"Yes," answered Godden. "What was the warning?"

"Don't know," said the officer-in-charge guardedly. "South coast, maybe. We'll get a lot of those before we're finished."

"Who's outside now?" asked Watson.

"Horrocks."

"Pal of yours, eh?"

"Yes. Last war."

Watson smiled. "Where you got that medal?"

"Yes." Godden smiled back, feeling ridiculously elated. He was back now in a world he understood, a world that had a use for him and didn't mind telling him so. Medals and old soldiers had been out of fashion for a very long time. Now they seemed to be climbing back into their place again.

He said good night, and crossed to the canteen hatch in search of a final cup of tea. Cuthbert, hollow-eyed, but still the tattered life and soul of the party, said:

"What cheer, ducks! How are the horrors of war?"

"All right," said Godden.

"I feel like one of them myself at the moment."

Godden did not contradict him.

The second warning, which came towards dawn, roused the depot from something like a normal night-time silence. Someone had got the idea of using the stretchers in place of beds, and the main hall was a dark carpet of sleeping figures, laid out in sprawling rows, with their kit close at hand. Once more there was a sudden burst of noise and movement as the alarm went. Godden, collecting his helmet and gas-mask, joined the others in the roughly sandbagged shelter; but it was hot and stuffy, and presently he slipped away and went out into the street. Wilensky, who was now the sentry, greeted him, and they stood side by side at the street corner.

It was just getting light: the air had a crisp freshness, the houses, emerging from the darkness, were solid and comforting. There were two cats staring at each other on one of the doorsteps. Somewhere a cock was crowing. It was the first war-time dawn, and a good one.

The same old couple, still shivering, still talking disjointedly, joined them on the corner.

"Are they coming again?" asked the old woman.

"Perhaps," said Godden.

"I think too light," said Wilensky.

"What's he say?" asked the old man.

"It's too light – too near daytime," explained Godden quietly. He looked at the old woman: her wispy hair seemed almost transparent, the skull showing through. "Why don't you go in, mother? We'll look after you."

"Eh?" said the old woman. She was staring up at the sky. "This terrible night," she mumbled. "They oughtn't to allow it."

"You'll be better inside."

"I thought we had to come out when the warning went," said the old man. "Didn't the newspapers say that?"

The All Clear siren sounded its long cheering note.

"What's that?" asked the old woman nervously. "Are they coming again?"

"No," answered Godden. "That's the All Clear."

"Eh?"

"It's all over. You can go in now."

"This terrible night," she repeated. "If we have much more of them I don't know what I'll do."

The old man led her away. Wilensky shook his head: there was compassion and anger in his face.

"Better that she was dead," he said harshly. "Like many others. War is too much for the old people."

"She'll be all right," said Godden, rather shocked. "Got to get used to it, that's all."

He went off duty at eight o'clock, strolling home slowly in the fresh morning sunshine, feeling the stiffness of his cramped body melting away gradually. The first night of the war, and Jerry hadn't come after all. . . . But he felt no sense of anti-climax; if not last night, then tomorrow or the next one: there'd be plenty to do, and the right sort of people to do it for. He'd been dead right to take this job, and he was going to make something of it. They all were: they'd be the best squad in the best depot in London.

He was happier that morning than he had been for many years.

2 · CHRISTMAS

THE depot was now a going concern, disciplined, organized, and settled down to its job. A routine for the day-to-day time-table was now properly worked out – so much time for drill, so much for practices and lectures, so much for the slightly unpopular fatigues, such as sweeping the mess-hall or swabbing out the lavatories, which they shared with the stretcher-bearers. The first process of shaking down together, as a body of men, was over: it had been aided by a change in the hours worked (now twenty-four hours on duty and twenty-four hours off), which allowed them time to know each other better and gave them a sense of solidarity. Actual physical conditions within the depot, too, had been much improved since the discomfort of that first makeshift night: there were now beds and blankets for every man on the shift, and some of the upstairs rooms had been taken over and converted into dormitories, so that the squads which were off duty could get a reasonable amount of quiet and sleep.

The canteen, with a proper full-time staff, also showed a distinct improvement, the unvarying fried bread, egg, and chips which was the sole menu for the first few weeks had been superseded by a full midday meal and a choice of supper dishes which went a long way towards brightening the evenings. The night-club singer, Cuthbert, had moved out with the egg and chips; he was rumoured to have gone down to one of the Chelsea depots, where they had murals, titled volunteers, and a better class of stretcher-bearer altogether.

He was not the only one to move on: there had been a certain amount of judicious weeding out which, after the come-one-come-all system of the first days of the war, had become glaringly necessary. The drinking types were the first to go: there were not many of them, but in this small close-knit organization they stuck out a lot – slipping out to the corner pub when they should have been on sentry duty, raising hell when they returned, keeping the off-duty squads awake, and initiating a slightly scandalous pile of empties in the mews. They did not last long. . . . Then there was an outbreak of petty thieving, which led to the dismissal of two more men, ingenious fellows, who built up quite a line in stolen gum-boots and bottles of iodine from the first-aid kits before they were traced. Another malefactor, more ambitious and more socially prominent, was taken off by the police: he adorned the headlines a few days later as a "Mayfair Man", with a mink coat on his conscience and a background of bouncing cheques and straying diamond bracelets, which made life at the depot seem very drab by comparison.

Isaacs also had been sacked, after a final collision with Watson over fatigue duty – his method of cleaning out the lavatories was to lock himself in with a newspaper for several hours on end, and his excuses were a blend of argument, protest, and straightforward lying, which could not hope to succeed more than a certain number of times. Wilensky's comment, when he heard of it, was: "I am a Jew, too – but not such a one," one of his few remarks on any subject which did not directly concern the job in hand.

Wilensky, indeed, was turning out to be one of the best workers in the depot. He picked up the technicalities of the job very quickly: he was willing and entirely trustworthy; and Godden, working alongside him on many occasions, felt all the time the force of a single-minded purpose, which would not let the other man rest until whatever they were doing was properly finished and rounded off. Obscurely, Godden knew what it was that drove Wilensky on, that made him concentrate all his abilities no matter how trivial the job. It was Poland – Poland by now submerged in a wave of horror and destruction, which seemed to have engulfed the whole country. Wilensky, the exile, was working to stem that wave and ultimately to drive it back; and as he wedged a shore in position, or made a competent job of rigging a derrick, he was thinking of it as a tiny part of the future's huge struggle to rescue and to reconstruct.

But they were all working hard, that Christmas-time, in the bitter weather, which turned the depot into a drab and draughty barracks. Though there was surprise at the continued respite from bombing, there had been no appreciable relaxing of the tension: the job still seemed a vital one, with the possibility of sudden action at any hour of the day or night, and after the initial period of learning and sorting themselves out they remained tuned up and on edge, ready and waiting to meet what lay ahead.

With their eye on that meeting the whole depot, rescue men and stretcher-bearers alike, was caught up in an intensive effort to prepare itself, not to be found wanting when the time came. The breathing space could hardly last much longer, and there was a lot to learn and to perfect; so all through those weeks and months, while the Western Front hung fire and the troops in the Maginot Line wondered what it was all about, they set to with a will. For the heavy and light rescue squads (the difference lay in the type of equipment they used rather than in any personal attributes) there were daily exercises, among themselves and in competition with the other depots: rigging various kinds of lifting gear, practising quick demolition work to get at the heart of a building, sending down a loaded stretcher (with no great rush to be the first patient) from the roof of the depot to the street-level. They were given their grounding in first-aid, shorn of some of its terrors in the form of Latin technical terms, which occasionally defeated the stretcher-bearers, but not the less useful for that. At times some of it seemed a trifle irrelevant. "It is important," said one lecturer, who was ploughing through the whole syllabus, whether applicable or not, "to distinguish carefully between the measures necessary to counteract the two main forms of bite – the bite of the dog, and the bite of the snake." ("Blimey!" said one awed rescue worker, "What does he think Jerry's going to drop on us?")

The stretcher-bearers had a full programme of training also. First aid certificates had to be won before their jobs were confirmed: "incidents" were organized, with six or seven patients to be dealt with by each squad, and marks given for diagnosis, treatment and handling of them: many of the stretcher-squads attended at nearby hospitals, which were evacuating their patients to the country as soon as they could safely be moved, and lent a hand, there. They kept the same hours as the rescue squads, so that the whole personnel of the depot, divided into two shifts, spent twenty-four hours at a time working together: when they went off duty at eight in the morning, feeling tired, looking "rough" and untidy after a night spent in their clothes, there was a sense of comradeship and communal purpose among them which made the tiredness and the discomfort seem worthwhile.

Nor was this community spirit confined only to the work they shared. Several football matches were organized that winter, with the other shift or with other London depots: the rules about drinking were relaxed so that a small proportion of them could visit the local pub at some time during their twenty-four hours on, and within the depot darts, dominoes, and a wave of shove-halfpenny tournaments all contributed to this solid sense of unity. For all of them, at this stage, it was not quite an ordinary life, and not quite an ordinary job: the long hours, the "disciplined" atmosphere, the very nature of what they were waiting for, together gave it a special quality. Above all, it was worthwhile, as a safeguard and an insurance against danger; and it might become of paramount importance at any moment.

Godden felt this quality more than ever, after three months on the heavy rescue side. He had worked hard, done his share and a bit more, made a success of the novelty of finding himself part of a team again. Since that first night, and the old couple he had tried to look after (they were in the country now, and the house was shuttered and empty), he had never ceased to find in the job the same special attribute that Wilensky felt, and the pacifist stretcher-bearer too: that it was part of something much larger, tremendously worth doing, and linked in some subtle fashion with the way people ought to behave towards each other, if the world was ever to be a decent place. To the depot, and the work he did there, and his ambitions for the future, he transferred all the love and care which would, ordinarily, have been centred on his own family and friends.

For things were no better at home; and always in the back of his mind was the feeling that this job would have had more point – would indeed, have had a sort of final justification – if he had had behind him the home life and the loving welcome which Edie used to give him when they were first married. But there it was – she *didn't* give him anything, except a running, nagging commentary on what she thought was little better than a loafing waste of time: as far as home was concerned he was on his own, and all that he might have felt towards his family was given towards this job, or kept in readiness for anyone who might need it in the future.

Certainly Edie was a trial. In fact she would have come near to spoiling the taste of the whole thing, if he had let her, and if the other feelings hadn't been so strong.

There was that business about the stretcher-bearers' show, for instance. Over that he'd come near to – well, to doing a lot of things that didn't bear thinking about in cold blood.

Godden hadn't been too sure about inviting Edie and Edna to the show which the stretcher-bearers put on just before Christmas; and looking at them through a crack in the curtains during the interval, he was even less sure about it. Edie, six rows back in the audience, was looking pretty sour, no doubt about it – that was because of his get-up in the Arab scene, probably, and Edna, dressed up to the nines in pale blue, was trying (trust her!) to get off with a couple of fellows farther along the row. Godden thought: you're the wrong side of the curtain, my girl, with all that stuff on your face; and he wondered what the rest of the chaps would say when they knew that this fluffy bit was his daughter, after all.

184

. . . Well, if Edie hadn't enjoyed it, just because he'd taken part in it and had a little fun, everyone else had: the laughter all the way through the first half, and the applause at the end of it, had been a riot.

It was the stretcher-bearers who had had the idea of giving a show at Christmas: they were doing most of it themselves, but they had co-opted several of the rescue men, Godden among them (after enormous persuasion), to take small parts and supply the spear-carriers generally. The costumes, where necessary, had been made by one of the girls from the local pub, who was also lending a hand with the make-up. The programme was the usual mixture: sketches, songs and choruses, a refined ballad singer, and a distinctly unrefined cross-talk act; but the audience – mostly "friends and relatives", strengthened by two rows of Borough Council worthies – had eaten it up, and now, with the interval here, the cheerful buzz of conversation was a good measure of its success.

Godden had only made one appearance so far, as an "Arab" in a snake-charming scene: the dusty make-up, flowing robes, and high turban had made him look rather a dashing character, in a religious sort of way, and the scene had gone down well. But the success of the show, so far, had been a domestic sketch with Hitler, Goering and Goebbels as the protagonists – ready-made characters for farce, and very much to the audience's taste. It finished up with the young pacifist, who played Hitler, standing on the table and making a rousing speech on the theme, "We have no living room", to be countered succinctly by a char-woman who popped her head round the back-cloth and remarked: "You wouldn't say we had no living-room if you had to clean the bloody place out!" This piece of homely philosophy had brought the house down.

Now as Godden peered through the curtain, they were getting ready for the second half of the programme. Edie was still looking annoyed about something, he noticed. Well, she'd get an eye-opener in a minute or two.

Someone bumped into him from behind, and he turned round. It was Horrocks, who had been roped in as an odd-job man and was now setting out some chairs on the stage. When he caught sight of Godden he laughed out loud.

"You look a proper sketch," he said cheerfully. "Hope your missus will like it."

Godden was quite sure that she wouldn't, but he didn't give a damn. He was enjoying himself enormously, in a way he had almost forgotten even existed.

There was something about the sheer fun of this evening, the excitement behind the scenes and the obvious enjoyment of the audience, that took him right back to the old days, to other Christmases before the last war when dressing up was part of the ritual, and there was ten times more colour in a single day than there was from one year's end to another now. This was more like a real Christmas party, this was more like the sort of life he had once hoped for; and here he was, right in the middle of it, and not exactly being coy about it either. . . . Godden was dressed, at that moment, for his part in the "Fairy Ballet", which figured later in the programme: the frilly white skirt and tight bodice gave his stocky figure a ludicrous air of virginity, the wreath of pink roses crowning his rather solemn face had an almost blasphemous inappropriateness, like Judas Iscariot, wearing somebody else's halo after a party. It had taken a good deal to persuade him to make up the number in the *corps de ballet*: he would never have done it, indeed, if there had not been seven others, equally daft, to join in. But what Edie would have to say about it when she saw him, was another matter.

"It's a bit cold, this get-up," he answered Horrocks. "Kind of draughty here and there. What do they think of the show out in front?"

Horrocks laughed again. Godden had never seen him in such good spirits during all the last few months: it was like coming round a corner and suddenly meeting the old Horrocks, cheerful and self-reliant and ready for anything. The

Old Firm might set up in business again, if he was getting back into this form. . . .

"They're loving it – eating it up," Horrocks replied. "Remember those old concert parties back at the base? Something like that, only of course you're keeping it a bit cleaner. . . . What have you got under that skirt, by the way?" he added, following a natural continuity of thought.

"Football shorts," answered Godden. "Only thing we could trust."

"Thank God for that."

The stage manager hurried on, and said: "All off, please – curtain going up."

"So long, Bill," said Horrocks. "I'm going round in front again. Good luck with it."

Godden looked down at his frilly skirt, and said: "We'll need it." Then he retreated into the wings.

The curtain went up, to a burst of clapping, and a St. John Ambulance sergeant began to sing "Trees", with an absence of any feeling on the subject, one way or the other, which would not have disgraced a civil servant in the Forestry Commission. He was followed by a tap-dancer, who lost the beat half-way through but continued to plough a lonely furrow right to the end – a manful effort, which earned a lot of applause and a shout of, "He can do it with music, too!" from a sarcastic onlooker at the back. Then it was the turn of the cross-talk act, two stretcher-bearers dressed as charwomen, relying largely on "family" jokes about the depot, which mystified some of the audience but went down well with their fellow-workers. And then it was time for the "Fairy Ballet".

This had been very carefully worked out and rehearsed till they were all heartily sick of the music – one of Chopin's waltzes. But the rehearsals certainly paid a dividend. The curtain rose on a group of fairies – the actual grouping borrowed wholesale from "Sylphides", but stopping right there as far as any other attributes were concerned. The volunteers for the ballet were of assorted types: big men who lumbered, skinny little fellows who hopped about like fleas, sturdy performers who shook a leg as if it were a length of two-inch planking; but they all wore the same frilly skirts and wreaths of roses, and they were all united in frowning determination over one thing – to follow the pattern and the music as they had been taught.

Their performance lasted for three and a half minutes altogether, and the audience rocked with laughter throughout. After a few preliminary twirls by the *corps de ballet*, the only male character (he was actually the only stretcher-bearer who was at all effeminate) struck an attitude of anticipation, and the Queen of the Fairies, artificially buxom, bounded on to the stage, jumping down from a box in the wings and landing with a thud which nearly jerked the record from its groove. Solemnly the *corps de ballet*, in their absurd frills, capered about them, their faces set and preoccupied: one of them, just behind Godden, was counting, "Hop two, three ... hop! two, three ..." in an urgent voice, which the music and the laughter only just drowned. The two principals had a set-to in the middle, sinews cracking as they went through the motions of enchantment and despair which the story (a confused one) dictated. Then, to end it, the *corps de ballet* formed up behind Godden and lumbered in solemn procession round the stage: the male figure took up a welcoming stance in the centre, the other dancers stopped in their tracks, breathing heavily, and the Queen of the Fairies, hurrying to join her partner for the fall of the curtain, over-reached herself in a final *entrechat royale* and landed in a sitting position with a crash that shook the hall. On this scene of transcendental beauty, as the programme notes would normally have had it, the curtain fell.

The ovation which this effort received made an encore imperative, and the whole thing was repeated, this time without mishap, but with a hard-breathing concentration, which showed that the effort, physical and emotional, was beginning to tell. That was almost the end of the show, except for another short sketch, and a chorus of popular songs in which the audience joined cheerfully – "Run, Rabbit, Run", "Somewhere in France", and "Hanging Out The Washing On The Siegfried Line", being among them. For Christmas, 1939, they seemed just the right note to end on. . . . The final curtain fell to thunderous applause from all over the hall.

Godden, changing back into his ordinary clothes, but keeping on the rose-petal head-dress as a mark of distinction (which indeed it was), joined the rest of the performers as they mingled with the audience afterwards. Making towards Edie and Edna, he knew instinctively that neither of them was going to be pleased. But it seemed somehow to have nothing to do with him personally; he was in such high spirits, and so firmly a part of the success of the evening, that any other influence could hardly touch him. Indeed, when Edie started on her outburst, he thought for a moment that she must be joking. But he was not long in doubt.

It was his opening remark, when finally he made his way over, that set her off.

"Here we are!" he exclaimed cheerfully. "Did you enjoy it?"

"Enjoy it!" Edie, who was standing up in the middle of the row waiting to move, drew in her breath with a sharp hiss, which should have warned him. "Enjoy it! I was never so ashamed in all my life. Dancing round the stage in that silly way. You and your rescue work. Is that what you do all day?"

"Go on," he said, still cheerfully. "I bet you were laughing as loud as the rest of them."

"There wasn't anything funny in what I saw," said Edie furiously. "And for goodness' sake take that thing off your head. Haven't you done enough fooling about already?"

"It made me feel funny all over," broke in Edna affectedly. "What ever made you do it, Dad?"

"It was just a joke," said Godden, ignoring her and trying to answer Edie. "What's the harm if there's a lot of us doing it?"

"A lot of grown men behaving like a bunch of kids doesn't make it all right, not by a long chalk." People near by were

189

turning round to watch them, and Edie lowered her voice till it was a fierce whisper. "You ought to think of the people you invite to watch it, even if you *don't* mind making a fool of yourself in front of everybody. If I'd known it was going to be like that, you couldn't have dragged me here!"

"It was SORFUL," exclaimed Edna, with a realistic shudder. "I wanted to run away and hide myself."

And that's what I felt about you, thought Godden, suddenly angry. By God, he hadn't been got up any worse than Edna was right now, with her paint and her skirts up round her neck! For the first time for years he wanted to hurt them both; Edna for her silly affected talk, Edie for the perpetual nagging which could turn even a night like this into the same old row at the end. A moment ago he had been on top of the world: now the whole thing was spoilt, and all because of their blasted bad temper and complaining. He hadn't really wanted them to come, anyway: thought he was giving them a bit of a treat; and now they made this sort of mess of it. And it wasn't just the show, it wasn't just tonight, either: it had been like this even since the beginning – everything to do with the depot came in for the same damned nagging and back-biting. In the back of his mind Godden knew Edie was jealous of him: jealous of what he was doing there, and what the depot had done for him. She realized, well enough, the difference it had made to him, to have a job he could be proud of, and a place where people treated him as a human being instead of a bit of furniture lying about the house. She knew how much he liked it there, and she hated him for it.

"Now look here, Edie," he was beginning, stung to the point of giving her a straight answer for once in a while, "I've had about enough –"

He stopped suddenly, as a hand clapped him on the back and Horrocks's voice said cheerfully:

"Good old Bill! I didn't know you had it in you."

Horrocks interruption fitted in so well with what Godden had been about to say, and with the general temper of the atmosphere, that an awkward pause ensued. Then Godden pulled himself together.

"Hallo, George," he said quietly. He turned to Edie. "This is George Horrocks. Remember, I used to talk about him? In the war. . . . This is the missus, George. And my girl, Edna."

Edie took a look at Horrocks and the old clothes he still wore, decided that he wasn't worth making an effort over, and nodded. Edna, from different motives, exhibited the same disdain. There was another pause, and then Horrocks said:

"Pleased to meet you, Mrs. Godden. Hope you enjoyed the show."

"Can't say I did," answered Edie shortly. She was still in a violent temper, and this shabby old chap wasn't going to change it.

"What, not even old Bill capering round like a two-year-old?" said Horrocks, surprised. "You ought to be proud of him. Quite the artist, he was."

"She didn't care for it," Godden mumbled.

"I should just think I didn't care for it!" Edie burst out again. "I told him he ought to be ashamed of himself dressing up like that, and I'll say it again to his friends."

Horrocks, red and embarrassed, said nothing. Godden, unequal to making a scene before a third person, muttered: "Steady on, Edie!" which only infuriated her further.

"It's you that ought to steady on, acting the fool like that at your age." She really was in a towering rage. "Catch me coming down here again. If that's what they teach you in the rescue, then God help us when the raids start. Strikes me they ought to get some *men* for this job, not a bunch of kids dancing round the stage." She pulled her coat round her roughly. "Come along, Edna – we'll go home, now we know the sort of place this is. I can't say I'm much surprised, either."

There was a silence after they had gone; Horrocks still embarrassed and Godden very much ashamed. Finally:

"Sorry, George," Godden mumbled. "Bit of a row before you turned up. Ought to have warned you, but I hadn't time."

"Stuck my neck out a bit, didn't I?" Horrocks laughed, beginning to recover his spirits. "Let's forget it . . . I had the best laugh for years, seeing you up on that stage. You deserve another medal for that."

Godden laughed in turn. "Well, you see what I got instead. . . . What about a cup of tea?"

"There's a bit of a party after they've cleared up here," answered Horrocks. "Borough Council's had some beer sent up, and the canteen are doing the sandwiches now. Proper Christmas do, it is." He patted Godden on the back. "Cheer up, Bill – forget about it. It's too good an evening to spoil."

That turned out to be true, not very much later. The crowded mess-hall, with the beer going round and the trestle tables loaded with sandwiches, was overwhelmingly cheerful; and Godden, as the rescue-squads' star performer, came in for a lot of good-natured chaffing, which pointed the fact that he was now accepted as a personality, and a well-liked one. Expanding in the warmth and comradeship, he forgot about Edie and all the rest of it, and slipped easily into the place he'd made for himself.

He was in a good job. He was twice the man he'd been a few months before. He was happy.

It was a grand Christmas after all.

3 · SPRING

In the asphalt courtyard enclosed by the school buildings Godden's squad was rigging a sheer-legs. This straightforward job, which comprised three scaffolding poles lashed together in the form of a tripod, with a block and tackle hanging down centrally for lifting any heavy weight below, was a favourite exercise with the rescue workers. They had done it lots of times, and they were good at it. As Number Three got busy on it now, the other squads, and some of the stretcher-bearers, formed a ring of spectators round them, enjoying the sun and the sight of someone else working, and offering comments and suggestions as the work progressed.

One of the Peters brothers, the least expert of the squad, was having trouble with the top lashing, and the remarks from the peanut gallery made it plain that they didn't think much of his efforts.

"What sort of a clove hitch is that?"

"That's the knot my old woman uses for the kid's nappies."

Peters looked up, his face red as he wrestled with the refractory knot. "You – yourself!"

"Not with that bunch of bananas, I won't." There was a ripple of laughter round the courtyard. "Call that a sheer-legs? It wouldn't lift a dog's hind leg."

Godden, bending down beside Peters, straightened his back. "Haven't you got anything better to do?" he asked shortly.

"Wouldn't miss this for a quid, Bill," said the most persistent of the interrupters. "Number Three squad goes into action. Stand clear, Adolf, you might get hurt!"

There was more laughter, good-natured and friendly. Godden bent down again, and took over the lashing from

Peters. He didn't mind the chaff, but it was his job to see that there was nothing to find fault with, as far as his squad was concerned.

For it was now his squad; he had been made a squad-leader a couple of weeks previously, to his enormous surprise. Indeed, he had hardly known what to say, when Watson called him into the control-room one morning, and asked:

"Think you can take over the squad from me?"

Godden swallowed and stared. "What, do you mean leader? What about you, then?"

"I'm off to another depot, taking charge of one of the shifts. I thought you could move into my job. You know the work all right. How about it?"

Godden thought. "Well, there's Wilensky."

Watson nodded. "He's good, too. But I think you'd be able to handle the squad better."

"Some of the chaps can't always understand what he's saying," remarked the officer-in-charge, who was also present. "It might make a difference in a crisis."

That seemed fair enough. . . . Godden grinned suddenly, and said: "All right, then."

Watson smiled in answer. "Makes you think a bit, doesn't it? But you'll get used to the idea.

And there he was – a squad-leader. "That'll worry Hitler," said Edie sarcastically, when he told her about it, "What do you wear now? Lace knickers?" What he actually *did* wear was the secret pride of his life at the moment: a white-painted steel helmet with a star and a big "R" on it, the badge of his leadership. As Watson had remarked, he *was* getting used to it: it had been a bit strange at first, and some of the others were inclined to resent the promotion and pass a remark or two, but he'd gone about it quietly, not chucking his weight about, and it seemed to be working out very well. It meant a lot to him, more than he could express even to himself: he remembered being made a corporal in the war, and how proud he had felt then, but this was somehow even better, after all the past years without any sort of distinction or any progress except the slow way downwards. Now he'd taken this terrific stride, back to self-respect and a position with a proper label to it. No wonder, as he directed the squad on their present job, that he felt ready to cope with whatever trouble they ran into. Number Three Squad had the right idea – and the squad-leader was all right, too. . . .

The sheer-legs took shape gradually: the block and tackle was rigged and secure, and Godden began to attach the ropes for hoisting it upright, while Wilensky, turning as always to the next part of the job, without prompting, paced out the spread of the tripod legs and laid them in position. Some of the onlookers wandered off, down to the end of the mews, where three ambulance drivers, girls, were cleaning their cars. The rescue men and stretcher-bearers always watched these girls at work, and talked to them when they had the chance; two of them were slim and rather pretty, in an immature, coltish way, and the sun was like a warm bond between them all, and it was part of the spring. To each other the men made remarks about them, coarse in expression, but not vicious in spirit: the girls were just kids really, but nice-looking ones, and they were there, in the hot sunshine, to be watched and talked about.

"Look good on a pillow, that hair would."

"Lovely pair that little one's got."

"Bet she's covered a bit of carpet in her time."

The girls were innocent, in fact, and they all knew it and it pleased them as much as making these remarks about them did. The pretence of their wantonness was all part of the same thing: looking at pretty girls, wanting them and yet not wanting them at all, being glad to be men with all this fabulous choice of women at their disposal; drifting along on a lazy, faintly erotic harmless tide of manhood which had no real desire to assert itself.

Spring had brought other developments to their corner of the world, besides this easy stirring of the senses. Some of the younger men had been called up, and those who came to replace them were mostly the same type – old soldiers, or small shopkeepers and stall-holders, whom shortages and the beginning of rationing were forcing out of business. There was a curious outbreak of minor sabotage among the stretcher-cars, which on two occasions had sugar tipped into their petrol tanks and were put out of action. It was thought to be nothing more sinister than a reprisal for an earlier dismissal: but it earned some fluent cursing from the drivers, who had to clean out everything – tanks, petrol pipes, and carburettors – before their engines would function again.

With the warmer weather, too, much of the depot's activity had moved out-of-doors. Exercises and full-scale "incidents" were arranged with a muster of all the other services – wardens, fire-brigades, first-aid parties, and mobile hospital units: when they were all collected in the park, and were running through the sequence of events, from the first bomb-damage to the final dispatch of casualties to the hospital, it was rather like an old-style field-day. The mobile unit set up its standard in one corner, and spread out its tables and stretchers: the casualties lay about in attitudes of abandon, to accord with their ticketed injuries: the men and their equipment covered a sizable area, through which Borough officials wandered, to ensure fair play and a reasonable standard of zeal: and rate-paying citizens hung about on the outskirts, watching their money being spent with a mixture of pride and alertness which did them equal credit.

It was very pleasant to work out-of-doors in the sun, after being cooped up for so long in the depot, where the rate of colds and mild flue had been high all through the winter. These exercises were enjoyable for another reason, too: there was a strong feeling of comradeship when all the air-raid services were collected together, engaged on different parts of the same job, and when, at the end, they gathered round one of the mobile canteens at the edge of the park, for a cup of tea, this comradeship made itself felt more strongly still. There were few enough compensations on this job: the pay was low, the uniform none too dashing, the living conditions inside the depot still fairly stark; but when they could meet like this they felt that they had allies after all, and they understood each other without effort – a shabby army talking the same language and waiting for the same signal.

Godden, satisfied at last with every detail of the layout of the sheer-legs, gave the order to hoist it; and as the squad tailed on to the ropes it rose slowly and evenly upright. The spectators gathered again to watch them and see that it was done properly: last week, for instance, Number Six squad had forgotten one of the steadying lines, and the whole thing had toppled sideways and broken a skylight. They might as well see how Number Three shaped, anyway, even if they didn't provide a bit of drama of that sort: the ambulance girls had gone back into their garage, and there was nothing else to look at or to do until the canteen had supper ready in a couple of hours. Till then, it was just waiting, as usual.

That was the trouble nowadays – the aimless waiting about. They knew by heart the work they did in the exercise hours, and when the day's routine had been completed, with perhaps a lecture or a first aid demonstration thrown in, there was nothing left for them. It was only just starting, that feeling, but it could be met, in embryo, all over the building: creeping into their job at the depot, against the tide of spring, was the beginning of boredom.

Six months of A.R.P.; three quid a week, and nothing to do but hang about. . . . That was what the neighbours seemed to think, anyway: some of them were always passing remarks, particularly about the Fire Service, which for some reason was pictured as nothing but a lot of girls in trousers gossiping over the tea-things. But it covered all the services really: here and there the whole thing was beginning to be thought of as a joke, and if you said you were in A.R.P. it was good for a laugh any time – and not always a pleasant laugh either. For, of course, the joke was a sight too expensive, if you think it out: costing the country thousands, it was, and nothing to show for it, except a few chaps loafing round the park and some silly old wardens creating about the black-out.... That was the kind of thing you heard, now and again, and before long it began to spread inside the depot. Perhaps the people outside were right, and they *were* just wasting their time.

"By God, I'm going to join up!" was the reaction to that: but you couldn't – you had to wait your turn. Private war, that was what it was: run by the bosses, all making hundreds a week, and you couldn't even get into it if you wanted to: you had to hang on in this flaming place, practising things that would probably never be needed in any case, and getting a lot of funny looks from the people next door when you came home in the morning. Some people left to get jobs outside, and they were the smart ones: there were good jobs if you only knew how to get them – six quid a week making tea in a shipyard, it was in the papers yesterday, it's a fact.... So, within the depot, the talk went on: making the boring job seem trivial and useless also, making the men who did it feel cheated of their share in the war. For whether they had joined the A.R.P. to help things along, or whether they saw the war as a chance of bettering themselves, they were not doing either, and weren't likely to if they stayed where they were.

Of course, it wasn't always like that: there were times, now and then, when the thing still seemed to have some sense in it, and the old spirit of the first few days of the war was as strong as ever. The full-scale exercises, too, were still a tonic. But it was getting harder to feel eager about the job, when there was so little to show for their enthusiasm, and so much that beckoned them from outside.

Perhaps this discontent, also, was part of the spring.

There it was, anyway – a sheer-legs, properly rigged and ready for use. The tripod stood steady and rigid, the block and tackle swung evenly from the centre, Godden was pleased: it had gone without a hitch.

It stood in the hot sunshine, with the ring of men round it, staring. Nothing wrong with it, as far as anyone could see. But what did it add up to now it was finished? It was just a sheer-legs, just another bit of practice, another hour gone.

Suddenly they were all bored with it. They left Godden's squad to unrig it and stow away the gear, and drifted off in search of tea.

4 · SUMMER

1

DENMARK and Norway fell, almost over the weekend. It came as a jolt, and the more so after the official description of our forces there as the most formidably equipped expeditionary force ever to sail from these shores. It came as a jolt – but it was only the first one, not really hard enough to cure that "phoney war" feeling or to make clear the impending hazard.

"What did Chamberlain mean about Hitler missing the bus?"

"Means he's made a mistake. Started too late or something. You'll see. We'll probably attack in France while he's mucking about up there. Finish off the whole lot of them."

"I'm not so sure," said Godden. "They may start something over here pretty soon. We'd better be ready."

"We've been ready for six months, and nothing's happened. This place is a lot of eyewash."

"If there's air-raids," said Godden, "they'll need us quick enough. We've got to be ready to help."

"Help who?"

"Anyone that needs it."

"Don't deserve it, most of them. They're just laughing at us half the time. Chap next door said to me this morning, 'They ought to call up more women, so that you fellows could go to Norway instead of hanging about.' I could have crowned him."

"Never mind what a chap like that says," answered Godden. "There's plenty more who don't say it – and don't think it either. It's them we've got to look after."

"Let 'em look after themselves."

"They can't all do that."

"You're too soft. Love of mankind, that is. Love of boloney. Who's for a cup of tea?"

Cups of tea. Practices. Waiting.

2

Chamberlain, faced by a revolt from the Left, and from a small proportion of Conservatives, resigned, and Churchill took over the Government.

"Now we'll see something," said the pacifist stretcher-bearer. "I'd rather fight for this chap than for the bunch of Tories who kept Chamberlain in power."

"Thought you wouldn't fight at all?"

The pacifist shook his head. "I don't know. It looks as though we might all have to."

"But it's the same lot bossing us about, isn't it? What's the difference now?"

"It won't be the same lot. There's a coalition of all the parties."

"What's that mean, exactly?"

"Conservative, Liberal and Labour all in one government."

"Proper mix-up, that's going to be."

"We'd better try something new, or we'll be missing the bus ourselves."

"Perhaps this is the real beginning of the war," said the pacifist. "We'll know pretty soon, anyway."

3

The Germans broke through into Holland by frontal assault, and overran it at spectacular speed with a new weapon – the Panzer formation of armour. Rotterdam was bombed, with the greatest slaughter of the air-war so far.

"They are devils," said Wilensky sombrely. "How can they do these things to unarmed cities?"

"Must have been like Warsaw, only worse."

Wilensky did not answer.

"What happens now, anyway? We'll have to watch out, or we'll be in a mess ourselves."

"Oh, we'll be all right. Gort'll see to that. He knows what he's doing. Remember that bit in the paper, a while back? 'It may be long, it may be short. It all depends on Viscount Gort.' He's the boy, all right, You keep your eye on him, not on all these frogs."

"I'm not so sure. If things go on like this they'll be all over us while we're still quoting poetry."

"They are devils," said Wilensky. "Just devils."

4

In face of the continued and lightning German advance, King Leopold of the Belgians announced that his armies were incapable of further resistance and had laid down their arms.

"Dirty bastard," said one of the Peters brothers. "Why didn't he tell us first, instead of doing it on his own?"

"Perhaps he didn't have time. Those Jerries are moving, you know."

"All the same, he could have warned us. It's put us in the cart properly."

"If they keep on like this, what's going to stop them?"

"There's still the Maginot Line. Don't forget that."

"Strikes me they've got round that, at the top, without having to attack it."

"But what's happening? What are we going to do? Are we just going to sit there and let it happen to us?"

"I know what I'm going to do – have a cup of tea."

Cups of tea. Wondering. Waiting for it.

5

The French armies fell back from Sedan. The Maginot Line was turned, broken, and left far behind: the blitzkrieg

202

stopped being a music-hall joke and became a tidal flood of steel and fire searing its way through France and Belgium. The British retreated, fighting their way through France and Belgium. The British retreated, fighting their way to the beaches. A new place came on to the map, and a new, proud idea into men's minds and memories – Dunkirk.

"Why didn't they let us help at the time, instead of telling us all about it afterwards?" said Horrocks. "God, I'd have gone over there in a rowing-boat, if I'd known what was going on. And how long are we going to sit here doing nothing?"

"We'll be busy enough before long," said Godden.

"Maybe. . . . Just think of it, Bill: the whole British Army brought off in those little boats. It must have been hell on those beaches."

"Like Ypres – and a bit more."

Horrocks shook his head. "I don't know that you and me saw anything to touch this, rough times and all. Those poor bastards on the beaches, in all that dive-bombing. . . . What happens next?"

"Maybe the French will hold them, and we'll go in again lower down the coast."

"Don't suppose we've got the guns – or the tanks – or the aircraft, or any bloody thing. Christ, where's all that money gone? I thought we'd been re-arming for three or four years! What did they spend it on?"

"Wrong things, I suppose. Horses, most like."

"Somebody ought to do a bit of explaining."

6

Hitler danced as Paris fell. Marshal Petain, talking of defeat and the need for regeneration through suffering almost before the reins were in his hands, refused to listen to Churchill's plea for another effort before the towel was thrown in. France surrendered, and was overrun.

"Those bloody Frogs!" said the younger Peters brother, the one who had always quarrelled with Isaacs. "They could have crossed to Africa, and carried on from there. Their army can't be finished already."

"They've taken the hell of a knock, these past weeks."

"No more than we have, and *we're* not finished yet."

"We've got the Channel – and thank God for that! It's just about saved us, this time."

"Think they'll try an invasion?"

"Bound to. Or else a lot of air-raids, every day and every night till something happens. Whatever it is, we'll have a job to do here, and about time, too."

"Strikes me there'll be a job to do everywhere. We're on our own now."

"Yes, we're on our own."

7

Two broadcasts stirring the nation – Churchill's summons to fight "on the beaches, in the streets", and Eden's call for the volunteers needed for that fight, the L.D.V.

"That's the thing we ought to be joining, not just sitting here waiting for the invasion."

"We'll be doing just as much good here," said Godden, "when the thing starts. It's a different kind of fight, that's all."

"You're right there – fighting the Borough Council for a few extra bob a week, that's all it is. I want to get into it properly."

"You wait," said Godden again, "you'll be busy enough before long. They'll be crying out for rescue squads and stretcher-bearers, before we're very much older. Then you'll see the sense in all this training and practising."

"Wish I thought it was worth it."

"The first chap we pick up after a raid will make you think it's worth it."

"Where do you get all these funny ideas?"

"I've been thinking," said Godden. He smiled. "Plenty of time for it, haven't we?"

"You're right there. . . . Who's for a cup of tea?"
Exercises. Cups of tea. Waiting and seeing it coming.

8

Battle of Britain. Terror over the coast and the fair southern counties: glory also, and courage to meet it. A mounting score of the enemy brought down every day, a yet more ferocious effort to beat a way through, a lonely battle by a few brave and skilful men.

A people watching the sky.

"London next," said Godden.

5 · SEPTEMBER

THE two stretcher-cars arrived first, racing up the street till they were waved to a standstill by a blue-overalled figure – the air-raid warden who had summoned them. They parked one behind the other at the kerb's edge, just short of a great patch of broken glass; as the stretcher-bearers jumped out, grabbing their blankets and first-aid kit, they looked round them quickly, like travellers set down on an untried, unknown shore. Then they filtered into the small crowd staring at the end house, and became part of the cruel etching of this street scene.

The end house had had it. All its windows were blown out, its front door sagged drunkenly from a single hinge, its shredded curtains flapped in a haze of dust and dirt which was still stirring. From it the desolation had spread along the row and across the street: the same shattered windows, splintered woodwork, and dusty, scarred fronts disfigured a dozen of the nearby houses, which stood like mute, lesser witnesses of the main violence. Structurally, the victim looked all right from the front: but through the gaping front door and upper windows it could be seen that the bomb had ripped off the whole back of the house, burying the slit of garden under a mass of rubble, leaving only the façade and the front slope of the roof untouched.

It had been a nice little house: somebody's pride and joy. Now it was not much more than a fairly simple problem in demolition. But first the human oddments had to be tidied away.

Some of these were ready for the stretcher-bearers when they arrived: passers-by injured by blast or flying glass, a man who had been in the lower front room and had been thrown across it, breaking an arm and a leg, a child whimpering over a torn wrist. These were attended to and taken off. In the back garden of another house two people had been killed: the stretcher-bearers brought them out and laid them on stretchers in the roadway, where they waited for the mortuary ambulance. Meanwhile the warden and the war-reserve policeman on duty, talking to the wounded and the onlookers, were trying to find out if there was anyone else in the house when the bomb fell.

"There's an old couple living in the basement," he told the stretcher-party leader. "But they used to go out quite a bit." He raised his voice. "Anyone know anything about the Timsons?"

"They were out shopping this morning," said a voice. "I saw them at the butchers'. Don't know if they got back or not."

"Anyone see them come back?" asked the policeman.

"Yes," said another voice. "About an hour ago. They might have gone out again, though."

Everyone looked at the heap of rubble and woodwork showing through the open door. If they hadn't gone out again the Timsons were somewhere there.

For the second time the warden climbed down the area steps and walked through into the front basement room. It was in ruins, as if an enormous wind had seared through it, stripping and wrecking everything in its path; and the roof at the far end sagged to the floor, blocking the way to the bedroom and scullery at the back of the house. In the air the dust still hung, mingling with a faint smell of escaping gas to form a thick, disgusting blend. . . . The Timsons might well have been in the bedroom or the kitchen, thought the warden: in which case they were still there. A search would have to be made in any case, as soon as the rescue squads arrived and could get to work.

When he reached the top of the steps again a woman came forward and said to him:

"I think they were in, Mr. Fenton. They had nothing to go out again for, not after that shopping."

"Looks like it," answered the warden.

"What's it like down there?" asked the policeman.

"A mess," said the warden briefly. "The back room's blocked: looks as though the whole ceiling's caved in. But we'll have to get to it somehow."

The policeman sucked his teeth. "There's no way in from the back garden – I had a look just now. Too much stuff on top. The rescue chaps will have to tunnel through from this side. Did you put in a call for them?"

The warden nodded, and then pointed towards the end of the street. "There's the lorry now."

"Stand back there," said the policeman. "Right back on the kerb." He waved the lorry up, and it came to a standstill alongside the stretcher-cars. Godden was the first to jump down from it.

Two minutes to get the hang of the situation, and the lay-out of the house: another five to assemble the gear in the basement room; and Number Three Squad went to work. Godden, going over his plan as he tripped off his coat, was satisfied with it. They would tunnel along the edge of the side wall, shoring up as they went, until they reached the division between the front and the back rooms: break a way through this if it was still standing; and go on tunnelling and shoring until they found something. It was possible that the ceiling of the back room, where the Timsons probably were, still held, in spite of the enormous weight of ruined brickwork on top of it; though if the front room was anything to go by, it wasn't very likely. But even if the back-room ceiling had collapsed, there was still a chance that the Timsons might survive – underneath one of the cross-beams, or in the angle between the wall and the floor. In any case, they had to find out. . . .

Godden and Wilensky, working in turn with picks and with their bare hands, were the spearhead of the attack; the rest of the squad were strung out behind them, ready with shores, crowbars, and baskets for the rubble as it was passed back to them.

They worked silently in the dusty, twilight room, with its foolish and shattered oddments of furniture – broken chairs, a sofa scattering flock and horsehair all round it, an overturned table, and a "Present from Margate" which still survived on the mantelpiece. Godden, plugging away methodically – hacking at the brickwork and plaster, picking up the bits and passing them back, chopping, wrenching, thrusting aside – felt full of confidence: at that moment it was the most important thing in the world to get through the mess and reach the Timsons, and he was sure they would do it. Indeed, it was more than confidence – it was sort of ecstasy of achievement: somewhere, not very far away, were people who needed his help, people to take risks for and fight to save, and he was going to save them. This, at last, was the job he had been waiting to do, through all the months of training; this, at last, was what he had been talking about when he told his squad: "There'll be people needing our help before very long."

At the end of his spell he straightened up and stepped back: with a grunt Wilensky reached for the pick and took his place at the wall tunnel. Good old Wilensky, thought Godden; he knows what he's doing all right, and he's not wasting any time either. . . . With the back of his hand Godden wiped the sweat and dust off his face, and then walked from the basement into the area, passing close to Horrocks, who said: "Don't kill yourself, Bill: take a bit of a rest." Out in the area, leaning against a wall and breathing deeply and thankfully in the fresh air, he stared up at the slit of sky overhead. It was clear blue and sunny; it seemed very peaceful and miles away from the stress and pain buried down here. . . . There were three heads visible, outlined against the sky, leaning over the railings at the top: the warden, the policeman, and the pacifist stretcher-bearer, watching and waiting like the rest of them up on the street-level.

"How's it going?" asked the warden.

"All right."

"You don't want another squad on it, do you?"

"No."

"We've sent all the other casualties off," said the stretcher-bearer. "Eight of them. I suppose we'd better stay on here, though."

"It'll be a bit of time yet," said Godden.

"Better wait, all the same. Anything I can do down there?"

"Not yet. We might need a couple of slim chaps a bit later."

"That's me, for one."

"Can you hear anything?" asked the policeman.

"No. Too far away still. . . . Tell you what we *could* do with – a few cups of tea."

"The mobile canteen's coming along soon," said the warden. "I'll have some sent down."

The All Clear went suddenly. The policeman straightened up, and his head disappeared from view. Godden said: "Well, that's something, I suppose," waved to the other two, and went back to take over from Wilensky.

The tunnel grew. At the end of two hours it was about nine feet long, and nearing the dividing wall between the front and back rooms. The shores and props placed at intervals to hold off the massive weight on top gave it a workman-like air; but from its entrance it dwindled in height until it was not more than four feet high at the far end. This economy saved time, but it meant working under very difficult conditions: kneeling down in cramped discomfort, swinging the pick at half-arm, elbows close to the sides, attacking the wall of rubble with quick short jabs, which made the sweat pour. . . .

Horrocks had now taken the place of Wilensky, who had had to give up working in the tunnel itself – the dust and close confinement had started fits of coughing which made it impossible for him to keep up the pace: but Godden worked on untiringly, picking at the rubble, prising out bricks and woodwork, passing the loose stuff back, working with a sense of timeless effort, automatic and continuous. He had to breathe through his nose to filter as much of the dust as possible: he had stripped down to a pair of trousers only, and the sweat, running in rivulets down his scratched, filthy chest, collected in a sticky band at his waist line. Occasionally he paused, listened for sounds beyond the tunnel, trying to quiet his own laboured breathing in order to catch any faint noise or movement ahead: but there had been no sign of anything so far, and each time he would fall to again, making up for the tiny delay with a sustained spurt of energy.

Once, when he backed out at the end of his spell to let Horrocks take his place, the latter said: "It's like the Old Firm again, eh?" Godden smiled without answering, but he liked the idea a lot: sipping his tea from the mobile canteen, he felt glad that the work was so tough and that he and Horrocks were leading this hard-driving effort of rescue.

It was Horrocks who reached the dividing wall, during one of his spells, and after clearing away the last of the rubble he crawled out to report the fact.

"It's not much," he said. He, like Godden, was dirty and streaked with sweat. "Two bricks thick, I should say. Won't take long to get through."

"What's the other side sound like?" asked Godden.

"Hollow, I think. Looks as if the wall had held up this end of the ceiling, same as in here."

"Won't be long now, then," said the warden, who was down in the basement with them. "I'll warn the stretcher-bearers."

"I take a turn now?" asked Wilensky.

"No," said Godden. "This bit is mine." He took the pick, and a short crowbar from Horrocks, and crawled into the tunnel again.

The time was now four o'clock – three and a half hours since they had started. Godden went at the last obstruction carefully, breaking away a brick at a time close to the side wall and the floor, making a sort of little rat-hole in one corner, to keep as much of the wall's support as possible. Presently he could put his arm right through up to his

211

shoulder, and when he did so, and reached round with his freed hand, he touched nothing. So far so good: this corner of the ceiling still held. He prised away a dozen more bricks, until the hole was big enough to crawl through: then he dropped the little crowbar and eased his body through the opening.

It was pitch-dark inside: no glimmer of light penetrated from anywhere. Godden lay on the ground half-way into the room, his legs still in the entrance-hole, and listened. All round him the blackness was still and silent: the air smelt acrid, and he could feel the thick brick dust settling in his nostrils. He stretched out his arm again, and felt all round him, to the full length of his reach: still he touched nothing. Then from somewhere in the room there was a vague stir, which might have been the rubble settling overhead. He cleared his throat, and called softly:

"Anyone there?"

There was no answer: not an echo, not the smallest answering resonance, relieved the loneliness of his voice. The darkness seemed to be crowding round him, the weight of the ruined house overhead pressing upon this small threatened space. Then there was a slurring movement from somewhere near by, and a sound which might have been a groan. Godden felt his scalp prickle, and the sweat drying cold on his body as he pictured what the darkness might hold He called again:

"Who is it?"

There was the groaning sound once more and a whimper which seemed separate from it, and then silence.

He turned his head back over his shoulder and called through the opening: "Horrocks!"

"Yes, Bill?"

"Get me a torch, will you?"

"All right. . . . Are you through?"

"Yes. Can't see anything, though. But there's somebody here all right."

There was a scraping sound along the length of the tunnel: it stopped as Horrocks bumped into his legs.

"Pass the torch through the hole," said Godden.

He felt Horrocks reaching out, and then the torch was in his hand.

"Thanks, George. . . . Wait here till I see what else I want."

He clicked the torch on, and slowly splayed it round the room.

The roof first. . . . More than half the ceiling was down, sagging to the floor with the laths sticking through the plaster like dusty ribs adrift from a skeleton. Only the corner by which Godden had entered was still clear, and the small section of the room underneath it was in ruins: the wood-work was scarred, the walls cracked and pitted, the single item of furniture – a settee – overturned and splintered. By this settee a woman lay, face downwards and groaning: she had a deep scalp wound, and her hair spread like a sticky red fan on the floor around her head. Farther away, where the ceiling met the floor, lay another figure, an old man: he had been trapped at waist-level by the roof fall, and his thin body seemed to grow out of the ruins like the centrepiece of some tawdry illusion. From him there was no sound: his eyes were closed, and his bony face and bald head seemed to have shrunk to a waxy skull.

That was the Timsons, anyway. . . . Godden's torch swung again, attracted by a nearby sound, and found a last sur-prise. Almost at his elbow, sitting on a stool with her back to the wall, was a child, a girl of about six. She was ob-viously terrified: her back was braced taut against the wall, her face seemed to have dwindled to a pair of enormous eyes, set above grey cheeks streaked with dust and tears. She was apparently unhurt – in body, at least; but when the torch reached her face she screamed and hid her eyes from it.

"It's all right, love." said Godden. He was deeply shocked. "I won't hurt you."

As he spoke there was a cracking sound overhead and some more plaster fell from the ceiling, landing close by his body. The child screamed again. Godden's torch swung upwards, exploring the battered arch above him: there was nothing new to be seen, nothing to add to the danger or to lessen its menace, but it was clear that he had very little time to play with. Of the whole house, there only remained this tiny corner which had not caved in completely; and by the look and sound of it, it would not last much longer.

"It's all right," said Godden again. "I've come to get you out."

The child said nothing. Godden crawled forward until the rest of his body was clear of the entrance-hole, and then stood upright. Into the small space round him the walls and ceiling seemed to be pressing tightly: it was like standing in a coffin.

Keeping the torch pointed away, he bent down and touched the child on the shoulder. She shrank away from his arm: under the thin jersey he could feel the small body convulsively jerking, straining against a total collapse with God-knows-what effort of self-control.

"It's all right," he repeated, for the third time. He felt quite inadequate: he had really forgotten how to talk to children, and perhaps he had never known how to talk to a child in so pitiful a state. "Can you find your way out, through the hole? That's the way I came. It's quite easy. You'll be outside before you know where you are."

Godden indicated the entrance-hole with his torch, and then swung the beam round until he could see the child again. She did not answer him, and she had not changed her position; there was no way of telling whether what he had said had got through at all, or whether the child was still too hopelessly dazed to take in anything. He tried again.

"Come on," he said gently. "Get down on your hands and knees, and see if you can crawl out by yourself."

He put out his hand to coax her, and then drew it back again as the girl stiffened, ready to cry out. She made no other move, and there was nothing to show that she had understood his words. Godden shook his head. This was getting him nowhere: he just wasn't the sort of person who could persuade her to any new action; indeed it was waste of time to try, in this black hole where the horrible thing had happened to her. And there were the others to be thought of, too. . . . A fresh series of cracks from the ceiling, another fall of plaster, reminded him of the true significance of this time-wasting: unless he got moving soon, the whole lot of them would be caught. Standing there in the gloom, exhausted by the physical effort of tunnelling, shaken by the child's condition and the two prone bloodstained figures, it was difficult to think of the right order of things. He took a grip on himself, put on the torch, and bent down to the entrance-hole.

"Horrocks!" he called.

"Hallo, Bill," came the answer. "Who was that calling out?"

"There's a kid in here."

"Lord!" said Horrocks. "Anyone else?"

"The other two as well. They're both knocked out. The old man looks as if he's gone: the woman's still alive." (But was she? There's been no sound, no movement of that clotted head, for sometime.) "Send a stretcher-bearer to move them out, anyway."

"What about the kid?"

"I can't get her to move at the moment. Shock or something. The stretcher-bearer better have a look at it too."

There was a pause, while Godden heard Horrocks at the end of the tunnel repeating the information, and a faint echo in which he could distinguish the warden's voice. The link with the outside world was tenuously comforting. Then Horrocks called again, a shade more anxiously:

"Do you need any gear, Bill? What's the ceiling like?"

"Not too good. But there's no room to shore up – and too much weight anyway if it starts to go. We'll just have to try getting them out, and trust to luck. . . . Send a couple of hurricane lamps through with the stretcher-bearer. I can't see much with just a torch."

"All right. Watch out for yourself, Bill."

Silence fell again. While he was waiting, Godden switched on the torch and went back to the Timsons. The woman had stopped bleeding, which he vaguely knew might be a bad sign: he had been ready to put on a tourniquet, like they'd been shown in the classes, but there didn't seem to be any need now. (How did you put a tourniquet on a head wound, anyway?) He could not tell whether she was still breathing; his own sounded too loud. Leaving her, he shuffled over on his hands and knees to have another look at the old man: clearly he was pretty far gone – the breathing imperceptible, the face like a thin paper mask with a line of dried froth at the mouth – and there was nothing to be done to help him. Godden didn't want to start pulling him out before the stretcher-bearer had a look at him: that was what he'd been taught, though it seemed a cruel thing to leave him there with all that weight on top of him. . . .

There was a scraping noise in the tunnel, and a thin line of light which grew until it spread over the whole corner of the room. A hand came through, thrusting two hurricane lamps into the open; then a head followed, wriggling and jerking like a moth leaving a cocoon. It turned towards the light. It was the pacifist stretcher-bearer.

He peered round him, and then his face broke into a grin. "Hi there, Bill!"

"Hallo, lad. Bit of work for you here."

The stretcher-bearer stood up, rather gingerly, and glanced round the room. "How long is this going to last?"

"Oh, it's not so bad." Dismissing the state of the ceiling with a carelessness he did not feel, Godden pointed to the Timsons. "Three of them to look at, with the kid there. See if she's O.K., will you, and we'll send her out first."

"All right."

As he knelt down beside the girl, Godden said: "She may scream."

The stretcher-bearer did not answer, but took the child's hand, and smiled at her. His face, grimy with dirt from the tunnel and queerly shadowed by the lamplight was not reassuring; but some quality of gentleness in him must have reached the child, for this time she did not cry out. Godden watched as the stretcher-bearer ran his hands swiftly over her body and made her stand up, talking all the time in a soft whisper, which seemed to fill the shattered room with comfort and confidence. It was wonderful to watch his concentration as he laboured to get through to the child's mind, and the way in which she gradually surrendered to him. Godden wished he had been able to do it himself, but he knew that could never be. He hadn't the trick of that sort of thing. It was something you were born with, most like.

Presently the stretcher-bearer stood up. "She seems O.K.," he said to Godden. "Shaken to bits, of course. . . . Now we want to get you outside," he went on, bending down to the child again. "Do you think you can crawl through the hole down there?"

The child followed his pointing arm, looked at the tunnel entrance for a moment, and shook her head. Godden thought: we'll be all night over this, and the roof will probably go before we're properly started. From the corner he stared at the pair of them, impatient, wanting to hurry them up, but knowing that he could do nothing: he could only stand by and wait, with no more part in the scene than the enormous crooked shadows the two of them cast against the ruined wall and ceiling. Sweating and half-stifled, feeling the drag of the minutes as they stretched out over the limit of safety, he listened to the curious, hurrying, half-whispered dialogue of the stretcher-bearer persuading the child to move, and the child delaying in terror. But Godden knew that, in spite of the critical circumstances, it *had* to be persuasion: unless she were willing to go, it would be impossible to force her down the tunnel without a grim and horrible struggle.

"Don't want to leave Granny."

"I'll bring Granny out in a minute. You go first."

"Where does it go to?"

"Outside the house. You'll be out in the sunshine in a minute."

"It's too small. It's a little hole."

"It's just big enough for you."

"It's too small for Granny."

"No, it's big enough for her, too."

"Will there be somebody there?"

"Yes, there's a nice man waiting for you outside." The stretcher-bearer called, and Horrocks answered faintly. "You see – he's all ready to help you."

"Who is it?"

"Just a nice old man. I expect he's got a bag of sweets in his pocket somewhere."

"What's he doing out there?"

"He's come to help you."

"Don't want to go by myself."

"Just go a little way, and you'll see him there waiting for you."

In the end, tearful, trembling uncontrollably she went. . . . Godden heard Horrocks saying: "Come on, love – here we are," heard the child start sobbing out loud as she reached the tunnel-end, and felt suddenly a huge surge of relief. At least they were free of *that* bit of the job.

Swiftly the stretcher-bearer turned to the old woman, examined her, started binding up her head and then putting a long splint on her broken thigh. As he worked, with furious speed, the roof overhead gave an enormously loud crack, and he looked up momentarily.

"Sounds as though the whole bloody issue is coming down. . . . How long have we got, do you reckon?"

Godden shook his head. He was beginning to feel slightly sick: it was obvious that their small bit of the ceiling would go at any moment. "Don't know, lad. . . . Not too long. . . . Have you finished?"

"Nearly." The stretcher-bearer, tying a knot at the bottom end of the splint, glanced over his shoulder. "We might as well leave him where he is . . . I'll put this old girl out: you follow me." He grinned suddenly. "Don't forget the lamps, will you? Council property."

"All right." But Godden knew already that he would not leave the old man until the very last moment. He could still be alive. It was worth a good try, at least.

After a moment the stretcher-bearer looked up. "O.K. – finished. It's as rough as hell, but it'll do for now. Give me a hand up to the entrance."

They half pulled, half carried the lolling figure to the tunnel mouth. More plaster fell as they moved, a last warning to speed their exit. At the open corner the stretcher-bearer made a long sling out of three bandages, looped it over the old woman's shoulders, and tied the ends round his own waist. Then he said: "See you later, Bill – don't hang about too long," and began to crawl out on his hands and knees, dragging the old woman after him like an unwieldy bundle at a rope's end. As she moved, inch by inch, the hacked-up floor scored her face cruelly. Godden, easing her body through the entrance, thanked God she was unconscious.

Left to himself, he crossed back to the old man, and peered down at the pale face. Not a flicker there. . . . But he must try, anyway: this was one of the people he was meant to look after. He took a good grip of the thin shoulders and heaved. The body gave a little, and then stuck. A fresh shower of plaster covered them both with a grey, choking cloud of dust.

Through the tunnel came Horrocks's voice: "What are you doing, Bill?"

"Getting the old chap out, if I can."

"Thought he was dead."

"Maybe not. Worth a try, anyway."

"Don't be a bloody fool," Horrocks's voice, unnaturally loud and strained, communicated its fear. "Leave him and come on out."

Part of what he said was drowned by a rumble overhead. Horrocks called sharply: "Bill!"

Godden, tugging again at the old man's body, grunted: "Yes?"

"For heaven's sake come out before it's too late. The whole house will be down in a minute."

"All right. I'll just have one more –"

He broke off suddenly. The roof *was* coming down: he felt the whole crazy structure start to sag. Up till now he had not been afraid: now a stab of panic shot right through his heart. With his arms still round the old man – the old man he already seemed to love so fiercely and tenderly – he gave a wild glance round the room. What a rotten place to die, what a little hell-hole of dirt and pain. . . . He heaved again at the body, feeling it inexorably stuck against something within the rubble, feeling the roof dropping like a wave slowly breaking over them both. One of the lamps went out, caught by a sagging beam: the space left was suddenly halved by a crashing fall of brickwork.

Horrocks's voice called "Bill!" on an extraordinary note of anguish.

Godden thought: "Poor old George. He'll be sorry."

The old man was torn out of his arms by a sudden cruel weight dividing them, and disappeared from sight, as if sponged out by a dirty cloth. With nothing left to save, Godden jerked backwards, making for the tunnel, but he did not reach it: as he stumbled across, the roof overhead split with a crack like thunder, unloosing a cascade of brick and woodwork, which thickened until it was a solid avalanche of rubble.

Its crushing weight bore down upon his back, beat him to his knees in total darkness, forced his body down and clamped it to the floor. Blood came into his mouth. The house fell upon him with repeated blows, but he was not alive to more than two or three of them.

WAR FICTION—AVAILABLE IN GRANADA PAPERBACKS

Ella Leffland
Rumours of Peace   £1.95 ☐

J P W Malalieu
Very Ordinary Seaman   85p ☐

Frederick Manning
The Middle Parts of Fortune   £1.50 ☐

Nicholas Monsarrat
H M S Marlborough Will Enter Harbour   £1.50 ☐
Three Corvettes   75p ☐

Theodor Plievier
Stalingrad   60p ☐

Erich Maria Remarque
All Quiet on the Western Front   £1.25 ☐
The Road Back   95p ☐
The Night in Lisbon   95p ☐
A Time to Love and a Time to Die   £1.95 ☐
Spark of Life   £1.95 ☐

GF2381

WAR FICTION—NOW AVAILABLE IN GRANADA PAPERBACKS

GF2281

TRUE WAR—NOW AVAILABLE IN GRANADA PAPERBACKS

Len Deighton
Bomber	£1.95	☐
Fighter	£1.95	☐
Blitzkrieg	£1.95	☐
Declarations of War	£1.25	☐

Norman Mailer
The Naked and the Dead	£2.50	☐

Alfred Price
The Hardest Day	£1.95	☐

Leon Uris
Battle Cry	£1.95	☐

James Webb
Fields of Fire	£1.95	☐

All these books are available at your local bookshop or newsagent, or can be ordered direct from the publisher. Just tick the titles you want and fill in the form below.

Name _____

Address _____

_____

Write to Granada Cash Sales
PO Box 11, Falmouth, Cornwall TR10 9EN.

Please enclose remittance to the value of the cover price plus:

UK 45p for the first book, 20p for the second book plus 14p per copy for each additional book ordered to a maximum charge of £1.63.

BFPO and Eire 45p for the first book, 20p for the second book plus 14p per copy for the next 7 books, thereafter 8p per book.

Overseas 75p for the first book and 21p for each additional book.

Granada Publishing reserve the right to show new retail prices on covers, which may differ from those previously advertised in the text or elsewhere.

GF2081